MAKE QUILTS NOT WAR

A Harriet Truman/Loose Threads Mystery

Arlene Sachitano

ZUMAYA ENIGMA

AUSTIN TX

2013

MAKE QUILTS NOT WAR
© 2013 by Arlene Sachitano
ISBN 978-1-61271-139-3
Cover art and design © April Martinez

"Zumaya Enigma" and the raven logo are trademarks of Zumaya Publications LLC, Austin TX. Look for us online at http://www.zumayapublications.com/enigma.php

Library of Congress Cataloging-in-Publication Data

Sachitano, Arlene, 1951-
Make quilts not war : a Harriet Truman/Loose Threads mystery / Arlene Sachitano.
    pages cm
  ISBN 978-1-61271-139-3 (print/pbk. : alk. paper) — ISBN 978-1-61271-140-9 (electronic/multiple format : alk. paper) (print) — ISBN 978-1-61271-141-6 (electronic/epub : alk. paper) (print)
  1. Quiltmakers—Fiction. 2. Mystery fiction. I. Title.
PS3619.A277M35 2013
813'.6—dc23
                                        2013001791

This book is dedicated to Colonel Henry Bohne, Medical Corp, US Army Reserve. In an age when his peers are traveling to resorts and golf courses, Hank has joined the army and put himself in harm's way to care for our injured soldiers. For that we thank him.

ACKNOWLEDGMENTS

Any endeavor that takes place over a period of time and requires a degree of effort, requires support from ones family, friends and acquaintances and writing a book is no exception. Thank you to all of you who have had your schedule or plans disrupted by my writing schedule or promotional travels; in particular, Susan, Susan and Annie.

I'd like to thank Katy King, my critique "partner" (we are all that's left of our group) who always gives me insightful comments and suggestions on my current manuscript.

Once a book is written, a lot of effort goes into promotion. I'd like to thank everyone who has hosted events for me or allowed me into their shop, booth, parking lot or bookstore. Special thanks to Vern and Betty Swearingen of StoryQuilts, Linne and Jack Lindquist of Craftsman's Touch Books, Ruth Derksen of Shop Girl Fabrics and Deon Stonehouse of Sunriver Books and Music.

As always, thanks to Liz and Zumaya Publications for making all this possible. Special thanks to April Martinez for the great cover work.

Last but not least, thanks to Jack and our offspring and their offspring.

Prologue

The shooter couldn't have planned better circumstances. Evenly spaced along the exterior wall of the large exhibition area were alcoves with life-sized statues representing prominent figures from Washington state's past. Captain Robert Gray was shown holding his spyglass to his eye. It was perfect.

The backlighting meant anyone looking away from the well-lit quilt display would see the silhouette of the statue, the spyglass pointing directly at the target, hiding the rifle of the killer concealed in its shadow.

The target, unaware she was taking her last breaths, stood on the far side of the show floor on a raised stage, a white glove on one hand to allow her to handle the quilt hanging behind her without fear of soiling it. The glove wasn't going to be any help, the shooter mused then sighted on the target and pulled the trigger.

Chapter 1

I t was a dark time," Mavis Willis said.

The Loose Threads quilt group sat spellbound around the table in the large classroom at the back of Pins and Needles, Foggy Point, Washington's, best and only quilt store.

"Cotton had once been king. Up until the early nineteen-sixties, something like eighty percent of the textiles sold in America were made of cotton. By the mid-nineteen-seventies, it was down to maybe thirty-five percent. Cotton was displaced by the scourge of the decade."

"Polyester?" Harriet Truman said in a hushed voice.

"That and worse," Mavis replied. "Synthetics of all sorts. Our fabric, our threads, our upholstery—the very warp and weft of our being was being supplanted by a poseur."

"What did you do?" Carla Salter asked, her eyes round. At twenty-three, she was the youngest member of the group and had never experienced polyester fabric firsthand.

"What *could* we do?" Harriet's Aunt Beth answered for her friend. "We used what was available. Our fabric was a cotton/acrylic blend, heavy on the acrylic."

"I think everyone made at least one polyester knit quilt, too," Mavis confessed with a small shrug.

"Yes," Beth agreed. "We all have them."

"Where?" Harriet challenged. "I've never seen yours."

"Would you display it, if you had one?" Mavis asked.

"Good point," Harriet said.

"I'm sure the colors were different back then, too." Robin McLeod said tactfully.

"If you mean avocado green, electric orange and mustard yellow, you're right, if the pictures in my mom's photo album are any indication," Lauren Sawyer added.

"Those were the colors of the times," said Aunt Beth. "Not just for quilts, either. Appliances and shag carpets also favored them."

"I guess I'm glad our house is historic," Harriet said, referring to the spacious Victorian home her aunt had given her, along with the long-arm quilting business housed within, when the older woman had retired.

"I wanted a harvest gold refrigerator in the worst way," Aunt Beth mused. "I was so jealous when Mavis got hers." She smiled at her friend.

"My mami was so thrilled when *papi* put Astroturf on our cement patio," Connie Escorcia said, rolling her eyes to the ceiling. "*Diós mio*," she added with a laugh. "Those were the days."

"How old were you in the sixties?" Carla asked Connie, blushing at her own boldness in asking such a personal question.

"Those were my glory days," Connie replied with a smile. "I was a teenager. I was born in nineteen-fifty, so I turned ten in nineteen-sixty. My mami taught me to sew on her sewing machine when I was twelve, but I didn't take up quilting until my babies were in school. By then, I'd gone back to teaching, so I didn't have a lot of time."

"When do we need to have our quilts finished?" Lauren interrupted. She looked at the clock on her phone. "I have to meet my client in forty-five minutes."

"The sixties festival opens in exactly four weeks," Harriet said. "They want us to have the quilts hanging in the exhibition hall by Friday of the week before."

"Yikes," Robin McLeod exclaimed. "I got behind when the power was out from the storm. I've got mine cut out, but I haven't sewn a stitch yet."

"You better get cracking," Mavis said. "They didn't do long-arm machine quilting back then, so Harriet isn't going to be able to stitch your quilt for you."

"I'm tying mine with yarn," Carla said.

"That was popular back then," Beth assured her.

"What are *you* doing, Harriet?" Lauren asked.

"I'm working with some cheater cloth," she replied, referring to a fabric that is preprinted with images of pieced quilt blocks. "I'm doing some piecing to go along with it, but I'm not sure I like what I've gotten done so far."

"I'll be done with mine by next week," Jenny Logan said. "I can help sew binding or..." She looked at Carla. "...tie knots."

"You made another quilt?" Lauren asked. "I thought I heard Marjory ask you to bring that quilt you have in your guest room. Didn't you say you made that in the sixties?"

Marjory was the owner of Pins and Needles and was chair of the textile show committee for the upcoming festival.

"Yes, but that was forty-some years ago. The fabric is faded and worn, and I was just learning to quilt back then."

"It looked like it was in pretty good shape when I saw it," Lauren persisted.

"I need to do something current. I wish I'd never shown it to you all. I wasn't a real quilter back then. The batting is an old blanket, and I made the blocks from old clothes. And I tied it with acrylic yarn." She shuddered with the memory.

"Marjory's not going to take no for an answer," Mavis told her. "She's looked at every authentic sixties quilt in our community, and yours was the only one that didn't have orange and brown in it. They want to hang it in the exhibit hall, and with those mustard-colored walls, orange just wouldn't work."

"I'm still not comfortable with it," Jenny said, tucking a stray strand of silver hair behind her ear then patting it into place.

"It captures the youthful spirit of the times," Harriet said. "Besides, anyone who attends quilt shows around here knows your quilting has improved dramatically since the sixties. If it bothers you that much, I'm sure you could ask them to leave your name off of it. Do you have a label on the back?"

5

"Of course not," Jenny snapped then reddened when Harriet and Carla stared at her. Her tone softened. "I mean, we didn't think of that back in those days. It was just a quilt meant to be used on a bed. And thank you, I will ask Marjory if they can leave my name out of it."

"I just hope all this effort is worth it," Aunt Beth said. "I know some of the other communities around here have had success with theme weeks during the dead of winter as a way to pull tourists in, but no one has ever done the sixties before."

"It does seem like that time period would better lend itself to a summer event—summer of love and all that," Harriet said.

"The committee thought people were burning out on murder mystery weekends, especially with what's been going on in Foggy Point the last few months," Mavis said.

"Langley isn't that far from here," Beth added, referring to the host community of a very successful mystery weekend held every year on Whidby Island.

She and Mavis had been on a planning subcommittee once the main group had decided to add a quilt show to the lineup of events.

"I can't imagine any theme they could choose that would boost my business. I'm in such a specialized niche tourism doesn't affect me at all." Harriet said.

"You got some additional work when we did the Civil War quilts last summer, didn't you?" Lauren asked.

"I did, but it was from you guys, not new customers, and then no one did new quilts for a month after that, so in the end it wasn't an increase at all."

"Well, at least the stores and restaurants will get a lift," Jenny said.

"I heard the newspaper was going to run a special edition, with headlines from the era," Robin said, rejoining the conversation. She and her friend DeAnn Gault had been concentrating on the binding they were hand stitching on a lap quilt they were making as a gift for Robin's elderly grandmother.

"They're offering very affordable advertising," Marjory chimed in from the kitchen across the hall. She came into the classroom. "The staff will help you tailor your ad to the theme. They got into their archives and made copies of representative advertising from nineteen sixty-eight."

"Wow, they're really getting into it," Harriet said.

"My mom is digging out a couple of macramé pieces she made for the county fair," DeAnn said.

Carla looked up, clearly confused.

"Macramé was a popular craft back in the day," Aunt Beth said.

"People braided polyester cord into intricate designs," Mavis added.

"They made hangers for potted plants, or sometimes you could put little glass or mirror pieces into them and make a hanging shelf," Beth continued. "We all tried our hand at it."

"People made belts and guitar straps and choker necklaces, too," Jenny said. "They usually used hemp cord for the bracelets and neck-wear, though."

"Sounds...interesting," Carla said, her cheeks turning pink as she spoke.

"They were interesting times," Mavis said.

"It was the Age of Aquarius," Connie said with a smile.

"It was also the age of assassinations, the age of the war in Vietnam, the cultural revolution in China and the six-day war in Israel," Lauren said.

"Every era has its share of sad things," Mavis said with a sigh.

"I'm surprised you didn't mention the invention of the computer, Lauren," DeAnn said.

"The computer wasn't 'invented,'" Lauren corrected. "A series of innovations allowed the computer to evolve into its present state."

"The sixties were definitely political times," Robin mused.

"And it was a time of good music," DeAnn said. "Marjory," she called in a voice loud enough to carry. Marjory had returned to the retail area of the shop.

"You rang?" Marjory said as she appeared at the classroom doorway a moment later.

"Someone told me you guys landed a big-name rock star for the grand finale," DeAnn said.

"As a matter of fact, we did. And not just for the finale. We're having a 'senior prom,' of sorts, and he's agreed to play at that, also."

7

"Don't keep us in suspense," Harriet prompted.

"We got Colm Byrne," Marjory said with a smile.

"Colm Byrne? The Irish rock star? That Colm Byrne?" Harriet asked. "How did you land him?"

"We have our ways," Marjory said and laughed. "Actually, Jerry Weber is on our committee, and he apparently knows him. I don't know if Colm has looked at real estate in this area with him or what."

Jerry owned and operated Foggy Point's biggest real estate office.

"All I know is, we decided we wanted music, and Jerry made a few phone calls, and suddenly we'd booked Colm Byrne and we're only paying a pittance." She turned and left the room.

"Wow," Harriet said and sat back in her chair.

"Wow is right," Robin agreed.

The group around the table fell momentarily silent.

"Did the Loose Threads go home?" Jorge Perez asked as he came into the room carrying a large insulated box. "I hear no one speaking. This can't be the Loose Threads I know and love." He laughed. "They are never without words."

"Marjory just told us the festival committee has landed Colm Byrne as the musical entertainment," Harriet said.

"Colm Byrne the Irish rock star?" Jorge asked. "I think Marjory is telling you stories."

"It's true," Marjory protested as she returned once again. "Jerry Weber has some connection to him or someone influential in his entourage."

"He will draw a crowd," Jorge said and smiled. He set his box on the table and removed the lid. "Now, who's hungry?"

The Loose Threads had arranged to use the classroom all day so they could make serious headway on the projects they were finishing up to make way for their sixties quilts. Jorge had agreed to deliver lunch from his Mexican restaurant, Tico's Tacos, so the group wouldn't have to go out.

"Here, Lauren," He said and handed her a brown paper bag. "Señora Beth said you have to leave early and wouldn't be staying for lunch."

"Thank you," Lauren said as she took the bag. She looked at Beth.

"You said you were dealing with your difficult client when I saw you yesterday. If it's the same one from before, they seem to have a nose for when we eat. I had Jorge make your food to go just in case—seems like I was right."

"You were, indeed," Lauren said and put her coat on, then picked up her sewing bag, tucking her lunch inside.

"What are we having?" Harriet asked.

"I brought cheese quesadillas, pork tacos and chicken burritos and, of course, chips, salsa and guacamole and…" He paused to take a plastic box from his big container. "…a chicken salad for Señora Robin."

"Thank you." Robin sounded surprised.

"You think I don't notice what everyone eats?" Jorge said with a wink.

"What are *you* doing for the festival?" DeAnn asked.

"I'm doing what I always do," Jorge said. "Making food. My restaurant is timeless, so I don't need to do anything there. I'm on the food committee for the festival. We're having a food court at the community center in the walkway between the exhibit hall and the auditorium where the music will be. I guess they're going to have the high school bands from Foggy Point and Angel Harbor playing music a couple of times a day before the big concerts at night."

"What sorts of food will be available?" Carla asked.

"We'll have tacos and hamburgers and hotdogs, but also we'll have a cart of foods from the era—fondue, peanut butter and Marshmallow Fluff sandwiches, on soft white bread, of course. We'll have spaghetti from a can, little pizzas made from round crackers with a slice of pepperoni and mozzarella cheese…" He paused to think. "Instant breakfast in a can, vegetable sandwiches with sprouts—that was toward the end of the era. Twinkies, Ding-Dongs, HoHo's, if we can find some."

He ticked these items off on his fingers.

"We're having brownies, but not with anything *special* in them, we'll have cans of Fresca soda, someone is bringing that gelatin that separated into three layers. And I'm sure there is more I'm not remembering."

"Lots of us were cooking perfectly normal food every day," Mavis said, "But those meals weren't especially memorable—or tied to a single point in time, for that matter."

"Isn't that when we got our first Julia Child cookbooks?" Aunt Beth asked.

"Maybe," Mavis looked at her longtime friend. "Or that could have been in the seventies." She sighed. "It all runs together after a while. In any case, Twinkies and Marshmallow Fluff were much more memorable."

"Can you stay and eat with us?" Harriet asked Jorge.

"I think I can spare a few minutes to eat," he said and glanced at his watch. "I don't have to sew anything if I stay, do I?"

Chapter 2

"Who needs a wig?" Harriet asked as she set a large shopping bag on the cutting table in her quilting studio.

Mavis and Beth sat in the two wingback chairs by the bow window in the reception area, each holding a mug of steaming tea. Jenny was in a folding chair to their left, a large black tote at her feet. Robin and DeAnn stood with Lauren at the short end of the cutting table, a pile of clothing between them.

"Sorry I'm late," Carla said, stripping off her wet rain coat as she came in from the outside parking area. "I'm sorry, did I interrupt?" Her cheeks, red already from the cold, reddened further.

"Harriet was just asking if anyone needs a wig," Beth told her. "And I'm pretty sure we were all going to say yes."

"Ewww, where did they come from?" Lauren asked. "You didn't get them from the thrift store, did you?"

"Maybe," Harriet said evasively. "I got a deal from a wholesale wig place in Seattle for six of them. I got four more from DeAnn."

She paused, and DeAnn took up the story.

"When Nana first got dementia and we didn't know what was going on, she went on a huge catalog shopping spree. It didn't matter what sort of catalog came in the mail. If she got it, she ordered something—or many somethings. She must have gotten a wig catalog at some point, because we found a box with five brand-new ones in it."

"That's handy," Lauren said. "What about the thrift store?"

"Okay, I did find three killer wigs at Trash and Treasures." Harriet reached into her bag and pulled out a handful of black fluff and held it up. "I found this afro, and it was too perfect to pass up. I washed it three times."

"Toss it over," Jenny said and held her hands up to receive it.

Harriet carried the wig around the table then lobbed it. Jenny caught it then turned it in her hands to orient the cap before pulling it onto her head.

"Is it me?"

"Tuck your hair in around the back," Lauren suggested, "unless you like looking like a skunk."

"Let me help you," Carla offered. She set the mug of tea she'd just poured on the big table and stood behind Jenny, tucking stray strands of hair neatly under the wig cap.

Harriet laughed. "It's perfect," she choked out. "Let me get a mirror."

She disappeared through the door into her kitchen and the house beyond. She returned a moment later with a hand-held mirror and gave it to Jenny.

"Oooh," Jenny said. "It's definitely me."

"What else do you have?" Mavis asked. "Anything in red?"

Harriet pulled all the wigs from her bag and passed them around. After a few minutes of trial-and-error, everyone except Lauren had chosen new hair.

"I'm going to go with my own," Lauren said and ran her hand through her long, straight blond hair, pulling out a hair clip that had been holding it away from her face. "I've been growing my bangs out ever since we started talking about this, so I can cut them just above my eyes like that singer Mary from that old sixties folk group."

"Well, honey, you're the only one in this group that could pull that off," Mavis told her.

"I hope Connie likes her bob," Jenny said.

"What's not to like?" Aunt Beth asked and laughed.

"Sorry I missed last week," DeAnn said. "The kids all had a stomach bug, and I didn't want to risk sharing it with you-all."

"And we thank you for that," Harriet told her.

"You didn't miss anything," Lauren added. "A bunch of people went to Seattle to shop for costumes, so only a few were left to work on their quilts."

"We weren't just shopping. We were picking up the posters and flyers and some other signs," Mavis informed DeAnn. "The committee got a donation from a big printing company. It worked out that we were able to do a little shopping for our costumes while we were there."

Jenny got up and dumped the contents of her bag onto the cutting table as Robin pushed the pile of clothes near her to the center.

"Dig in," Aunt Beth said. "Mavis and I put the stuff we thought you ladies would be interested in on the table, but we have several more bags in the garage. The organizing committee asked us to bring back some selections for them, too."

"Where did you find all this stuff?" Harriet asked.

"We found two vintage clothing stores that had a lot of sixties stuff that was reasonably priced. Then, we went to a theatrical costume store. The fringed vests and beaded headbands came from there; some of the bell bottoms, too," Mavis reported.

"I brought some things from the church clothing drive closet," Jenny said. "We've been pulling out anything that looks to be of that vintage and setting it aside for this event."

"And we hit a military surplus store on our way back," Aunt Beth added.

"Is everything here up for grabs?" Jenny asked as she held up a long-fringed cowhide vest.

"Yes," Beth replied. "Mavis and I already have our costumes."

"That vest will be killer with your 'fro," Harriet said.

✂- - - ✂- - - ✂

"Can I interest anyone in brownies?" Harriet asked when everyone had decided on an outfit and either taken it to her car or stowed it in her stitching bag.

"Even I won't say no to chocolate," Robin said.

"I'm not sure why you bother to ask," Lauren added and got up to follow Harriet to the kitchen.

They returned with a large platter of chewy brownies and a stack of pink paper plates and matching napkins.

"Anyone need a refill on their drink?" Harriet asked. "I got some of that holiday spice tea on sale at the Steaming Cup yesterday if anyone wants one last cup of it before it goes away until next Christmas."

Lauren retrieved the coffee carafe from the drip machine in the kitchen and topped off the cups of the three people who were drinking coffee while Harriet did the same with hot water from the electric kettle for the tea drinkers.

"Can we see a copy of the flyers you picked up?" she asked when she and Lauren were through with their hostess duties.

Mavis reached into the canvas tote on the floor by her chair, pulled out a trifold brochure, and handed it to Harriet.

"Oh, nice. Look, Jenny, your quilt is on the front." She held up the flyer for all to see.

"I wish they hadn't done that," Jenny said, the color draining from her face. She pulled the flyer from Harriet's hands and examined it. "I told Marjory she could display my quilt, and I didn't *really* want to do that. She didn't say anything about putting it on her advertising materials."

"You must have let them take the picture," Lauren pointed out.

"I let them take a few pictures, but Marjory said it was just for layout and planning purposes. No one said anything about using it for anything else."

"It's a pretty quilt," Carla said in a soft voice. "And it looks like it's in really good condition."

"That's not the point," Jenny snapped. "It's ancient history, and it isn't anything like what I do today."

"I think that's the whole point," Mavis said. "And if you feel that strongly, I'm sure Marjory will take it down and give it back to you."

"It's a little late for that now." Jenny handed the flyer back to Mavis then stood and pulled on her leather jacket. "I've got to go," she said, and left without another word.

"Well, that was weird," Lauren said, breaking the silence that had ensued.

"Something's going on," Harriet agreed. "She's been weird about that quilt ever since Marjory asked her to let them hang it in the show."

"I agree," Robin said. Being an attorney, she was usually careful in her opinions, so her statement carried weight with the group. "She didn't have to keep the quilt in a place where we could all see it at her house, and even then, she could have said no when the committee asked."

"Yeah, but she's the nice one of this group," Lauren pointed out. "Every group has one member who is nicer than everybody else, and she's our designated nice person, so she probably *couldn't* say no. It would ruin her reputation."

Harriet looked at her.

"You're nuts," she said.

"Maybe she didn't make it herself," Carla suggested. "Did she ever say she was the one who made it?"

"Good point." Lauren looked at Beth. "Do we know the answer?"

"Now that you mention it, I'm not sure the question ever came up," Beth replied.

"Why would it?" Harriet asked. "I mean, when I visit any of you and see a homemade quilt on a bed, I just assume you made it. I would never ask you if you'd done it yourself."

"Clearly, there's an issue," Mavis said. "I'm sure Jenny will tell us all in good time."

"We aren't going to solve it today," Aunt Beth said. "So, how is everyone doing on their quilt? Does anyone need help?"

"All I have to do is the yarn ties on mine," Carla said.

"Mine's done," Robin volunteered.

"I'm binding mine," DeAnn added.

The rest of the group reported they were similarly close to being done.

"Don't forget, we need the hanging sleeve to be four inches deep to accommodate the metal pipes they're using to make the hanging racks," Mavis reminded them.

"All right," Beth said. "We've got our wigs and costumes, and our quilts are nearly done. I declare the Loose Threads ready for a return of the nineteen-sixties."

"Far out," Harriet said.

Chapter 3

He didn't tell you anything about your date except you should wear something smashing and be prepared for something big?" Lauren asked for what seemed like the hundredth time.

"No, and if you ask me another hundred times, I still won't know anything else," Harriet snapped.

She didn't like surprises. When she was growing up, the word *surprise* in a letter or phone call from her parents usually preceded an announcement they were sending her to a new boarding school, or that she had to join them at some conference where they were going to be interviewed and wanted to come off like devoted parents. It was never good. Not once.

"You don't have to bite my head off," Lauren shot back.

She'd come by to go through the bags of costume pieces, claiming she wanted to see if there was a better blouse choice. But the tunic she'd already chosen was perfect, and they both knew she was there because Harriet had let it slip the day before she would be getting ready for a big date with Aiden Jalbert this afternoon.

"I'm just having a hard time believing you agreed to this gig without any more information than that. I mean, it's no big secret there's been trouble in paradise this winter."

"I guess I won't know if I don't go, will I?"

"What if he's making the grand gesture because of the reappearance of Tom? Would you want him to be committing to you just because another guy is showing interest?"

"Let's not get ahead of ourselves. Not that it's any of your business, but things have been better with Aiden the last few weeks. And there is no reason to believe that his 'grand gesture,' as you put it, has anything to do with commitment or anything else."

"He's sending a limo to pick you up, and he told you to prepare for something big. That sounds like a little more than a dinner out to me."

"And you're suddenly the expert on romance?"

"Just because I don't currently have a boy toy doesn't mean I've never had one. Besides, I read romance novels."

"Really?"

"We all have our weakness," Lauren said. "What jewelry are you going to wear with that?" She pointed at the little black dress Harriet had laid on the ironing board in her studio.

"I'm still debating. You want to look at the choices?"

Harriet loaded her dress back onto its padded hanger and led Lauren through the connecting door into the kitchen and upstairs to her bedroom. She hung the dress on the closet door and opened a wooden jewelry box that sat on top of her dresser.

"Oh, my gosh!" Lauren said. "Is that stuff real?"

She pointed at the neat lines of jewel-encrusted gold and silver necklaces that lay on the velvet surface of the top tray. Harriet opened the first drawer of the box, revealing three strands of pearls. She sighed.

"Yeah, my parents thought jewelry could make up for their absence on the holidays." She held up a pearl choker with a diamond-and-ruby clasp. "I wanted new riding boots one year for Christmas, but I got this instead."

"That would look really good with your dress," Lauren gasped, ignoring Harriet's musings. "Did you get earrings to match?"

Harriet pulled open the middle drawer of the box, revealing a tray of earrings. She removed a pair of pearl teardrops with diamond-and-ruby accents. Lauren took them and held them up.

"You *have* to wear these," she said, turning them until the rubies caught the light. "I've got to go back to my computer now, but tomorrow I have to meet Robin at noon. I'll come by on my way, and I want a full report. If anything big happens, call me tonight. I'll be up until at least midnight."

"I'd have never pegged you for such a romantic."

"Romantic? What are you talking about? I just love a good train wreck."

Lauren set the earrings back in the jewelry box, turned and left. Harriet was still standing in her room when she heard the kitchen door open and close again.

"Are you up there?" called Aunt Beth. "Lauren said you were in your room."

"Do you think I'm walking into a trap?" Harriet asked her aunt when the older woman had ascended the stairs and plopped her ample self into the red overstuffed chair beside Harriet's bed.

"What on earth are you talking about? Aren't you going on a date with Aiden? Or did I miss something?"

"Yes, I'm going on a date. No, you didn't miss anything. Lauren stopped by to give me a pep talk. I think."

"Well, that explains it," Beth said.

"I accused Lauren of being a romantic, and she said she just wanted a ringside seat to the train wreck my date is sure to be. She thinks Aiden is reacting to the threat of Tom."

"Tom Bainbridge? Why would Aiden be threatened by Tom? He was in Foggy Point during the big storm in December, but didn't he go back when the slide was cleared?"

Harriet and the Loose Threads had met Tom when they'd attended a retreat at his late mother's folk art school in the community of Angel Harbor early the previous year, and had renewed their acquaintance when he'd been trapped in Foggy Point by a landslide that had blocked the highway.

"He did." Harriet turned her back to her aunt as she began rearranging her sock drawer.

"Have you been seeing Tom?"

"Define *seeing*," Harriet said in a careful tone.

"Oh, honey, tell me you're not using Tom to pressure Aiden into making a move."

"I'm not using anyone to do anything. Tom and I have had coffee a few times. He is well aware that Aiden and I are working on our relationship, and he is fine with being friends."

"Does Aiden know you're still seeing Tom?"

"It's none of his business—or yours, for that matter—but yes, everyone knows about everyone else. I'm starting to get a bad feeling about this whole surprise date thing, and not just because of Lauren, either. Even you think it's not on the up-and-up; I can hear it in your voice. You think he's asking me out on a special date because of Tom."

"I didn't say that. I was just *asking* you if that's why. It's entirely possible he's making a grand romantic gesture because he wants to knock your socks off. Maybe all the trouble you've been having lately has made him realize he could lose you, all on his own, without help from anyone."

"Still, that's not a good reason to make a grand gesture. And I'm afraid of what that gesture might be. He's been afraid of any sort of commitment. What if he swings to the other end of the scale?"

"You think he plans on *proposing*?" Aunt Beth asked, the color draining from her face.

"I don't know. That's the problem. And why does the idea make you look so pale?"

"Oh, honey." Beth patted her hand over her heart. "It just seems sort of sudden, given everything. And what would you say?"

"Let's not get ahead of ourselves here. It's equally likely he's just taking me to a good restaurant for a romantic night out. I could cancel. Then you and Lauren wouldn't have to worry about it."

"I raised you better than that," Beth scolded.

"Did you come over for something besides my tortured lack of a love life?"

"Yes, I came to see if we had a pair of bell bottoms in a size sixteen. DeAnn's mother is going to help take tickets at the quilt show, and she's got a tie-dyed shirt but needs something to wear with it."

"I think there might be a white pair," Harriet said. "The bags of clothes are down in the studio." She glanced at the clock radio on her nightstand. "I've got time. Shall we go look?"

✄ - - - ✄ - - - ✄

"Are you sure you don't want me to wait with you until Aiden comes to pick you up?" Aunt Beth asked Harriet when they'd found the jeans for DeAnn's mom and then had tea.

"You don't need to stay and hold my hand. Besides, Aiden isn't coming to pick me up—he's sending a limo to take me to wherever it is we're dining."

"Call me tomorrow and let me know how it went, either way."

"I know, and if it's really exciting, you'll be up till midnight. I got the same instructions from Lauren."

"Mavis and I are playing Bunko at Marjory's tonight, so we *will* be up late…if you want to call." Beth smiled and put her coat on.

Chapter 4

The limo Aiden had promised arrived at seven sharp.

"What do you think, Fred?" Harriet asked her fluffy gray cat as she twirled in a circle and came to a stop in front of the mirror in her front hall. The sleeveless black crepe cocktail dress skimmed the top of her knees. "Are the earrings too much?"

She held her hand over one ear, blocking the sparkle of the diamonds as she turned her head from side to side, evaluating each option in turn.

The doorbell rang, ending the debate.

"Enjoy your night alone," she called to Fred.

She'd taken Scooter, her little dog, to Connie's house for an overnight visit. Scooter had recovered dramatically after being rescued by Aiden from a hoarding home. He'd been well enough to leave the animal hospital several weeks ago but still required medication several times a day.

Connie and her husband Rod had agreed to take him for an overnight visit so Harriet wouldn't have to come home early to administer his nightly dose.

She opened the front door to a short middle-aged man with gray hair. He was dressed in some sort of formal livery. Harriet wondered if Aiden had paid extra for the costume.

"Ms. Truman?" he asked. "I'm Mr. Jones, your driver. Your car awaits."

"Let me get my coat," she said and grabbed her black dress coat from the antique rack by the door.

"May I pour you a glass of champagne?" Mr. Jones asked when Harriet was seated in the white leather passenger area of the limo. He'd picked up a chilled bottle from an ice bucket, wrapping it deftly with a white towel.

"No, thank you, I'm good." Harriet's palms were beginning to sweat. She was happy that Aiden was making an effort, and excited to see what came next, but at the same time, she worried this whole limo-and-champagne routine was a little over-the-top.

"Let me know if I can do anything to make your journey more enjoyable," Mr. Jones said, and when no requests were forthcoming, he closed the door and got into the driver's seat.

If the limo was taking her anywhere in Foggy Point, it would be a short ride, Harriet thought. It soon became clear that Mr. Jones was driving a serpentine route around town, finally arriving at their destination precisely thirty minutes later.

The limo came to a stop, and a moment later, Mr. Jones opened the door. Harriet recognized the location immediately. They were in Smugglers Cove at a restaurant owned by her friend Harold's buddy James. Harold had brought her to the place when she'd first returned to Foggy Point.

She had known from the moment Aiden asked her on this date that whatever he had planned would happen someplace where there would be a good chance someone she knew would bear witness. Foggy Point just wasn't that big, and its selection of event worthy restaurants was limited.

James not only owned the restaurant Aiden had chosen but was also the head chef. There would be at least one witness.

Mr. Jones led Harriet from the parking lot to the door of the eatery, opening it and then handing her off to the hostess.

"I hope you're having a wonderful time," the thin redheaded woman said with a smile. "Your table is ready."

She picked up a leather-bound menu and led Harriet to a table that overlooked the cove marina. Harriet tried to interpret the meaning of the single menu. Either Aiden was waiting at the table or, more likely, hadn't arrived yet. Being a veterinarian, it wasn't unusual for him to have to deal with last-minute emergencies.

Her stomach clenched as the hostess seated her at an otherwise unoccupied table.

The woman offered to bring her a drink, and Harriet asked for sparkling water with lemon. When fifteen minutes had passed without any sign of Aiden, a waiter—Joshua, he said—clad in black trousers and vest and a white open-necked shirt, brought a small white plate with thin-cut carrots and celery and several small pieces of cheese.

"Compliments of Chef James," he said as he set it in front of Harriet. "Can I bring you anything else?"

"No, I'm good," she mumbled. Anyone with eyes could see she wasn't good, but Joshua left without saying anything.

At thirty minutes, Joshua brought warm crusty Kalamata olive bread and fresh butter. Harriet went to the ladies room and splashed cold water on her face, hoping her absence from the table would cause Aiden to arrive but knowing in her heart that she was indulging in magical thinking.

Forty-five minutes brought James to her table.

"Hi," he said. "Do you mind?" He pointed at the chair opposite hers.

"Please," she said, waving absently at the chair.

"This is awkward," he began.

"Oh." Harriet sat straighter. "Do you need this table?"

"No, no, I didn't mean to suggest...I'm sorry, what I meant to ask is, can I do anything? Call someone? Dr. Jalbert made the reservations, and I assume he sent the limo for you, which means you're stuck here until he shows."

"You're assuming he's going to show," Harriet said, her face flaming red.

"I'm sure he's just been detained at the animal hospital," James offered.

"And he's alone, without a phone or anyone who could call for him?"

"I'm sorry," James said again, and looked down at his hands.

They sat in silence for a moment.

"I didn't bring my cell phone," Harriet finally said.

"Would you like to use mine?"

"No. If he's so busy he can't call me, I'm not going to bother him."
A dark part of Harriet wondered if this had been the plan all along.

"I can take you home, if you'd like," James offered.

"I can't let you do that," Harriet said. "You've got a restaurant to run. I'll call my aunt or one of my friends. Do you mind if I sit here a few minutes to steel myself for the explanations?"

"At least stay long enough to eat. I cooked a special beef dish just for you."

"I'm sorry, I can't possibly eat dinner."

"How about some Death by Chocolate?" he offered. "It might be just what you need."

Harriet sighed.

"I'll take that as a yes," he said. "Be right back."

True to his word, in less than five minutes, James came back with two dishes of the warm, dense chocolate cake.

"I hope it's okay that I'm joining you," he said.

"Thanks for not making me suffer through this alone." She took a bite of cake.

"I'm sure there's a reasonable explanation," James started.

"Can we not talk about it?" Harriet took another bite of cake. "I'm going to have to go through all this until I'm ready to scream with the Loose Threads, and then I'll still have Aiden to deal with whenever he surfaces. And frankly, at the moment, I can't think of any excuse that's going to make this okay."

"Can you taste the hint of chili in the cake," James asked her with a crooked smile.

"Tell me about it."

Chapter 5

I f you don't mind waiting until the dinner rush is over, I can take you back to my place," James said, stabbing his fork into the last piece of cake on his plate. "Not for anything," he added in a rush. "I mean, if you want to hide out for a while. This all might be easier to face in the morning, or next week." He gave her his crooked half-smile.

Harriet reached across the table and touched his hand; her own shook in spite of her effort to steady it.

"Thank you, that's very sweet of you, but I'm afraid this won't get easier with time. If I'm not home tonight, it will only make things worse. Besides, it's not exactly the end of the world as we know it. I was stood up. It happens to people all the time, maybe without quite this spectacular of a setup but all the time, nonetheless. If you don't mind, I'd just like to sit here a few more minutes and then call a cab."

"At least let me have someone drive you," James pleaded. "You shouldn't be alone right now."

"Thanks, but I think an anonymous taxi is what I need."

"You do realize that nothing's anonymous in Foggy Point, don't you?"

"You're right, but I don't know the taxi guy yet. And thanks again for this." She pointed at her now-empty dessert plate.

"It was the least I could do. I would have never done this to you or anyone else, but somehow, since it happened at my place, I feel like a coconspirator or something."

"You've been wonderful," Harriet said and looked at him. "I mean it. This could have been so much worse if you weren't here trying to make me feel like less of a loser."

"Well, the next time the good doctor calls for a reservation, he's getting a table by the kitchen door."

Harriet looked toward the kitchen.

"You don't have a table by the kitchen door."

"I'll set one up just for him," James said and looked at Harriet. "Was that a smile?"

She tried to look serious but failed and ended up laughing.

"See, you *have* made it better."

The hostess came in their direction, hovering a discreet distance away and clutching a stack of menus to her chest.

"I think you're needed," Harriet said with a nod to the hostess. "I'm going to go powder my nose, and then, if you could call the taxi, I'll be out of here."

"As you wish." James stood. "Call me if you need anything."

Harriet went to the restroom and, after using the facilities, splashed her face with cold water again. She was not looking forward to the next hour. If she didn't call her aunt and Lauren by midnight, they would call her, so there was no getting around it. They'd made it seem like it was up to her, but she knew they expected a report.

She looked at her face in the mirror. She was pale, with two unnaturally bright spots high on her cheeks. Tears came unbidden to her eyes. She'd been a fool to agree to such a big date, given how things had been between her and Aiden these last two months. She should have known. She'd never make a mistake like this again. She sighed. There was no more stalling.

She went back out into the restaurant.

"Harriet," a soft female voice called to her from just outside the restroom door.

"Carla?" Harriet said. "What are you doing here?"

"Aiden's not coming," the young woman said, looking everywhere but at her.

"Yeah, I figured that out."

"I came to get you," Carla continued. "I'm sorry, I would have been here sooner, but I had to take Wendy to Connie's house first." She referred to her toddler.

"Oh, great, so Connie knows already?" Harriet said.

"I'm sorry," she repeated. "I didn't think I should bring Wendy with me this late."

"No. No, you shouldn't. You shouldn't have come at all. I've got a taxi coming."

"I told the lady at the front that I was here to get you, and she went to the kitchen and talked to the guy, so I think he didn't call the taxi."

"Aiden sent you to get me?" Harriet said a little too loud.

Carla looked down.

"Can we talk outside?" she murmured.

Harriet looked around and realized that people were staring at her. She turned and went to the door, brushing past the hostess before she could hold it for her. She heard Carla apologize to the woman before following her outside.

"If Aiden didn't send you, why are you here?" Harriet asked as she rounded on Carla. "No offense, I guess I'm glad you're here. What I meant to say is, why *didn't* Aiden send you?"

"Aiden has his hands full—"

"Aiden always has his hands full," Harriet yelled. "He can't ever seem to pick up the phone and tell me himself that he won't be coming. He could even text me. Or he could have called James."

Carla stared blankly at her.

"James owns this place. The point is, I'm important enough for Aiden to send a limo to bring me here, just not quite important enough for him to call when he decides to call it all off. Or maybe it was the plan all along. If he wanted to make it clear we're not going to make it as a couple, this did it."

"It's not like that," Carla said, her face turning red. "He wanted to be here."

"Now you're going to defend him?"

"No, I'm not defending him, but you don't understand." Carla hit the button on her key fob, and the doors to her car unlocked.

Harriet went around to the passenger side and got in. Carla joined her and started the car.

"He *couldn't* come," she said. She left the car in park. "He was getting ready for your dinner. He'd laid a tuxedo out on his bed and was polishing his shoes when Michelle called—"

"Of course it would be Michelle. She's been the problem all along."

"She's in the hospital."

"What?" Harriet sank back into her seat, her fury deflated. "What happened?"

"I'm not sure anyone knows for sure, but Aiden was getting ready and his cell phone rang and Michelle said she was at the end of his driveway and she said goodbye and he ran out and went to her car and she was unconscious. He called nine-one-one and they came and got her. He said there was an empty prescription bottle on the floor of the car. He's at the hospital."

"That's all?" Harriet asked. "No explanation as to why she did this?"

"Wendy and I went out to wait with him for the ambulance, and she was moaning and talking, but she didn't make any sense. When they were gone, I went back in the house and gave Wendy her dinner, and when I took her upstairs to get her pajamas, I saw his tuxedo and realized you were waiting for him. I called your house, and when you didn't answer, I was going to call your aunt, but I didn't think you'd want me to."

"Thank you for that," Harriet told her.

Carla turned her face away and continued.

"I went into his office and looked at his scratch paper. He has this big tablet on his desk, and he writes notes about everything he does. There were three different restaurants listed; I got lucky on the second call."

"Exactly what did you say to the restaurant?"

"I told them the truth," she said. "I said I was trying to find my friend, who was waiting for her date, and that he had been called away on a family emergency."

"I'm sorry. I don't mean to take this out on you. I really do appreciate you coming and getting me. And I'm sorry Michelle is in the hospital. I don't like the woman, but she's obviously disturbed if she staged a suicide attempt in her brother's driveway."

"She really did take the pills," Carla protested.

"I know. I'm sure she did. It's just that she did it in such a way there was no chance she wouldn't be found before it was too late. She made sure Aiden was home and nearby before she took the pills, didn't she?"

"I guess so," Carla said. "That's really sick, isn't it."

"Indeed, it is," Harriet agreed.

Carla drove her home in silence.

"You want to come in for a cup of tea?" she asked when Carla had parked.

Carla hesitated and then agreed.

"I guess Connie won't mind a few more minutes."

"I'm sure whatever time you arrive, you're going to have to pry Wendy out of Rod and Connie's clutches."

"I'll start the water," Carla said and headed for the kitchen.

"I'll get the cups and tea," Harriet said and followed her.

Chapter 6

Harriet sighed for the third time, and Carla looked at her through the curtain of dark bangs that skimmed her eyebrows. Neither woman wanted to reopen the wound that if not yet healing was at least not bleeding as profusely, so they sat in Harriet's yellow kitchen, hands wrapped around mugs of tea, steeling themselves for what was to come; whatever that turned out to be.

A soft knock sounded on the quilt studio's exterior door, followed by the noise of the door opening.

"Honey, are you home?" called out Mavis.

"We're in the kitchen," Carla replied immediately.

Harriet smiled to herself. Carla knew her too well; she probably thought Harriet would try to pretend she wasn't there, but Mavis would have seen Carla's car and know they were inside.

Mavis came through the connecting door, followed by Connie and Aunt Beth. Connie busied herself dumping the hot water from the kettle and refilling it before setting it on the stove to heat. Aunt Beth set her purse on the counter and started digging in the cupboards for mugs and tea. Mavis went to Harriet, sat down in the chair beside her and enclosed the younger woman in her arms. Carla got up quietly and drifted over to the sink.

"Grandpa Rod has Wendy tucked in," Connie told her in a quiet tone

"Why don't you let her spend the night with us so you can go back to Aiden's to see what you can find out about Michelle? We'll take her out for pancakes and drop her back by around eleven, if that works for you."

"She'll be thrilled," Carla replied in a hushed voice. "Thank you."

"You know we'll be as thrilled as she is to have her stay over."

"Should I go by the hospital?" Carla wondered.

"No," Beth interjected. "Maybe you could call Aiden on his cell phone. Ask if there's anything you can do. There's no need to draw attention to the fact you went racing out into the night to clean up his...whatever this is." She gestured toward Harriet.

"Let us know if you find anything out," Connie added.

Carla quietly slipped into the studio then left the house.

Tears slid down Harriet's hot cheeks. Aunt Beth went to the half-bath and got a washcloth from the cabinet, wetting it with cold water before returning to the kitchen and handing it to her.

"Here," she said. "Wipe your face and pull yourself together, and let's see if we can make any sense out of this mess."

Harriet took the cloth, but she couldn't see how a person made any sense out of being set up and humiliated.

"Carla only told us she had to go rescue you because Aiden had been called away on a Michelle emergency," Connie said, giving her a starting point to grab on to.

Harriet was pretty sure Carla had told them exactly what she'd told *her*, but she appreciated her friend's efforts to help her regain control of the situation.

"Apparently, Michelle drove to Aiden's, parked at the end of the driveway, took a bottle of pills and then, before she passed out, called Aiden and told him what she'd done."

"I guess that explains why he didn't make it to dinner," Mavis said, and before Harriet could protest, added, "But it doesn't explain why he couldn't call you after he called nine-one-one."

"Or after the ambulance came," Connie said.

"Or even from the hospital," Aunt Beth finished.

Harriet sagged back into her chair.

"So, you all can see it. Why can't he?"

"That girl is a master manipulator," Mavis said. "This is a little extreme even for her, though."

"If it was just one incident, I could get past it. Yes, he left me in a restaurant full of people who all saw me arrive in a chauffeur-driven limo and then be dumped or stood up or whatever it was that happened, but it isn't the first time we've had to cancel our plans so he could run to his sister's side. And usually, it's yet another scheme for her to get money from him. He says he can see it, and that I'd understand if I had a sister, but it doesn't change his behavior."

"He needs to see a counselor," Connie said. "That's not a natural brother-sister relationship. She's using him, and he's letting her."

"He and I have had that discussion, too. He doesn't think their relationship is unusual, so he rejects the idea of talking to anyone. I suggested we talk to Pastor Hafer, but he won't even do that."

"Him leaving you without a call or anything is not acceptable," Aunt Beth said. "I don't care who or what that snake Michelle is to him. Or what new game she's up to."

Mavis got up from the table.

"This calls for something stronger than tea," she announced. "Anyone want a cup of coffee?" She took the carafe from the coffee machine and started filling it with water.

"Sure," Connie said. "We're not going to sleep anytime soon, so why not?"

Aunt Beth and Harriet agreed. Connie collected the empty tea cups and took them to the sink to rinse.

✂ - - - ✂ - - - ✂

The phone rang, and Harriet jumped, spilling hot coffee on her hand.

"Here, honey," Mavis said, handing over her napkin and getting up to fetch another from the holder on the kitchen bar.

"Let the machine pick it up," Beth ordered and went to stand by the phone. When she heard Carla's voice, she picked up the receiver. "What's happening?...Uh-huh..." She said several more times as Carla related her update. "Well, keep us posted, and we'll see you tomorrow at the show."

"What?" Harriet asked, seeing the look on her face. "Whatever it is can't be any worse than being stood up in such a flamboyant way."

"Anyone need a refill?" Mavis asked, allowing Beth time to get seated. Beth waited while she picked up the coffee pot and topped everyone's drink then sat down again.

"Apparently," she began, "this was all a ploy to get Aiden to let Michelle and her kids move in."

"That's what Carla said?" Harriet asked.

"Well, not in so many words, but that's the obvious conclusion. She had her kids in the car, and it turns out she'd only taken six sleeping pills—two is the normal dose. In other words, she took just enough to be real sleepy."

"So, she was never in any danger," Harriet stated.

"No, she wasn't," her aunt confirmed. "She wanted Aiden to think she was. Carla said the kids told her their dad kicked their mom out. A nurse Aiden knows was just getting off work and offered to bring the kids back to his house. She left when Carla got back home, and the kids immediately called their dad in Seattle and asked him to come get them."

"Diós mio," Connie exclaimed. "What a mess."

"It's embarrassing, but I'll live," Harriet said. "You ladies have been very kind, helping me lick my wounds, but it's really not necessary for you to stay any longer. An emergency happened, and as a result, I was stood up. Yes, it hurts that Aiden couldn't spare two minutes to call and let me know, but I'll live to date another day."

"Well, aren't we just being a grownup about all this," Aunt Beth said in a teasing tone.

"I'm just tired," Harriet said. "I don't do drama well."

"Are you going to talk to him tomorrow?" Connie asked.

"I think the real question is am I going to talk to him ever," Harriet replied.

"That's my girl," Mavis said. "I was getting worried there for a minute."

"I'm angry and hurt, and more than a little embarrassed, but I'm not going to let him keep hurting me by dwelling on it. We have a quilt show to set up tomorrow, and I'm going to concentrate on that."

"That sounds like a plan. We've got a busy week coming up," Mavis said. "Shall we meet here around one and drive over to the exhibit hall together?"

"Sure," Harriet said. "Parking close to the building is probably going to be tight. If we take my car, we can all fit."

"I'll call Lauren and see if she wants to come with us," Connie volunteered. "Robin and DeAnn are going together, and I think I heard them making arrangements with Jenny, too. I can talk to Carla tomorrow when she picks up Wendy."

"Are you sure you'll be okay if we leave?" Aunt Beth asked. "I can stay, if you want."

"I'm fine, really. I appreciate the support, but I'm okay. I think I'll read my book and then go to bed and try to pretend this day never happened."

"I'm really sorry your big date ended the way it did," Aunt Beth said.

"You know, it would be a little easier if you didn't phrase it that way," Harriet said with a tired sigh. She got up and began carrying empty cups to the sink.

Connie got her purse and coat then went to Harriet and pulled her into a warm hug.

"Just remember, we all love you," she said.

Mavis joined them, patting Harriet on the back.

"If there's anything I can do, I'm just a phone call away," she said.

"That goes for me, too," Aunt Beth added. "I know you're tough, but even the strong need support sometimes."

Chapter 7

Harriet woke up early the next morning. She'd actually slept well the night before, probably because her dog had slept over at Connie's. Scooter usually got up at least once each night to go outside, and he woke crying in the night several times a week. She could only imagine what sort of treatment had left him with nightmares.

"Hey, Fred," she said when she'd come downstairs and scooped some of the rubbery glop Aiden had prescribed into her cat's ceramic bowl at the end of the kitchen bar. "I know this isn't your favorite, but you have to admit your dandruff has improved."

It hurt to think of Aiden, but she pushed the thought to the back of her mind. Today was a new day, and she'd need all her concentration to be on quilts and the upcoming festival.

She went into the quilt studio and unlocked the door to the outside. No one, including the paper delivery man, used the formal front door to her stately Victorian home. The paper man generally slowed and pitched her paper out without coming close to a full stop, leaving it anywhere from the flower boxes on either side of the small porch to the bushes on the opposite side of her driveway. She opened the door this morning and was surprised to find it lying neatly on the steps beside a white box with a gold bow. She bent to pick it up as a car pulled into her driveway.

"I see I'm not the first one to think of leaving a present on your doorstep," the driver called through the open window of his car.

Tom Bainbridge parked and got out, a flower vase in one hand. Three red roses surrounded a single origami flower that matched a bouquet he had made for her when he was stuck in Foggy Point by the storm.

"Tom?" Harriet met him at the bottom step. "What are you doing here?"

"Good morning to you, too," he countered and handed her the vase.

"What are these for? Have you been talking to the Loose Threads?"

"No, I haven't. You want to invite me in for coffee and tell me what they would have told me if I *had* talked to them?"

"Would you like to come in for coffee?" Harriet asked with a mock bow. "But, no, I don't want to talk about the Threads." She turned and went back up the steps.

"Don't forget this," Tom said and picked the white box up off the porch where she'd set it when she'd taken his flowers. He followed her into the house.

Harriet tried to appear casual as she flicked the small card on top of the box open to see if Aiden had sent a peace offering, but her expression gave her away as she read the name inside. Not Aiden.

"Have I come at a bad time?" Tom asked. "Whatever's on that card clearly wasn't what you were expecting."

For one fleeting moment, she'd allowed herself to believe Aiden had acknowledged what he'd done the night before—but he hadn't. James had sent her a box of his handmade chocolate truffles. *In case you need some chocolate to drown your sorrows in*, the note read.

"You're wrong," she lied. "This box is full of handmade chocolates personally crafted by the owner of the place where I went to dinner last night. He sent them in appreciation of my patronage."

"Do I have *another* rival for your affections? Someone who knows how to make truffles? That will be a hard act to compete with."

"James is just a friend. He's actually a friend of a friend."

"Who clearly wants to be more if that's what he gives you after you eat at his place."

"Could we just drop it?" Harriet asked as she led the way back into the kitchen and filled the coffeemaker carafe with water.

"Sure, whatever you say." Tom sat down at the bar and watched as she emptied the water into the tank of the coffee machine.

"What brings you to our fair town?" Harriet asked, trying for a light tone and falling just short.

"The sixties festival committee asked me to bring some stuff from Mom's school," he said, referring to the folk art school his mother had operated in Angel Harbor. "One of the ladies had taken pottery classes there and knew Mom had a collection of pots from when she first opened the place. They offered me a table in the vendor area to advertise the school in exchange for bringing them, so I agreed."

"So, you'll be around for the whole festival?" she asked.

"You say that like it's a bad thing." He sounded hurt.

"No!" She reached across the bar and put her hand on his arm. "I like having you around. Don't mind me, I'm just in a bad mood."

"Do you want to tell me about it?" Tom took her other hand, drawing her toward him. When his face was inches from hers, he leaned in and kissed her gently on the lips. "Let me make it better."

"You already have." Harriet smiled and pulled her hand from his. She poured coffee into two mugs and gave him one. "Do you have a costume?" she asked, changing the subject.

"As a matter of fact, I do. Mom was a bit of a hoarder when it came to clothes—she had plenty of storage space at the school, so I guess she figured 'Why not?' Lucky for me, she saved choice items from my dad's wardrobe, too. I've got several pairs of bell bottoms, a white patent leather boot-and-belt combo, and a sweet baby-blue leisure suit."

"I see you've been growing your hair out, too."

"It's driving me crazy. Enjoy my luscious locks while you can," he said and ran his hands through his hair. "I'm getting it buzzed as soon as this is all over."

"Buzzed? Really?"

"Well, maybe not that short, but the locks are leaving." He took a sip of coffee. "You sure make a mean cup of coffee, for someone who drinks so much tea."

"Thank you, I think," Harriet said and then proceeded to fill him in on all the plans her community had made for the festival.

"Can we meet for lunch or dinner while I'm here?" he asked when they'd exhausted the topic.

Harriet paused.

"Forget I asked. I told you I wouldn't pressure you about our relationship, and I won't."

"It's not you," she said.

"Aiden's making this way too easy. Maybe you'll decide you can tell me about whatever it is that's got you so upset. And don't try to tell me it's nothing. I can see *something's* happened, and it doesn't take a psychic to figure out Aiden was involved."

"I'm not talking about Aiden with you, but we can do lunch. I have to figure out what all my work shifts are going to be at the show. I'll have to let you know."

"Fair enough," he said. "I've got to go deliver my pots." He stood up, and she joined him. "Enjoy the flowers."

"Thank you," Harriet said. "I'm being rude. It was very kind of you to bring them to me."

"You're very welcome." He leaned in and gave her another quick kiss before turning and going out the door.

"Well, Fred," she said when the door had closed behind Tom. "*He's* good for your mama's bruised ego."

Chapter 8

et me get this straight," Harriet said as she drove her carload of Loose Threads to the exhibit. "We have to hang some of the quilts in the auditorium where the music and other entertainment will be going on?"

"And a few brave volunteers are allowing their quilts to be hung outside on the walkway where the food vendors are," Aunt Beth added.

"Is anyone besides me worried about how well the quilts will be protected in those two places?" Harriet pressed. "What about the white glove people?"

She meant the volunteers who wear cotton gloves to protect the quilts from body oils when they turned the edges of displayed quilts up to reveal the back side for anyone who asked.

"I suppose they'll have a group of volunteers willing to tolerate loud music," Aunt Beth speculated.

"I know Marjory asked for utilitarian quilts to hang in the food area," Mavis said from the back seat. "I brought her one that Curley chewed when she first came to live with me. I cleaned it and repaired the corner. Marjory said that was fine."

Curly was the rescue dog Mavis had adopted.

"There's Robin's car," Connie said and pointed out the side window as Harriet turned into the Foggy Point Exhibition Center parking lot. She found a spot two spaces away from Robin's minivan. DeAnn and Robin got out of the van when Harriet's car stopped.

"Hi, everyone," Robin called out. "We weren't sure where to go, so we decided to wait for you all to arrive."

"Where's Jenny?" Harriet asked.

"She called and said she'd drive herself," DeAnn said. "I guess she has somewhere to go afterward." She shrugged.

"That's weird," Mavis said. "She told me her husband was on a trip with her son, and she was looking forward to having no obligations for the next week."

"Well, that doesn't mean she wasn't going to plan anything until he got back," Aunt Beth said. "She just doesn't have to serve scheduled meals."

"Oh, she gets to live like you and me, huh?" Mavis said, and the two friends laughed in a knowing way.

"Popcorn and pickles," Harriet added.

Carla looked confused.

"What's that mean?" she asked and blushed.

"When I was growing up and was sent to stay with my aunt, we would have popcorn and pickles for dinner at least once each time my uncle Hank was away on a business trip."

"Why would you do that on purpose?" Carla asked, still obviously confused. "My mom and I ate combos like that just before we ran out of food."

No one knew what to say. Carla's face got redder as she realized she'd said something wrong, but still didn't understand what.

Aunt Beth put her arm around the young woman.

"They wouldn't, sweetie. It's a poor joke by two people who've never wanted for food in their lives. We should be more sensitive."

"So, did you eat that or not?" Carla pressed, still confused.

"Yes, we did," Harriet said. "Not because we had to, though. I'll tell you all about it later. You want to help me unload a couple quilts from the back of my car? When they put out the call for quilts for the food area, I got to be one of the drop-off points."

"Did I miss anything?" Jenny asked as she walked up to the back of Harriet's car, her quilt held tightly in her arms.

"We just got here," Harriet said. "These are some of the quilts Marjory rounded up for the food court."

40

"I'm supposed to meet with the two volunteers who are going to stand with my quilt when I'm not there. They're also helping hang quilts, so we thought we'd meet here." Jenny said.

"We better go inside," Aunt Beth called with a glance at the darkening sky. "It looks like it's about to start raining."

✂ - - - ✂ - - - ✂

Harriet and the Threads joined the women assembled in the exhibit hall, where they were divided into groups and given instructions on how to hang their assigned quilts. Jenny took hers and followed the two volunteers and another woman from the show committee.

Her quilt would be hanging in a place of honor in an alcove created from black curtains and with a raised plywood platform. Jenny or one of the other volunteers would stay with it and answer questions about not only about her quilt but pieced quilts in the sixties in general.

"Hey," Lauren said to Harriet an hour later. She'd just come into the building, shaking the rain from her jacket as she took it off. "I had to work with my client," she explained. "Did you know Colm Byrne is setting up in the next building? Not his flunkies, the man himself."

"Really?" Carla said.

"Would I lie to you?" Lauren shot back.

"Can we go see?"

"It's your lucky day, honey," Mavis said. "Marjory's bringing a cart full of quilts for us to take to the auditorium and hang."

"I'm going to see if Jenny's done," Harriet said. "This may be our only chance to see Colm Byrne." She went to find their friend, returning minutes later with Jenny in tow.

"Is that little guy tuning the guitar Colm?" Carla whispered when the group had reached the auditorium.

They stretched their first quilt open and held the edges of the hanging sleeve so that Mavis and Connie could slip the rod that would suspend the quilt into it.

"I have to admit, he looks bigger on TV," Mavis said. "Not that I've spent a lot of time watching him, mind you, but he's been interviewed on all the local morning shows this week."

"I must have missed that," Jenny said, unfolding a cathedral window quilt made from small-scale floral prints in mauves and pinks. "Then again, I was never into that sort of music."

"Not even in the sixties?" Harriet asked.

"Not even then," Jenny said and cringed as someone struck a loud and discordant note on a guitar. "I wanted to grow up to be a concert pianist. I listened to classical music."

"Wow," Carla said.

"I listened to a lot of classical music when I was young, but only because it was part of my parent's carefully orchestrated plan for my education," Harriet said. "I also had to learn how to play piano and cello. I listened to grunge bands whenever no one was looking."

"I thought *my* childhood was weird," Lauren said, "but you definitely have me beat."

"What was so weird about your childhood?" Harriet asked.

"We're talking about you, Miss I Played Piano and Cello While I Was Still in Diapers."

"Hey, it wasn't my fault I was an overachiever by proxy."

"He's staring at us," Carla said in a hushed voice.

"No, he's not," Lauren said. "He's practicing his come-hither look. It's kind of creepy, if you ask me."

"Can you gals help us here?" Aunt Beth asked.

"If you can tear yourself away," Mavis added.

"Why do you have to have so many helpers?" Carla asked Jenny as they prepared a red-and-yellow patchwork crib quilt to be hung.

"The committee chose several quilts that represent the styles of the times to be displayed on those raised platforms. We all have to answer questions about the style of our quilt and quilting in general during the sixties. They finally found a polyester double-knit quilt that looked decent and wasn't too heavy to hang without sagging. One of the Small Stitches quilt group had one that was four-inch squares in crayon colors that had been tied with yarn. The yarn ties were also crayon colors that coordinated with the squares."

"That sounds kind of cool," Harriet said.

"It wasn't actually done in the sixties," Mavis said knowingly. "Joyce's mother had cut all the squares but never made it up. Joyce put it together and did the yarn tying."

"Still sounds interesting," Harriet said.

"Do you have any more wigs with the costume leftovers?" Jenny asked. "The Small Stitches are all wearing polyester outfits and doing their hair up in beehives. My two teammates want to coordinate, and they were hoping to find afro wigs like the one I have."

"I do still have wigs, and if we comb the curls out, they'll match. Tell them to drop by, and I can fix them up."

"Thanks," Jenny looked around to see if the other two were still in the auditorium, to no avail. "I'll let them know."

The music got louder as they continued hanging quilts.

"Can I borrow you ladies for a minute?" asked a skinny man with three lip-rings and a graying goatee that sported two small braids with a turquoise and silver bead at the end of each one, giving him a devilish look. He wore a black T-shirt with *Colm Byrne* written in large orange letters diagonally across the front and a schedule of tour dates on the back. His bare forearms were covered with blue butterflies, Indian gods and, on his left arm, the word *peace* with a stylized peace symbol inside the C. Harriet guessed he was a manager of some sort.

"We need a row of people so we can fine-tune the lighting angles. We're used to playing much bigger venues, so we have to experiment a little and see if we've toned it down enough."

"I think our star couldn't stand it that we didn't immediately drop our quilts and run to the stage as soon as he strummed his first chord," Lauren whispered.

"We'll finish hanging our last two quilts, and then we'd be happy to help you out," Connie answered for the group, using her best first-grade-teacher voice.

The man turned and went back to the stage, proving that even a road-hardened tour manager wasn't immune to its effect.

"I'm going to go find the restroom," Jenny said when the last quilt was up and the group had started toward the stage.

"I've never been in the first row at a rock concert," Harriet said and sat down in the middle of the row.

"I've never been to a rock concert at all," Carla answered in a hushed voice.

"Not even at the county fair?" Lauren asked.

Carla's face burned scarlet.

"We never had the money when I was little, and then I had Wendy."

"We're going to fix that," Lauren said, not bothering to whisper. "And I don't mean this aging has-been." She gestured toward the stage, and Harriet reached out and pushed her hand down.

"Would you be quiet! He can hear you."

"And I care why?" Lauren shot back. She turned back to Carla. "When someone really good comes to the Tacoma Dome I'm getting you tickets. If Terry isn't in town, I'll take you myself."

Carla's boyfriend Terry was in some sort of military intelligence group that meant he came and went at unpredictable times, doing things he couldn't talk about.

Lauren settled back into her seat.

"Since when did you take over Carla's social education?" Harriet asked her.

"Since you're too busy with all your boyfriend drama to help her out. And I can't see your aunt or Mavis taking her to a concert."

"That's the truth," Mavis affirmed.

Further conversation was made impossible as Colm Byrne strode onto center stage and strummed the opening chords to one of his hit songs, dramatically raising his arm after each stroke. A black-and-orange dragon covered most of his arm; a stylized peace symbol was worked into the dragon's shoulder. He pranced and danced and belted out song after song, one running into another, while the sound man adjusted speakers, and the lights bounced behind him and in front of him and twice hit the quilters straight in the face, blinding them momentarily.

Harriet wondered, and not for the first time, why Irish and British singers didn't seem to have an accent when they sang, and yet were sometimes almost unintelligible, their accents were so thick, when they spoke. She decided that if she got the chance to talk to the manager again, she was going to ask.

The show went on for a full twenty minutes before the skinny man raised his arm, made a circle in the air and then drew his hand across his neck. The music stopped as quickly as it had begun.

"Everybody good?" he asked, looking first at the men gathered around the soundboard, located in an enclosure halfway up the center seating section, and then into the wings and to the back of the auditorium at the lighting managers.

"Okay, then, there'll be a taco bar set up in the big truck at seven. Until then, try to get some rest—we've got a full schedule coming up."

Byrne went off the left side of the stage, only to reappear in the far aisle at the seating level moments later.

"What did you ladies think?" he asked as he approached Harriet, Carla and Lauren, who were still in their seats. Mavis and Connie and Aunt Beth had gone the opposite direction to straighten the last quilt they'd hung before being drafted as audience. The words rolled off his tongue with a charming lilt.

"That was great," Carla gushed, her face lighting up.

"We were just discussing the fact that Carla's never been to a rock concert before," Lauren said. "You're her first."

"I hope I didn't disappoint," he said with a slight bow.

"It was...amazing," Carla stammered.

"I'm surprised someone of your..." Lauren searched for a word.

"Renown," Harriet supplied.

"Yes, someone of your renown would come to such a small town event as our sixties festival," Lauren finished.

"Normally, I wouldn't," Colm said with a practiced smile. "As you can see, we're equipped for a much larger venue, but when an old friend calls, what can you do?" His Irish accent seemed to get stronger as he spoke. "Wait here a second."

He jogged to the side door to the stage, opened it and spoke to someone on the other side. He returned with three lanyards, large yellow cards swinging from their ends.

"Here you go, ladies," he said. "They're good for any of the performances. Come back beforehand and meet the band before we go on."

"Thank you so much," Carla said, gushing enough for all three of them. Harriet said a polite thank-you, and Lauren managed a tight smile.

"I suppose this means we *have* to go now," Lauren said when Colm was gone.

"What an ingrate," Harriet shot back. "Lots of girls would toss their panties on stage for this privilege."

Lauren hit her shoulder, but Harriet just laughed.

"Where have you been?" Lauren demanded of Jenny when they had rejoined the group. She had just come up from the back of the auditorium.

"I ran into the quilt history chairman, and she wanted to go over our information with us again. Now she *formally* wants each trio to dress alike. And she wanted to be sure we didn't overlap on our stories. I tried to reassure her that I didn't have the slightest inclination to talk about mustard-yellow polyester or peach-colored shell shapes, but I guess the trio with the Amish quilt wants to tell the entire history of hand-quilting and how their quilt fits in the whole picture."

"Are they wearing Amish costumes?" Harriet asked.

"They are, and before you ask, no, none of them is Amish."

"Isn't that sacrilegious?" Lauren asked.

"Perhaps," Jenny said. "But fortunately for the organizers, there aren't a lot of Amish in northwest Washington to call them out on it."

"I'll be glad when this is all over," Connie said with a sigh. "I've got to make baby quilts for the unwed mothers group. We've got three girls having their babies next month, and one is having twins. And this bunch didn't take to quilting the way our Carla did."

"I think we're done here for the day," Aunt Beth announced. "Everyone ready to split?"

Harriet looked at her aunt.

"I'm practicing the lingo of the times, honey," she said and laughed.

Harriet shook her head. It was going to be a long week.

Chapter 9

"Are you sure you're okay with me leaving?" Aunt Beth asked Harriet for what had to be the tenth time.

"I'm *fine*. My tables are all set up, which I know you know because you and Mavis helped me. I've got my box of quilting samples right here." She pointed to a large plastic tub sitting by the studio door. "I have my business cards, order forms, a paper printout of my current calendar, and two thousand pens with *Quilt As Desired* and my phone number on them.

"I also have a baggie full of cheap tape measures with the same info, only to be given to people who seem serious about having me stitch their quilt. Am I forgetting anything?"

"Do you have some bottles of water? And a healthy snack?"

"You know I do. Now, go, help Jorge. He actually needs it."

"You're sure?" Beth asked, causing Harriet to roll her eyes and sigh loudly.

"I haven't been twelve for a long time, and having a fight with Aiden didn't change that."

"I'm not sure why they decided to start this shindig at five o'clock on a Wednesday," Beth grumbled as she put on her coat then wrapped her scarf around her neck.

"I think it was something about wanting to shake out any problems before the out-of-town crowd arrives on the weekend."

"Couldn't we have done that Thursday morning when it would have been light out?"

"I'm just guessing here, but I'll bet someone thought that Twinkies, Bugles stuffed with cheese from a can, and cocktail weenies were a hard sell as breakfast fare."

"I suppose, and I guess it would have been too hard to make a brunch out of Instant Breakfast."

"Jorge told me he's been working on a few modern twists on the old classics. Something about dipping Twinkie slices in chocolate. Ritz crackers, too."

"Sadly, that isn't a new idea. The crackers, anyway. Ten or fifteen years ago, everyone and their brother were dipping any salty snack they could get their hands on in chocolate—potato chips, pretzels, peanuts. You name it, I've had it delivered to my door by a well-meaning friend on a decorative holiday plate."

"Was any of it good?" Harriet asked hopefully.

"That's beside the point," Beth said and glared at her niece. "Just because you *can* do something doesn't mean you should."

"Oh, live a little, Auntie."

"I'm going to gain five pounds just working in Jorge's booth."

Harriet laughed. Her aunt counted calories like an anorexic both for herself and her niece, but somehow it didn't seem to result in any noticeable reduction in her aunt Beth's comfortably plump girth.

"See you there," Beth called as she went out into the rain.

✂- - - ✂- - - ✂

Harriet was surprised by the size of the crowd that showed up for the festival opening. The aisles of the vendor hall had a steady flow of people browsing from booth to booth.

"Harriet," Lauren said in a bright voice, "this is Kathy Ramsey. She lives in Sequim and is interested in having you quilt her latest project."

Lauren handed her a blank order form and a pen on a clipboard. Harriet took them and guided Kathy to a chair at the back of the booth. She pulled the box of quilting samples from under the table and began discussing possible patterns for the quilt top Kathy described.

"Thanks for helping me in the booth tonight," Harriet said to Lauren when Kathy had placed her order and moved on to the next booth in their aisle.

"It's purely selfish. Things were dull in this town till you moved in. I'm enjoying my front row seat to the train wreck that is your love life. I don't want you to pull up stakes and move."

"Thanks, I think," Harriet said and shook her head.

"Isn't that that stage manager guy?" Lauren asked and pointed to the other end of the aisle and the small man with the beaded braids in his beard.

"Looks like it. I wouldn't have pegged him for a quilter, though."

"If long-haul truck drivers can be quilters, why not roadies?"

"I'm still having a hard time picturing those hulking, tattooed, beer-bellied truckers quilting at the truck stop between loads. I know it's true, but still I can't quite get the right visual on that one."

"Incoming," Lauren announced and stepped into the aisle to snare her next target.

An hour passed before the crowd thinned again.

"Do you need a break?" Robin asked. She and DeAnn had been waiting in the aisle for the last customer to move on.

"We're fine," Harriet said.

"Yes, we need a break," Lauren said at the same time.

"Go," DeAnn said. "We can hold down the fort here. Most of the people are migrating to the food court, so you shouldn't be busy. The food vendors are doing a sort of happy hour."

"Each food booth has some offering for a dollar," Robin said. "You should go while they still have everything."

"Okay, then. If anyone comes by and is interested, just put their name and number on an order form, and I can call them back to schedule a time to talk about it."

"We can handle it," Robin assured her.

"Let's go see if Jenny wants to come with us," Harriet suggested. "We have to walk through the main exhibit hall to get to the food court, so it's not out of our way."

"Sure," Lauren said. "Maybe we can invite the Amish group and the Vienna Boy's Choir while we're at it."

"Would you stop it? We're just going to get Jenny. She needs a break, too."

49

"Connie and Mavis probably already took her."

"Geez, listen to you. We have to walk right past her area. What's the problem?"

"Besides having to be on our best behavior? Can you imagine her eating a chocolate-covered Twinkie? Or a cocktail weenie?"

Lauren did have a point. Jenny's silver pageboy haircut was never out of place, her outfits always coordinated, and Harriet had never seen her take more than a taste of junk food—just enough to not offend the others by being too perfect.

"Okay, just promise me you'll have a Twinkie with me, no matter what Jenny does or doesn't eat."

"I just have to dodge my aunt."

"I'll distract her, and you buy two of them from Jorge."

"Agreed," Harriet said and led the way to the door that connected the south vendor hall with the main exhibit hall.

"Is that Jenny?" Lauren whispered as they approached Jenny's quilt. With her Afro wig, tie-dyed tunic and large round-lensed sunglasses, the person standing next to the quilt was unrecognizable.

"How's it going?" Harriet asked when they stopped in front of her.

"I can tell I'm going to get real tired of saying the same words over and over again," Jenny replied.

"You're not going to make it if you're crumbling after two hours," Lauren said.

"I didn't say I was crumbling. People so far have asked the same questions over and over, starting with 'Is this really a quilt from the sixties?' and usually going on to 'Did you really make this quilt?'"

"Can't they match your name tag with the sign?" Lauren asked, pointing to the quilt and the prominent sign pinned to its edge, stating it was made by Jenny Logan.

"Apparently not," Jenny said with a smile.

"Can you take a break?" Harriet asked.

"I'd love one. Let me tell Pamela she's on." Jenny walked to the opposite side of her display area and spoke to a slender woman sitting on a chair watching the crowd.

"Can you take over for a few minutes?" she asked.

"Sure, let me get my wig and sunglasses on." Pamela Gilbert was wearing a tunic that also appeared to be tie-dyed.

"Your costumes are great," Harriet said with true admiration.

"We found three similar tunics, and then my daughter over-dyed them in rainbow colors," Pamela said proudly.

"We weren't sure which one of you was which until Jenny spoke," Harriet marveled.

"I'm happy to take a turn," Pamela said brightly.

"I won't be gone long," Jenny removed her glasses and pulled her wig off. She'd pinned her own hair into two bun-like curls behind each ear. "I wish I could take these hairpins out," she complained. "Between the pins and the wig, it feels like bugs are crawling over my scalp." She pulled a small triangle scarf from her skirt pocket and centered it over her hairdo, tying it at the nape of her neck. "These little scarves were real popular back in the day."

She patted her head with her hand.

"The food is going to be gone if we don't get moving," Lauren prodded.

"I can catch up if you want," Jenny said. "I need to stop at the restrooms on our way. They're right by the door out to the courtyard."

"Okay, we'll meet you outside the main doors," Harriet said and headed for the front of the building.

"Jenny seems tense," Lauren commented when she and Harriet were outside. The scent of frying food floated on the slight breeze. "For whatever reason, she didn't want her old quilt in the show. They almost bullied her into participating. I don't know what the problem is or was, but it's clear there was one."

"There must be a line in the restroom," Harriet said and looked at her watch. More than five minutes had passed.

"I told you we should have just gone ourselves," Lauren shot back and resumed rocking from her toes to her heels.

Someone screamed as the main double doors burst open and a crowd of people pushed out into the courtyard. Another loud shriek followed, then a man's voice shouting for someone to call 911.

"What's going on?" Lauren pushed past Harriet, heading for the open doors.

Harriet grabbed her arm.

"Don't go back inside until we know what's going on," she cautioned.

"Jenny's in there," Lauren said, dragging Harriet with her as she continued toward the door. "You're the one who always wants to stick her nose into everything. Don't you think we should see if she's okay?"

"I'm trying to mend my ways, since jumping into the middle of things hasn't worked out so well."

"What do you mean?" Lauren stopped suddenly, her progress blocked by a crush of people filling the doorway. "The bad people we've encountered have ended up in jail—that's a pretty good result, if you ask me."

"Easy for you to say—I'm the one who's been bashed in the head, had a shoulder injured and had to hobble around on crutches for weeks."

"Oh, wah-wah-wah. Always thinking of yourself, aren't you?"

"Since when have you wanted to risk anything to help anyone in trouble?"

Lauren turned and stared at her.

"I've done more than my share in your little adventures, if that's what you want to call them."

"I didn't say you haven't been helpful. It's just that you're usually the one trying to talk me *out* of getting involved in other people's business."

If Lauren made a biting retort, it was lost when Jenny was forced out the door by a large woman who was determined to leave and was willing to shove anyone who got in her way. She bumped into Lauren, almost knocking them both to the ground; only Harriet's proximity to a support post prevented them all from falling over. The cement column slammed into her spine with bruising force.

"What's going on in there?" she asked Jenny when they had all taken a step apart and regained their balance.

"I don't know. I was in the restroom, and when I came out everyone was screaming and heading for the door. There was nothing to do but go along with the flow."

"Did you hear anything else, or smell smoke or anything?" Lauren asked.

"No, the restrooms are so close to the front, I couldn't see anything but the backs of the people surrounding me. And the only noise in there was screaming, and someone calling for anyone with a phone to dial nine-one-one."

"Maybe someone had a heart attack or something," Lauren said and turned toward the food booths. The sound of sirens approaching became louder.

"I want to go check on my quilt," Jenny said.

"I'll come with you," Harriet said, "but I think we're going to have to wait a minute until the crowd clears."

Lauren gave Harriet a questioning look. Harriet shrugged. Jenny's behavior seemed a bit insensitive to her, but then, everyone reacts to shock in their own way. Who were they to judge?

"I don't know if you noticed, but there are life-sized statues of historic figures every so many feet around the outside walls of the main room. There are exit doors between each pair of statues. The one nearest my quilt was propped open to let some air in."

"Okay," Harriet said and turned. "Let's go see if it's still open."

It took a few minutes, and they had to scale a thigh-high cement support wall, but the trio found the door Jenny had described, and it was still partially open. Jenny pulled it wider and stepped inside.

"No!" she screamed, over and over again.

Harriet and Lauren hurried through the door, pushing her aside so they could see. Someone was lying on the platform in front of Jenny's quilt.

Jenny made her way to the small stage, and as a few people recognized her, they stepped aside. Harriet followed and could see Pamela flat on her back, a paramedic kneeling beside her, lifting first one eyelid then the other, shining a pocket penlight in each eye in turn. He pulled away from the body and shook his head from side to side, once.

Pamela was gone.

Chapter 10

I t was never a good thing when the first responders stopped moving quickly and started picking up their refuse. That was what was happening as Harriet watched Jenny run her hand over her quilt.

Pamela had been standing beside it when she was shot, but now, as she lay on the stage surrounded by torn packages and discarded tubing, there was at first little evidence that anything out of the ordinary had happened. She could have decided to take a nap, aside from the small dark hole in the middle of her forehead and an expanding halo of blood.

Jenny had neatly sidestepped Pamela's body when she went up the stairs to the platform. She hadn't looked at the body since; her eyes had remained fixed on her quilt.

"You ladies need to leave." Officer Hue Nguyen approached the stage where Harriet and Lauren waited for Jenny to finish her inspection, if that's what she was doing.

"We were just checking on Jenny's quilt," Harriet explained. It sounded strange to her, so she could just imagine how weird it seemed to Officer Nguyen. A woman had been murdered, and they were checking on a quilt.

"We'll leave now," Lauren said. "Come on, Jenny, we have to leave so the officer can do his job."

Jenny didn't appear to have heard.

"Jenny!" Harriet said in a firm tone. "We have to go now."

Jenny shivered then turned and came down the steps, rejoining her friends. The trio started to leave, but Nguyen stopped them.

"Are you three involved in this?" he asked without a hint of friendliness in his tone. He had been the responding officer several times in the past when Harriet was involved in misadventures. It was amazing to her that he treated them as if they were the criminals every time, even though it hadn't once been true.

"No," Lauren said and turned toward the door they'd come in through.

A part of Harriet wanted to follow her without saying anything else, but she couldn't.

"This quilt is Jenny's. Until a few minutes ago, she was standing on this stage and answering questions about it," she said. "Lauren and I went outside, and Jenny was in the restroom when this..." She gestured toward Pamela. "...happened."

Lauren poked her in the arm.

"Don't volunteer anything," she whispered.

"I've got your names," Nguyen said, tapping his notebook against his palm. "The detectives will contact you for your statements."

"We don't have statements," Lauren said. "We weren't here, and we didn't see anything."

Nguyen glared at her.

"I know, don't leave town," she said with a smirk. "I watch TV."

It was Harriet's turn to take Lauren by the arm and pull her to the door. Jenny followed silently, her face blank.

"We better find Aunt Beth and Mavis and tell them what happened," Harriet said as they circled around the building and on to the courtyard. The crowd was buzzing with talk of the shooting.

"What on earth happened in there?" Aunt Beth asked when they made their way through the line at Jorge's food cart. "People've been talking about someone being shot in the exhibit hall. I didn't recognize the name they said, and I'm embarrassed to say I was relieved that I didn't."

"It was one of Jenny's substitutes," Harriet told her.

"I'm so sorry," Beth said to Jenny, who had still not said anything.

"It's very sad, I'm sure," Jenny said in a flat voice. "I didn't really know her. We only met a few days ago."

"Well, it's a shame. I hope it doesn't scare people off our event." Aunt Beth made up three snack sampler plates, including the chocolate-coated Twinkies. "You all probably need a little chocolate after this," she said and handed them each a plate. "It's on the house," she added when Jenny started to dig in her purse. "Go find Mavis and tell her what happened before you go back," she said as they turned to go.

"Will do," Harriet said and followed Lauren to a table under one of the open tents that had been set up just beyond the food carts.

"Did Pamela have problems?" Lauren asked Jenny as she popped a slice of Twinkie into her mouth.

Jenny stared into space.

"Jenny?" Harriet asked when she still hadn't answered after a long moment. "Are you okay?"

"No, I'm not okay. That could have been me...or Sharon. We all three had the same outfit, hair and glasses. Whoever shot Pamela wasn't close by. Someone would have seen them if they were. How do we know they were after Pamela?"

"How do we know they weren't" Lauren challenged.

Jenny glared at her but remained silent.

"Jenny," Harriet said gently, "are you in some kind of trouble?"

"I don't want to talk about this anymore," Jenny said and stood up. "They aren't going to let us near my quilt anymore tonight. I think I need to go home."

"Do you want me to drive you?" Harriet asked.

"No, I'll be fine. I'll talk to you tomorrow." She turned and left the food court.

"Well, that was weird, even for the Loose Threads," Lauren said.

"We better find the rest of the Threads and let them know what's going on. Jenny's going to need support, and I'm not sure we're the ones who can give it to her."

"She's got some explaining to do, if you ask me," Lauren said. "These Twinkies aren't bad." She popped a second slice into her mouth before tossing her empty plate into a garbage bin.

They found Mavis at a booth in the north vendor area, on the opposite side of the exhibit hall from where Harriet had her booth.

She was selling raffle tickets for a quilt, which would help fund improvements to the restrooms at Fogg Park that the homeless people who lived in the park had access to. The Methodist Church was organizing the project and had several fundraisers planned. They hoped to add an indoor shower and a coin-operated gas stove and tables in a covered outdoor eating area.

The quilt was composed of a combination of blocks that depicted trees, cabins, mountains, birds and other country-related images, with vines and flowers connecting them into a whole. It reminded Harriet of a block-of-the-month quilt she'd seen at a show in Tacoma.

"How's it going at your end?" Mavis asked when she saw her friends approach.

"Haven't you heard?" Lauren asked.

"Heard what?"

"Someone's been shot in the main exhibit hall," Harriet explained.

"What? How could someone be shot in a room full of people? Who was it, and did they catch the shooter right away? Was anyone else hurt?"

"Whoa," Lauren said and held her hands up.

"First, it wasn't anyone we know," Harriet said. "It was one of the women attending to Jenny's quilt. They didn't catch anyone. Judging by the hole in her forehead, I'm guessing she was shot from across the room."

"We were outside when it happened," Lauren added. "Jenny was inside, but in the bathroom."

"As far as we know," Harriet said.

"What do you mean?" Lauren turned to look at Harriet to see if she was serious.

"All I'm saying is, we were outside, so we have no way of knowing if Jenny was in the bathroom or not. She told us that's where she was going, but we were outside before she went in."

"Oh, honey, you don't think she had anything to do with this, do you?" Mavis asked. She started to take off the deep-pocketed apron she wore while she was selling tickets. "Where is she? She needs us if she's involved in some way."

"No rush," Lauren said. "She took off already."

"Does she know the family?"

"She claims she didn't know the woman until they were teamed up by the committee to show her quilt," Harriet offered.

"Why would she go running off if she didn't even know the victim?" Mavis asked. "Her husband is on a hunting trip in Africa, so she's not going home for comfort."

"The exhibit hall is closed for the rest of tonight, so she said she wasn't needed and left," Harriet said.

"She was acting really weird, even for a Loose Thread," Lauren told Mavis.

"Yeah," Harriet agreed. "She told us that since they were all dressed in the same shirt, wig and glasses, the bullet could have been meant for any of them."

"That sounds like she had some reason to believe it could have been meant for her," Mavis said thoughtfully. "Did she give any indication as to why she said that?"

"No, but I have to agree with Lauren—she was acting weird. When we went back to see if her quilt had been damaged, she stepped past Pamela like she was a bag of trash on the rug."

"Yeah," Lauren jumped in. "Then she was fondling her quilt like *it* was the one who had been shot." She finished with a shiver. "It was kinda creepy."

"Do the rest of the Threads know?" Mavis asked.

"No. I mean, *we* haven't told them," Harriet said. "Aunt Beth had already heard, but Robin and DeAnn are watching my table in the south vendor hall, and we haven't seen Connie or Carla yet."

"Connie and Carla are here, two rows over, helping people arrange precut fabric into patterns that other ladies are sewing into blocks for baby quilts for the hospital. I'll go talk to them while you two go tell Robin and DeAnn. We all need to talk."

"Where shall we meet?" Harriet asked.

"Do you mind us coming to your place? It's too cold to sit outside here for very long."

"Sure," Harriet agreed.

She and Lauren went back outside. There was a door at the back of the room that led into the exhibit hall, but Harriet assumed the police wouldn't be letting people through that way for the time being.

"What's going on?" Robin asked as soon as they were in earshot.

"Someone said there's been a shooting," DeAnn said.

"Yeah," Lauren answered, "the woman who took over for Jenny when we took her for break."

"Is she badly hurt?" Robin asked.

"If you consider dead to be badly hurt, then, yeah."

"Stop," Harriet said and glared at Lauren. "Mavis suggested we meet at my house after we finish here. The woman who was shot was one of Jenny's replacements—they were all dressed alike. And Jenny's been acting odd since the shooting."

"I'm sure she's upset," DeAnn said. "Did she know the woman very well?"

"She says not," Harriet answered. "But then as soon as we were outside, she took off. And Mavis says her husband is out of town, so she's going to an empty house."

"If she's *going* home," Robin said thoughtfully. "Why would she run off like that if she didn't know the woman? I mean, I'm sure any of us would be upset if someone we worked with was shot, but we'd want to talk it over with the rest of the group, not run away."

"Maybe she's worried that she was the intended victim," Harriet suggested. "It was *her* quilt, after all, so most people who had seen the advertising would expect that she'd be the one talking about it, especially on the first night."

"She's been acting weird ever since the committee first asked if they could feature her quilt," Lauren pointed out.

"I agree," Robin said. "Her reaction to being asked was way off. Think about it. What would you say if they had asked you for one of your first quilts? It might not be comparable to something you'd make now, but would it freak you out?"

"Good point," Harriet said. "But who knows what memories that particular quilt might hold for her. Maybe her dead mother helped her make it."

"Or she cried on it when her first boyfriend dumped her," Lauren added with enthusiasm. "Or—"

"We get the idea," DeAnn said, cutting Lauren off. "But even if that was the case, it's been—what?—forty, forty-five years since that quilt was made? How upset can you still be over a lost boyfriend?"

"We aren't going to get any answers standing here," Robin said. "I'm going to swing by home and make sure things are under control. I'll come by after that."

"Me, too," DeAnn said. "David is with the kids, but I should check in if I'm going to be gone longer than I told him."

"I've got to wait until they close the vendor hall so my stuff will be secure," Harriet said. "Let yourself in if you get there before me." She had changed the locks on her house after it became apparent that Aunt Beth and her friends had given keys to half of Foggy Point when Beth had owned the house. Several of the Loose Threads had keys to the new locks; the rest used a key hidden under the planter box next to the door.

"So, what do you really think is going on?" Lauren asked Harriet when DeAnn and Robin had left.

"I don't know."

"But if you had to guess…"

"If I had to hazard a guess, I'd say Jenny knows something she's not telling the rest of us."

"That's what I'm thinking. I have no idea what that could be, but there's something there."

"Do you know how long she's lived in Foggy Point?"

"Now that you mention it, I don't. I just assumed she was descended from a serving wench on Cornelius Fogg's pirate ship, like almost everyone else in town."

"She talks about her son and daughter-in-law a lot, and I know her son went to school with Aiden." Harriet's stomach spasmed at the mention of Aiden's name, and she tried to block the flood of emotion that came with it.

"You're pathetic," Lauren said and shook her head.

"What?" Harriet felt her face coloring as she said it.

"It's like junior high with you and He Who Shall Apparently Not Be Named Without You Getting All Weepy. You need to work on shielding your emotions a little better if you don't want to share all with the Threads."

"Thanks for the advice. I suppose you're an expert?"

"The fact that you don't know tells you that I am. At least as far as blocking emotions goes."

She had a point, Harriet thought. She had no clue about Lauren's love life.

"Back to the topic at hand," Lauren continued. "I can do some digging on the computer after our meeting. Maybe I can find something."

A woman wearing a pink T-shirt with *she* who dies with the most fabric wins emblazoned across the chest in purple came up and asked about Harriet's long-arm quilting service, ending the discussion.

Chapter 11

There were several cars parked at Harriet's house when she pulled into her garage, but her aunt's silver Beetle was not among them.

"Beth decided to stop by Jenny's house and try to get her to come here with her," Mavis explained when Harriet came into the kitchen. "I hope you don't mind I'm making coffee and tea."

"Of course not, you know you don't need to ask."

"Do you have anything we could put out for people to nibble on?"

"I have hummus and could cut up some veggies."

Mavis looked at her over the top of the reading glasses perched on the end of her nose.

"Or I have some brownies in the freezer. It would only take a minute to thaw them in the microwave."

"That would do nicely," Mavis said and continued putting coffee into the filter basket on the coffee machine.

"Does anyone know the woman who was shot?" Robin was asking when Harriet entered her studio carrying a plate of warm brownies and a stack of paper napkins.

Carla and Connie shook their heads no.

"She used to come in the video store," DeAnn said, referring to her family's business. "I haven't seen her lately, but then again, I haven't been working much since we got Kissa."

DeAnn and her husband had adopted a baby girl the previous fall and that, along with her two sons' activities, meant she was too busy to help out at the store on a regular basis.

"I don't remember anything out of the ordinary. She generally rented from the new-arrivals shelf," She shrugged. "Not that movie habits tell you anything."

No one else knew Pamela, and the group sat, each one lost in her own thoughts, as Harriet carried the brownie plate to each one in turn, handing out a napkin as she went.

Mavis came in with the coffee carafe a moment later.

"This is decaf, and there's hot water in the teapot if anyone prefers that," Mavis said as she filled cups and handed them around.

The outside studio door opened, and Aunt Beth came in followed by Jenny. Harriet got up and took their coats, while Mavis handed them cups of hot coffee. Connie pulled two more chairs into the loose circle they had formed in the middle of the studio space.

"Did Jorge sell a lot of food?" Mavis asked.

"He did okay," Beth answered. "Most people left early."

The group fell silent again.

"Jenny," Aunt Beth began, "can you tell us what's got you so rattled?"

"A woman was killed tonight," Jenny said, her voice tight.

"Everyone knows how upsetting that is," Harriet said. "But if I understood you right, you didn't even know her."

"If you had come five minutes later, that could have been me."

"Or the killer could have had to wait five more minutes," Harriet said gently. "If you didn't know Pamela, how do you know she wasn't the intended target?"

"I don't, I suppose."

"Would you like us to contact your husband?" Mavis asked.

"He and Mark are on a hunting trip in Africa. They've been planning it for two years. I'm not going to interrupt them for this. I'm just a little shaken. I'll be fine after I've had time to process this and rest a little."

Robin had been silently studying Jenny, Harriet noticed. As a lawyer, she had probably had more experience deciphering whether people were being truthful or not.

"When I was in law school," Robin finally said, "we had a class on body language. You know, to help us tell if a witness was being truthful or not."

"I am not some kind of criminal," Jenny snapped and started to rise.

Mavis stilled her with her hand.

"I'm sure that's not what Robin is saying," she said.

"Actually, I'm not saying you're a criminal," Robin said to Jenny, "But I am saying you're not being truthful. We're not the police, and I'm not your attorney—we're your friends. If you're in some kind of trouble, maybe we can help you. We can't do anything if you don't tell us what's going on."

"I don't know what's going on," Jenny said.

"That I believe," Robin said.

"There must be something that's got you spooked," Harriet said.

"It's the clothes," Jenny finally said, a single tear slipping down her cheek.

"The clothes?" Harriet echoed.

Aunt Beth got up and crossed to Harriet's desk, where she picked up a box of tissues and brought it back, plucking out two and pressing them into Jenny's hand.

"I had an outfit very like the one I was wearing tonight," Jenny began. Harriet noticed for the first time that she had changed from her sixties outfit into a silver velour jogging suit.

"And?" Lauren prompted.

"And I hope you all will still want to be my friends after I tell you all this."

"You know there is nothing you can say that will cause us to not be your friends," Mavis assured her.

"I've been lying to you all for a very long time." She paused and took a deep breath. "Not exactly lying, but being dishonest, all the same. I've let you believe certain things and not corrected you when you came to the wrong conclusions. In fact, I led you there."

"Honey, you're going to have to tell us a little more than that," Mavis said.

"I know, I'm sorry, I–it's just hard after all this time." Jenny sipped her coffee, stalling. "I'm not from Foggy Point."

"Well, that's hardly a crime," Lauren said.

"I've lived here for some time, but not as long as I've let you believe. I didn't graduate from the University of Wisconsin. In fact, I didn't graduate from anywhere—not even high school. At least, not in the normal sense.

"I grew up in a commune in Georgeville, Minnesota. It was started by a couple of assistant professors from Smith College. They'd been fired for their liberal views so they 'tuned in, turned on and dropped out,' as the saying went back then. They did value education, so we were educated, but they didn't believe in 'the man,' or 'the system,' so we were never tested by the state or given real diplomas."

"Who were 'we?'" Harriet asked.

"All of us at the commune who were school-aged. I thought I'd put that time of my life behind me years ago. I moved on. I have a wonderful husband and son. I don't like thinking about those times." She started crying again. "This whole festival has brought it all back."

"Honey," Mavis said in a soothing voice, "nothing you've told us is anything to be ashamed of. That all happened a long time ago; it's not who you are today. You're right. You have a wonderful family and a group of friends who care a lot about you."

"You still haven't told us anything about why you would think that bullet had your name on it," Harriet said.

"Shush," Aunt Beth told her. "Jenny is upset enough. We don't need to hear anything else tonight."

Harriet looked at Lauren. She could see there were at least two people in the room who wanted to hear more tonight. But then, maybe that was because they were the two who had seen Jenny step past Pamela's body as though it didn't exist.

"Is there anything about your time living in the commune that would cause you to worry about our festival forty some years later?" Robin asked.

"No," Jenny said.

Harriet looked at Lauren and could tell they were thinking the same thing. You didn't have to be a lawyer or a body language expert to tell Jenny was still lying.

"Did you sign up any new customers?" Aunt Beth asked Harriet, ending any further discussion of Jenny's past.

Harriet gave a detailed accounting of her time in the booth, complemented by snide observations from Lauren. Robin and DeAnn told them about the customers they'd helped, but it was clear the Loose Threads were only half-listening.

Harriet was still thinking about Jenny's commune revelation. She wondered if she'd be more shocked about it if she'd come of age in the sixties. She just couldn't understand why Jenny was acting like being raised in a commune was such a horrible stigma.

"I told Jorge I'd help him dip more Twinkies in chocolate in the morning before the festival opens, so I better get going," Aunt Beth said finally. "Are you ready to leave?" she asked Jenny.

Harriet was pretty sure Jenny'd been ready to leave since before she arrived.

The group all assured her they supported her and loved her, and they each gave her a hug before she made her way out the door, followed by Beth.

"Anyone else think she's lying through her teeth?" Lauren asked when the door was closed again.

"Lying might be too strong a word," Robin said, "but I agree—she's still holding something back. And I don't for a second think she's just embarrassed about her educational background."

"I'll see what I can dig up on the Internet," Lauren said.

"Her quilt doesn't look like the rest of the quilts on display," Carla said, her cheeks turning red. "I mean, it sort of does, but that big piece in the middle doesn't."

"Quilters have always made use of recycled fabric," Mavis pointed out. "In pioneer days, people used their worn-out clothes to make quilts because they had limited access to fabric, but after the Depression was past, I think people did it as a way of remembering favorite clothes, often from their childhood. In the sixties, people were just starting to rediscover the idea of recycling. The center of Jenny's quilt looks like men's shirts did back then."

"I still don't get why she's so weird about that quilt," Lauren said.

"If Jenny lived on a commune back then, who knows what sort of memories it brings up," Mavis said.

"Yeah," Connie added. "There were communes...and then there were communes, and that's probably still the case today. I don't want to talk out of turn, but a lot of them were also cults."

"Do they even *have* communes today?" Harriet asked.

"People still live in group settings, but I don't think they call them communes anymore," Robin answered.

"They call them senior living," Lauren added with a smirk.

"Jenny didn't say anything about having escaped a cult," Mavis cautioned, ignoring Lauren. "Let's not borrow trouble."

"But there is something she'd not telling us," Connie countered. "Maybe she *did* escape a cult."

"I'll see what I can find out about the commune in Georgeville, Minnesota," Lauren said. "Assuming she was telling the truth about it."

"Anyone want another brownie?" Harriet asked and held up the plate.

Everyone did.

Chapter 12

*H*arriet *could hear the pounding of her heart over the roar of the sandstorm. She was crouched behind a dried clump of sagebrush, watching the shadowy form coming ever closer. He wasn't large, but the knife in his hand was.*

The chorus of an old song floated on the night air; something about not having seen anything yet. She felt sweat trickle down her back. The sweat felt like sandpaper against her skin...

And then the desert disappeared, and the sandpaper turned into Fred's tongue.

"Get away," she said and pushed him from her back, pulling her sleep shirt down as she did. Fred slapped Scooter as he slid past, causing the little dog to yelp in protest. She glanced at the clock on her bedside stand.

"You guys need to learn to sleep in a little," she complained. "There is no reason for any of us to be up at six-thirty in the morning."

Scooter whined, his indication that he wanted to go outside to do his business. Something he probably could have waited another two hours for if it hadn't been for Fred.

"Arghhh," Harriet said and rolled out of bed to start her day.

✂- - -✂- - -✂

"You two behave yourselves," Harriet instructed her pets an hour later.

She'd walked Scooter, fed both him and Fred, and taken her shower. Now, she clicked the pet gate across the opening from the kitchen to the hallway that led to the stairs. She shut the door into the dining room; she was thankful her Victorian house was old enough to have doors between almost all of its rooms, making dog management easier.

"Uncle Rod is going to come by and walk you at lunchtime," she told the little dog as she laced her black hiking boots over her black tights. She had on a floor-length skirt she'd made from an old crazy quilt that had been irreparably damaged years before. "And I'll see you later on."

Connie's husband Rod had volunteered to provide dog-walking services for the duration of the festival and quilt show for the rescue dogs several of the Loose Threads had adopted the previous fall.

Harriet planned to stop by her favorite coffee shop for a cup of hot chocolate and a muffin before continuing on to the quilt show. She needed some time to think, and she wasn't due at the festival for two hours.

The Steaming Cup Coffee Shop provided several seating options. Harriet was carrying her cocoa and muffin toward one of the overstuffed chairs in front of a glass-fronted artificial fireplace when she glanced at the long table that had a bookcase with embedded power strips running down its center. She changed her mind and headed for one of the chairs at the computer table.

Most mornings, Lauren could be found here, her laptop connected to the power. With any luck, she'd show up before Harriet finished her breakfast and have some results from her background check on Jenny. She had no doubt Lauren had done her search as soon as she'd gotten home the night before.

Harriet was staring into her nearly empty cup when Tom Bainbridge stopped at the chair opposite hers.

"This seat taken?"

"No, sit, please."

"You here by yourself?"

"The kids woke me up early this morning, and with everything that happened yesterday, there was no hope of going back to sleep."

"The kids?" He raised his left eyebrow.

"My cat and dog. They're running my life these days."

Tom sat down, smiling and shaking his head.

"You laugh, but that's just because you don't have any pets."

"Not true," he said. "I have a quite elderly cat, but he's very independent. As long as his food is in his dish on time, he's happy. When you come visit me, I'll introduce you."

"I'll look forward to it," Harriet said and took a sip of her cocoa.

"I heard there's been a shooting. Was it someone you knew?" Tom broke off a piece of his blueberry scone and popped it into his mouth.

"Not exactly," Harriet said, and then explained Jenny's connection to the victim.

"She must be shaken up,"

"She's shocked that the person who replaced her got shot right after she left for her first break, but her reaction was a little weird, and then she revealed she'd been raised in a commune and had been lying about it for all these years. I'm not sure why she felt the need to lie to the group, other than being embarrassed about her lack of traditional education."

"Interesting she chose now to come clean. You never know—"

Harriet never found out what wisdom was to follow.

"You didn't let my chair get cold, I see." Aiden towered over her, his hands on his hips, fire blazing in his ice-blue eyes. "I thought you said you were going to back off," he said to Tom and then turned back to Harriet. "You didn't even give me a chance to explain. What? You called him to take my place without any discussion? You're so insecure you can't be by yourself for a couple of days while I deal with an emergency?"

Harriet could feel her face burning. She clutched the edge of the table, speechless.

"Sorry I'm late," Lauren said and put her arms loosely around Tom's neck. Tom stood and swept Lauren into his arms, dipping her slightly and kissing her.

"No problem," he said when he'd finished. He kept his arm around Lauren's shoulders. "You want your usual?" He headed for the coffee bar.

"Have you been struck dumb?" Michelle asked Aiden as she joined the group. He'd frozen when Lauren came in and hadn't moved or spoken since. No one had noticed his sister come up beside him.

Michelle grabbed his arm and half-dragged him to the upholstered chairs.

"I need to know..." She continued talking at Aiden until they were out of earshot.

"I hate that woman," Lauren said and sat down in the chair next to Tom's.

"I hope your regular is a vanilla latte with two shots," Tom said when he came back to the table, a coffee cup in one hand and a bag with an orange-cranberry muffin in the other.

"Thanks, that works. Can I pay you for it?"

Tom waved her off.

"That was well worth the price," he said.

"You two are good," Harriet said. "Or maybe I should say bad."

"I can sympathize with a guy being mixed-up about how he feels," Tom continued. "And I can even understand having a difficult family, but there is no excuse for bad behavior. He's lucky all I did was help Lauren scam him. Next time, I might have to give him an attitude adjustment."

"I appreciate your help, but I can deal with Aiden," Harriet said.

"Come on, admit it," Lauren said with a wicked smile. "Didn't you enjoy that just a little?"

She smiled. "I did."

"My report is going to be anticlimactic after all this," Lauren went on. She pulled her laptop from her canvas messenger bag and plugged its power cord in. "Jenny is the invisible woman. She has nothing on the Internet, and I mean nothing. You have to work really hard to have that low of a profile.

"Of course, 'Jenny' might not be her legal name. Her husband's name is on everything I can find—tax rolls, car registration, address and phones. She must have a driver's license with her legal name on it, but unless we can figure out what that is, it's a dead end. And before you ask, I checked the obvious possibilities—Jennifer, Jeanette, Janelle, everything I could think of, but no dice."

"Thanks for trying," Harriet said.

"I'm not through here."

"Sorry. Continue, please."

"I also checked out that commune. As she reported, it was founded in the late nineteen-sixties by a couple of liberal ex-university professors. I can't find anything to indicate it has any cult ties, so at least that's good. They were more successful at truck farming than the local community expected—nothing too exciting. An exhibit has been created around them and is traveling to several museums around the country. That's new. Even if someone saw her picture in the exhibit, I can't imagine why that would be a problem, I mean, they would have to have been there themselves to know her from the commune, so what would the big deal be?"

"There's something wrong about Jenny's whole story," Harriet said. "I'm not sure the commune explains why she was so antsy about doing this event, but it definitely doesn't explain why she's so sure she was the real target of the shooting or why she was so frantic to check out her quilt afterward."

Her cell phone rang, and from the ringtone, she knew it was her aunt.

"I'm at the coffee shop with Lauren and Tom," she said after they had exchanged greetings. "I'd be happy to pick up more tortillas at Jorge's on my way to the festival."

She listened to her aunt's instructions about where to find the tortillas Jorge needed and told her to give Jorge's cook fifteen or twenty minutes to get them packed before she went to Tico's Tacos.

"Did Lauren have any news?" Aunt Beth asked.

Harriet relayed what Lauren had reported and rang off.

"I'm going to have a cup of tea," she announced. "I have to wait on a box at Jorge's."

She got up and went to the coffee bar to place her order. She could feel Aiden staring at her as she crossed the room. She glanced his way, and he quickly averted his gaze.

"Just who I wanted to talk to," Detective Jane Morse said from behind her in line; Harriet hadn't seen her come in. "Officer Nguyen mentioned you were hanging around the crime scene when he arrived. Please tell me that was a coincidence.

"You were involved," she continued when Harriet didn't speak. She looked up at the ceiling. "I don't need any complications, please."

"Lauren and I were there," Harriet explained, "but not when the shooting happened. Our friend Jenny made the quilt that was hanging on the stage where the woman was killed. I know it sounds shallow, but I think our friend wanted to see if her quilt had been damaged."

"Jenny Logan," Morse said, looking at the small notebook she'd pulled from her pocket. "She's your Jenny? Jenny from the Loose Threads?"

"Yes, our Jenny."

"I need to talk to her, too. Do you know where she is?"

"Probably at home. She'll be back at the festival today. Assuming your guys are letting people go back in."

"We had people working all night to clear the scene so we wouldn't interfere with the festival. It's our community, too, you know."

"I didn't mean to imply otherwise," Harriet said.

"I know," Morse said and rubbed her hand over her face. "I'm sorry, I'm just tired."

"Can you join us for a few minutes," Harriet asked her when she'd ordered her tea.

"Sure, let me get my coffee."

✂ - - - ✂ - - - ✂

"You know I can't tell you anything," Morse said when she'd taken a seat at the computer table. "But if you guys have any ideas, I'm all ears, particularly if you know anything about the victim."

"So far, none of the Threads knows her except in passing," Harriet said.

"I did a little checking on the Internet," Lauren volunteered. "I was curious," she added.

"And?" Morse prompted.

"It appears Pamela Gilbert was going through a contentious divorce," Lauren said. "You probably already know she had a restraining order against her husband and some woman."

"I didn't know that yet, and I'm wondering how you do."

"Some of my clients deal with security issues—criminal background checks, workplace security and monitoring—so I have to be current on what information can be accessed and how to do that," Lauren replied. "It's all legal."

"If you say so," Morse said.

"Don't you guy always look at the family first?" Harriet asked.

"We do. Unfortunately, most murder victims are done in by someone they know, usually a loved one. People are tracking down the husband as we speak."

"Are you going to increase security?" Lauren asked.

"We *will* have an increased presence, but the victim doesn't appear to be random, at this point, so it isn't likely anyone else is at risk."

"Let's hope not," Tom said.

"I better go get Jorge's tortillas." Harriet stood up.

"I'll walk you out," Tom said with a glance across the room at Aiden and Michelle.

Aiden glared at him, but Michelle was talking, and he didn't get up.

"Are you okay?" Tom asked when they were outside. "I don't know what's happening with you and Aiden, but clearly, his sister is making trouble again."

"I don't want to talk about it," Harriet said as tears filled her eyes.

"Come on, now." He put his arm around her shoulders, pulling her to him. "I didn't mean to make you cry."

"You didn't," she snuffled against his shoulder.

"Okay," he said. "Can I do anything to make it better?"

Harriet swiped at her eyes with the heels of her hands and shook her head. Tom gently kissed her on the forehead.

"I've got to go," he said. "Will you call me if you need anything? Even if it's just a shoulder to cry on?"

Harriet nodded, part of her wishing it was Aiden kissing her, in spite of everything.

Tom put his fingers under her chin and tilted her face toward his.

"Do you promise?"

"Yes, I promise."

"Okay, let me walk you to your car." He turned her around, keeping his arm across her shoulders. "I'll come by your booth at lunchtime, if that's okay with you. Just to see how you're doing."

"I'd like that."

When they reached her car, he pulled her into his arms for a hug and then turned and went back to his own car. Harriet watched until he'd gotten in and driven away.

Chapter 13

The stop at Tico's Tacos, Jorge's Mexican restaurant in down-town Foggy Point, had been uneventful. It had, however, meant that Harriet had to park farther back in the exhibition hall's parking lot. She spotted Jenny when she got out of her car and had her hand half-raised to wave when she realized Jenny wasn't alone. A man with matted hair and a tribal tattoo across half of his face was arguing with her.

Harriet continued around to the back of her car, where she could hear Jenny and the man without being seen, and slowly began loading the box of tortillas onto her fold-up handcart.

"Take it," Jenny shouted and pushed a handful of what had to be money at him.

"Don't think you can just shove a few bills at me and send me on my way," he yelled back.

"Scream all you want, but this is all I have," Jenny said and turned her back on him before striding to the entrance of the exhibit hall.

The man picked up a camouflage backpack and swung it onto his thin shoulders then limped off in the opposite direction.

Harriet locked her car and wheeled her box up to Jenny's car. An assortment of bills littered the pavement on the driver's side. She picked them up and stuffed them in her sweatshirt pocket.

"Thank you, honey," Aunt Beth said when Harriet arrived at the food court with the box of tortillas. "Are you okay?"

"I could have done without running into Aiden this morning, but besides that, I just saw something weird in the parking lot." She told her aunt what she'd witnessed.

"Are you going to say anything to her?" Beth asked.

"I picked up the money." She reached into her pocket and pulled the money out, counting it as she straightened the bills and aligned them into a stack. "Geez, there's two hundred-forty dollars here." She folded the bills and put them back in her pocket. "I'm going to give the money back to her and see what, if anything, she says about it. I'll let you know if I learn anything interesting."

Aunt Beth glanced at her watch.

"You better get moving if you're going to talk to her and get to your booth on time,"

"I'll talk to you later," Harriet said and strode off toward the exhibit hall.

"Hey, Jenny," she said a few minutes later when she found her friend, fully decked out in her afro wig and sunglasses, standing beside her quilt.

"Oh, hi, Harriet, how are you doing this morning?"

"Wow, it's like nothing ever happened here," Harriet said, looking around.

"The show must go on, I guess," Jenny said with a half-smile.

"Hey, when I was walking past your car, I found this money on the pavement beside the driver's side door." Harriet pulled the folded bills out of her pocket and tried to hand them to Jenny.

"That's not mine," She stepped back and held her hands up. "Someone else must have dropped it." When she realized she was still holding her hands up she dropped them abruptly and then nervously smoothed the sides of her tunic.

"No problem," Harriet said. "They must have a lost-and-found here. Maybe they can take care of it."

"That sounds like a good idea," Jenny said and turned away.

✂- - - ✂- - - ✂

Harriet talked to a steady stream of potential customers during the morning, two or three of whom she thought might actually follow

77

through. The rest loved her work but wanted to pay a fraction of her lowest rate. Most of them were new enough to quilting to not realize how much work it was to quilt a bed-sized quilt, no matter what sort of machine you used.

"Anything interesting happen while I was gone?" Lauren asked when she arrived just as the last customer of the morning was leaving the booth. She had on hip-hugger denim bell bottoms with a white patent-leather belt and a red-and-white-striped long-sleeved T-shirt.

"Nice get-up," Harriet said.

"I'm still going for the folksinger look. Did I make it?"

"Your long bangs and pageboy are right there, but I'm not sure about the shirt."

"The bangs are driving me nuts, but they did sort of define that era, don't you think?"

"Definitely," Harriet said and laughed.

A series of half-hour talks about the culture and history of the nineteen-sixties would be starting in the auditorium in a few minutes and continue until just after lunch. Traffic would be light in the vendor area for the duration.

"I need a distraction after the morning I've had," Lauren said, changing the subject. "I swear some people should have their license to operate a computer revoked."

"You want to talk about it?"

"Not really. You're probably one of them."

"I saw an interesting encounter this morning on my way in," Harriet said, ignoring the dig.

"Do tell."

Harriet related the scene she'd witnessed between Jenny and the tattooed man.

"Well, that is interesting. Any clue as to who he is?"

"None at all, and Jenny was no help. I tried to give her the money—like I'd just found it by her car when I went by. She shied away from it like it was poison. After my ruse, I couldn't easily go back and tell her I'd seen her arguing with tattoo guy and had seen her drop the money."

"Well, that wasn't very clever of you," Lauren said.

"I know that now, but thanks for pointing it out. I suppose you could have handled it smoother."

"I was just saying—"

"I wish we could find tattoo guy," Harriet said.

"Why can't we?"

"Time, space, too many people. Stop me if any of this resonates."

"I'm not sure that's true," Lauren said. "Think about it. He's not here—we don't have a big enough crowd yet to conceal someone so unique. If he was trying to get money from Jenny and wasn't successful, he's probably still around."

"You're right," Harriet said. "If he's sticking around, he'll either end up at the youth hostel downtown or the homeless camp at Fogg Park."

"Or he could be hanging out around Jenny's place waiting for her to show."

"If he knows where she lives, wouldn't he have gone there this morning instead of looking for her here?"

"I have an idea," Lauren said and pulled out her smartphone. She tapped a message into the device and sent it.

"Who were you contacting?"

"I teach classes to a group of computer geeks who hang out at the internet cafe downtown. I asked if anyone has seen our tattoo guy and, if yes, to text me. They'll go out and look. It's just the sort of mission that appeals to their inner nerd."

"Then what?"

"Then we go talk to him, of course." Lauren said and smiled at Harriet.

"Can you watch the booth a minute so I can see if Connie can come babysit when the call comes?"

"Yeah, but let's not count our chickens and all that."

"Don't you have faith in your nerds?"

"Yeah, but still…"

"You're right. Someone like that will be obvious, and your guys are perfect. He'll never suspect them of spying on him. Everyone always ignores geeks."

"I think I resent that remark. Technically, I'm one of them," Lauren said.

"You are not a geek, Lauren. I don't care how much you know about computers."

"Thanks, I think."

"I'll be right back."

Harriet was halfway across the exhibit hall when she saw Connie approaching from the north vendor area.

"We closed down the raffle station, since everyone's gone to the lectures or lunch," she said when they reached each other.

"I was just was coming to see if you could watch my booth in a little while." Harriet explained the scene she had observed with Jenny and about the plan Lauren had set in motion.

"I feel bad that Jenny doesn't feel like she can talk to any of us about whatever it is she's dealing with," Connie said.

"And she's clearly dealing with something," Harriet noted.

"Maybe you should go get a snack for yourself and Lauren so you'll be ready when the call comes," Connie suggested.

"Only if you'll let me get you something, too."

"I never turn down food," Connie said with a smile. "You can surprise me."

"Let Lauren know, will you?"

"Sure." Connie continued on toward the south vendor area.

"I need food for Lauren, Connie and I," Harriet said when she reached the head of the line at Jorge's taco stand.

"You ladies need something healthy," Jorge said. "No more chocolate Twinkies."

"That's not very fun," Harriet said and smiled. "I think you've spent too much time with my aunt. Her food police ways are rubbing off on you."

"It will be a long week, and there will be many opportunities for treats," he said and smiled back at her. "And I do have to keep the Señora happy, too. I brought some chicken burritos from the restaurant for you and your friends." He lifted a paper bag from an insulated box. "Let me get you some guacamole from the cooler." He put a white container in a smaller paper bag of chips and handed her both bags.

"You are too good to us. Thank you." She tried to pay, but he refused, reminding her that her aunt was providing free labor at his food cart all week.

"Any calls yet?" Harriet asked Lauren when she'd returned to her booth.

"Geez, you've been gone, what? Ten minutes? My nerds are good, but they can't breech the time-space continuum. It'll take awhile for them to mobilize. And Jabba is going to drive by the homeless camp."

"One of them is named Jabba?" Harriet asked, incredulous.

"His parents were *Star Wars* fans, what can I tell you? And no, he doesn't look like a cross between a slug and the Cheshire cat. He's tall and skinny."

"I wasn't going to ask." Harriet said. She knew all about parents and names.

"That's a terrible thing to do to a child," Connie proclaimed.

"He seems to like it," Lauren said. "And the other guys are all jealous and think he has cool parents. He goes by JB when he's out in the real world."

"I don't care what his name is if he finds tattoo guy," Harriet said and handed out the burritos.

"This doesn't seem like sixties food," Lauren said.

"I'm sure people ate burritos in the sixties," Harriet said.

"Only if they lived in northern Mexico," Connie said and laughed. "I think burritos are more popular in America than they are in most of Mexico."

"Mmmm," Lauren said around a mouthful of chip and guacamole. "He does make great guacamole. Did they have that in the sixties?" She looked at Connie.

"I think the Aztecs invented it," Connie informed them. "It's been around forever."

"So, it qualifies," Lauren said.

"I wish we knew who tattoo guy is," Harriet said, changing the subject. "It's hard to imagine how Jenny could be connected to him."

"Is it?" Connie commented. "What do we really know about each other?"

"We know a lot about the Loose Threads," Lauren answered. "Most of them have lived in Foggy Point forever."

"Not really," Connie countered. "Most of us have lived here a long time, but not forever. Very few of our group were born and raised in Foggy Point. Our lives before coming here are taken at face value. Whatever we tell people about ourselves is what is accepted as truth."

"You mean Harriet didn't really grow up all over Europe? She really lived in Columbus, Ohio, before coming here?" Lauren said.

"Harriet did not grow up in Ohio," Connie said. "But yes, that is the idea. Jenny clearly had another life we don't know about, including being raised in a commune, and it wouldn't be a big surprise if she knew more than one tattooed person from that life."

"Most of us don't do that, though," Harriet said. "Sure, everyone embellishes some, but the core of what we share is true. At least, I choose to believe that most people are honest and upright."

"I think we all know you're a little more naive than the average quilter," Lauren said.

Lauren's phone rang before Harriet could come up with a cutting response.

"He's where? Thanks, I owe you guys one," Lauren said and then pocketed her phone. "He's in Annie's," she said to Connie and Harriet.

"Let's go," Harriet said and they gathered up their purses and coats and headed to the parking lot.

✂ - - - ✂ - - - ✂

"What's the plan, Kemo sabe?" Lauren asked as Harriet pulled to the curb and parked a block away from Annie's coffee shop on Ship Street.

"I thought we could go in and get drinks."

"Well, that's brilliant."

"Oh, hush, and let me finish. We get drinks, and then on the way to our table, we 'notice' the guy then pull out some of the money Jenny dropped and say we thought we saw him drop it in the parking lot."

"And if he demands the rest of the money?"

"I'm not giving him all of Jenny's money."

"Are you going to tell him we know Jenny?"

"Not if I don't have to. We don't know who he is or what their relationship is. Our goal is to find out without revealing any more than we have to."

"Okay, let's get this over with." Lauren unbuckled her seatbelt and got out of the car.

Annie was a retired county librarian who had spent years making people toss their drinks before they came into her building. The day after her last day of work, she bought her coffee shop, lining the walls with books so people could drink coffee and read to their hearts' content.

Harriet and Lauren entered the shop and casually dropped their coats on chairs at a table near the tattooed stranger. Lauren made a show of choosing a book while Harriet walked up to the library table that had been converted into a counter. She ordered two mocha drinks and joined Lauren at their table. Annie herself delivered the drinks, asking about the festival before returning to the coffee bar.

"I thought she'd never leave," Lauren whispered. "By the way, see that guy in the gray cardigan sweater and black-framed glasses?"

Harriet looked across the room at a young man bent over a large book that lay open on the table in front of him.

"He's one of mine."

"Good to know," Harriet said and took a deep breath. "Show time. I guess."

"Don't blow it," Lauren cautioned.

"Thanks for the vote of confidence," Harriet replied in a low tone then stood up, pulling two bills from her pocket as she went. "Excuse me," she said when she'd reached tattoo man's table.

He jumped like he'd been shocked.

Close up, Harriet could see that not only did he have a lot of ink on one side of his face but he had a bar sticking through the top of one ear, metal barbells through the eyebrow on the tattooed side, and a large hole in the earlobe on that same side was held open with a black ring. His foot tapped a silent rhythm on the floor.

"I was at the sixties festival this morning, in the parking lot," she said, clearing her throat. She could feel sweat forming at her hairline.

The man stared at the surface of his table without saying anything. His clothes gave off the sweet-smoky odor of marijuana,
leaving little doubt about what he'd been doing since she'd seen
him.

Harriet held the money out to him.

"I found this on the ground. I thought I saw you talking to a
woman there. I thought maybe you dropped it."

The man looked up at her for the first time. Harriet nearly did a
double-take, but forced her face to remain still. He was much older
than his wiry frame, tattooed face and straggly hair had made him
appear at first glance.

"Do I know you?" he finally said. "What makes you think this
would be mine?"

It was her turn to stare.

"This is a small town," she finally said. "We don't get many people with facial tattoos on just one side of their face. I guess I was
mistaken. Sorry I bothered you." She started to draw the hand with
the bills toward her, but he reached out like a snake striking and
snatched them from her before she could put them back in her
pocket.

"Maybe it was me," he said.

Harriet didn't move.

"Thank you," he said finally and went back to staring, this time
at the coffee in his cup.

"I'm Harriet," she said and offered her hand.

"Bobby," the tattooed man said without looking up or taking her
hand. He busied himself straightening the two bills she had given
him before slipping them into a wallet he pulled from the dirty
camo colored backpack that was on the floor next to his chair.

"His name is Bobby," she reported to Lauren as she sank back
into her chair. She grabbed her mocha and took a big gulp of the
hot liquid, burning her tongue.

"And?" Lauren prompted.

"And that's it. He wasn't very communicative."

"Bobby? That's all you got for forty dollars? Bobby? How's that
supposed to help us?"

"Grilling a stranger is harder than it looks. He didn't want to say anything. I couldn't exactly get out the bright lights and rubber hose."

Lauren sighed.

"Do I have to do everything?" She pulled a handful of papers from the messenger bag she took nearly everywhere and slipped them into the book she'd taken from the shelf.

"What are you going to do?"

"Hide and watch, grasshopper, hide and watch."

She got up and made her way to the bookshelf beside Bobby's table. She browsed the books, reading the authors' names on the spines. She used her fingers to make a space between two of them and turned her book around in her hand as if she were going to put it back on the shelf. At the last moment, she fumbled the book, dropping it on Bobby's table, knocking his coffee into his lap and sending the papers from her book flying.

"I'm so sorry," she said and pulled a handful of napkins from the dispenser on his table. She handed them to Bobby, who immediately began dabbing at his lap. She set her book back on the table at the same time.

"Let me buy you another coffee," she offered and took her book back. Without waiting for a reply, she bent and started gathering her papers. "What would you like?"

"One of those fancy drinks," he growled at her. "I don't care what kind."

Lauren dropped her papers in front of Harriet and continued on to the table to order Bobby's drink. Harriet picked up the stack and began straightening them. Neatly hidden between the third and fourth pages was an identification card, the sort that fit in the clear plastic sleeve on suitcases and backpacks. It belonged to one Robert Cosgrove, who lived at 1561 Alaskan Way S, Seattle, Washington, zip code 98134, and listed a phone number with a Seattle area code.

"I'm impressed," Harriet said when Lauren returned from ordering and paying for Bobby's drink.

"That's how it's done. Does it look useful?"

"Assuming it's his, it's a start," Harriet said in a quiet voice, watching Bobby the whole time to see if he was paying attention to them or his backpack. He wasn't

"*Assuming* it's his?" Lauren whispered in a tone that was more like a hiss than a whisper. "Are you crazy? This is a major clue. Why would he have someone else's name and address on what is probably his only possession? Of course it's him. Besides the fact that he told you his name is Bobby and this ID card belongs to a Robert."

"Let's wait until we get back to the show, and then we can look up his address and phone," Harriet said. "We need to look casual and finish our coffee so he doesn't get suspicious."

"I know how to research a person, and it's more than looking up his address and phone number. Those are just starting points. And I'm not sure if you noticed, but the man is barely conscious."

"Even so, we need to be careful."

"Whatever," Lauren said and picked up her now-tepid mocha. "I suppose I have to drink this."

Harriet rolled her eyes but didn't say anything.

Chapter 14

I thought I'd come keep Connie company while you two were out sleuthing," Mavis said. "Did you find the guy you were looking for?"

"We not only found him, but Lauren was able to get his name and address."

"So, who is he?" Connie asked.

"We have a name and address," Lauren reiterated. "We won't know who he really is until I can do some research."

"He's a lot older than he seems at first glance—mid-fifties, at least. Maybe even in his sixties," Harriet said.

"Course he looks like he's led a hard life. He's a druggie," Lauren said with conviction. "That could add a decade to his looks."

"I wonder what he wants with Jenny," Connie said, more to herself than the others.

"Money, if what Harriet saw is any indication," Lauren said.

"But why would he think Jenny would give it to him?" Mavis said.

"Hopefully, that will become obvious when Lauren checks him out," Harriet stated.

"Is anyone going to the dance party tonight?" Connie asked.

"Not me," Lauren said. "I saw the list of dances from the sixties and, except for the twist, and maybe the monster mash, I didn't recognize any of them."

"You mean you never learned the Watusi or the Hully Gully?" Mavis asked with a smile.

Lauren turned to Harriet.

"Don't look at me," Harriet told her. "I learned ballroom dancing at boarding school and a little salsa. Miss Nancy would have had a stroke at the thought of those pagan dance steps being done at her school."

"I'm taking my tired feet home and sitting in my recliner with Curly," Mavis said.

"Rod and I are going to a talk about the history of the war in Vietnam," Connie said.

"I'll be researching our friend Bobby, plus I have to do some work for my paying customers," Lauren said.

"I haven't decided what I'm doing." Harriet glanced at her watch. "Thirty more minutes until closing. You all don't have to wait with me. All I have to do is cover my tables."

One by one, Connie, Lauren and Mavis took their leave. Harriet was alone straightening her samples when Tom stopped at her table.

"Are you doing anything tonight?" he asked.

"I'm torn between going home and seeing one of the movies."

"Funny you should mention the movies. I was just going to see if you wanted to go with me."

"What do you want to see? They're running three double features at the same time in the exhibit hall conference rooms."

"If I don't choose the right movie, are you going to turn me down?" he asked with a grin.

"No, but I've been trying to talk someone into coming to see *Psycho* with me, and so far no takers. Hope springs eternal, though." She raised her eyebrows up and down in encouragement.

"I would love to go see *Psycho* with you. Can we get a bite to eat first?"

"As it happens, *Psycho* is the second movie after *The Graduate* in Room A."

"Do you mind if we eat somewhere besides here?" Tom asked. "The sixties fare is fun and all, but I need some real food."

"Jorge brought us lunch from his restaurant today, but I agree."

"Italian?"

"Sure."

He drove them to Aberto's, a mom-and-pop place on the far side of Miller Hill. Dinner was scallops with angel hair pasta and green salads, with a basket of warm crusty bread.

"I assume you've seen the movie at least once," Tom said when they had finished their meals.

"Hasn't everyone? I thought it was a rite of passage in America."

"I think I saw it for the first time at a junior high school Halloween party."

"It's been so long I don't remember all the details."

Tom looked at his watch.

"Let's go refresh our memories."

✂- - - ✂- - - ✂

A car door slammed loudly as they crossed the parking lot on the way to Harriet's car after the movie. She jumped and leaned into Tom; he put his arm around her shoulders.

"Don't worry, I'll save you," he said and laughed. "Not that there are any crazy guys with big knives out here."

"I wouldn't be too sure about that, the way things in Foggy Point have been going lately."

He tightened his arm around her.

"If we're going down, we're going together." He leaned in and kissed her lightly on her lips. "Isn't that your friend Jenny?"

He pointed with the hand that was on her shoulder. She looked where he was pointing. Two men in dark coveralls looked like they were attaching chains under the front bumper of Jenny's Mercedes. Jenny stood to one side watching.

"I wonder what's going on," Harriet said.

"Can't be anything good if a tow truck is involved."

"Do you mind if we check and see if she needs help?"

Tom sighed, and Harriet could tell he was seeing any hope of alone time with her slipping away.

"Sure," he said and led the way across the empty lot.

"What happened?" Harriet asked, but then saw the problem when she looked at the tires. All four had been slashed multiple times and were very flat.

"Where are the police?" Tom asked. "Are they gone already?"

"I didn't call them," Jenny said quietly.

"What?" Harriet asked her. "Why not?"

"It's not that big a deal."

Tom looked at Harriet. She gave him a slight nod. Jenny had been unwilling to tell her anything so far; maybe she'd talk to Tom.

"One tire might be teenagers or a prank, but all four? Someone is angry. What might have happened if you'd come out when they were there with knife in hand, slashing? You might have ended up dead."

"Especially after what happened opening night," Harriet added. She paused a moment to let her words sink in. "Instead of nine-one-one, how about we call Detective Morse? If she thinks it's not a big deal, that will be the end of it." She knew that would never happen. Morse was going to be all over this like spray starch on appliqué grapes.

"Can't we just drop it?" Jenny pleaded.

"'Fraid not," Tom said. "You know the tow drivers are going to talk about it, and then the police will come for you anyway. Wouldn't you rather control the situation by calling it in yourself? Or if you want, Harriet can call Detective Morse."

Jenny stood in silence—weighing her options, if the emotions flitting across her face were any indication. Harriet and Tom waited, equally silent.

"Okay," she agreed. "Make the call."

Harriet pulled her phone from her purse, found Detective Morse in her contacts list and made the call. As she'd expected, Morse instructed her to tell everyone to stay put until she got there.

"I'm afraid you're going to have to stop what you're doing for now," she informed the tow truck drivers.

"Is this going to take a while?" the older of the two men asked. They looked like they might be a father and son—both had barrel chests and slight beer bellies. And two unrelated people couldn't possibly share that same hooked nose. "We just got another call," he continued. "They're over near the high school. We could be back in an hour or so."

"Go," Tom said. "I'm sure we'll still be here when you're done."

"Surely not," Jenny said. "Slashed tires can't possibly warrant that much attention."

"I'll wait with your car if you're done before then," Tom offered.

Harriet pressed the face of her phone again while Tom was talking.

"Are you in your jammies yet? You are? Can you please meet me in the parking lot in front of the exhibit hall? Jenny has had a little car trouble. I think she might appreciate the support." She turned to Tom. "Aunt Beth's back at the restaurant with Jorge, prepping food for tomorrow."

"Did you have to call your aunt?" Jenny asked. "I was hoping we could just keep this between us."

"Us and Tom and the tow drivers, Detective Morse and whoever she brings with her," Harriet said. "Jenny, whatever is going on, you're going to have to talk about it, and I suggest sooner rather than later, before anything more serious happens. I thought you might like the support of the Loose Threads when you do."

Chapter 15

Jorge's pickup stopped a discreet distance from Jenny's car, and he got out, coming around and opening Aunt Beth's door before helping her down to the pavement. Aunt Beth strode over to Jenny and pulled her into a silent hug. Jorge came to stand beside Tom and Harriet.

"The fun never ends around here, eh?" he said with a grim smile. "Do you have any idea what happened?"

"None at all. We went to one of the movies, and when we came out, there was a tow truck hooking up to Jenny's car, and she hadn't told anyone," Harriet said in a quiet voice.

"Harriet thought Jenny might need some moral support, so she called her aunt. Jenny agreed to let us call Detective Morse instead of nine-one-one," Tom added.

"This is getting to be a habit," Detective Morse said as she got out of her car ten minutes later. She'd stopped behind Harriet and Tom. "Are there any crimes in Foggy Point you're *not* in the middle of," she asked Harriet.

"Not on purpose," Harriet protested.

"So, what happened here? The Cliff Notes version, not the novel."

"We came out after the movies, found Jenny here with all four tires slashed and a tow truck. We called you. That brief enough?"

Morse turned to Tom.

"You have anything to add?"

He held his hands up as if to protest.

"Nothing. It's like Harriet said."

Aunt Beth guided Jenny over to the group.

"Do you have any idea who would do this?" Morse asked Jenny. "Do you have any enemies? Anyone been bothering you recently?"

"Someone tried to shoot her," Harriet said. "Isn't that enemy enough?"

"I'm sorry, Detective Truman, I didn't realize you'd joined the force," Morse said sarcastically.

"Jane," Aunt Beth said, "what's gotten into you? You know Harriet's just trying to help. You wouldn't even be here if she hadn't insisted Jenny call."

"You're right. I'm sorry. It's just that there's a lot of pressure to solve the murder before the big festival weekend events. The city council members have each come to the department and spoken to my boss."

"This should help, then," Harriet said. "Another try at Jenny should help focus the investigation, right? Weren't you still investigating the victim's background?"

"Quite the opposite, actually. The victim does have some issues, but this just clouds things. If Jenny was the target of the sniper, and he realizes he killed the wrong person, why would he slash her tires instead of shooting at her. If that person knew where her car was parked, he'd wait for her to come out here and take a second shot."

"Oh," Harriet said.

"Yeah, snipers are not tire slashers—ever."

"So, what does this mean," Aunt Beth asked.

"I don't know," Morse admitted. "It could be a complete coincidence, it could be related in some way we can't see yet, or it could be that whoever killed our victim did hit the right target and is trying to muddy the waters by harassing Jenny."

"So, if this is unrelated to the murder, it would be important to figure it out as quickly as possible, right?" Harriet asked, staring at Jenny the whole time she was speaking.

Jenny's shoulders drooped, and she let out a big sigh.

"It was probably my brother," she said. "I talked to him this morning, and we didn't part on civil terms. It would be very like him to have a tantrum and slit my tires."

"What did he want?" Harriet asked.

Detective Morse glared at her.

"Sorry," she said and took a step back.

"What did he want?" Morse repeated.

"What he always wants," Jenny said. "Money."

"But he wouldn't *take* your money," Harriet said. "That's what I saw in the parking lot, isn't it?"

Morse glared at her again but then turned to Jenny to hear the answer.

"He wants—or needs—a lot more money than I could give him. He's always one deal away from the big score, and he never has quite enough money to pull it off. I haven't seen him in years, and I didn't want to know what he needed the money for."

"Do you want to take out a restraining order against him?" Detective Morse asked.

"I didn't even want to report the tires, if you'll remember. I certainly don't want to take out a restraining order. I want to go home, put my feet up and forget that the last two days ever happened."

"Unfortunately, it isn't that simple," Detective Morse said. "Unless we bring your brother in and talk to him, we won't know for sure it was him. I can't promise, but depending on what else I find in the system, and what we can prove or not prove, he can probably get out of this without doing any jail time."

"I would appreciate it if you could help him. I know he slashed my tires and all, but he is my brother."

"I take it he doesn't live here. Did he tell you where he's staying?"

"I have no idea. I don't think he's living in Foggy Point," Jenny said. "I hadn't seen him until this morning, and he's hard to miss."

"How so?" Morse asked.

Jenny described Bobby's tattoo.

"Okay, I think we're through here," Morse said. She made a few notes in a tattered notebook she'd pulled from her pocket. "You can go ahead and bring the tow truck back."

"My offer still stands—I'll wait for the tow truck if you want," Tom said.

"I'll keep you company," Jorge offered. "If Harriet will take her aunt and Jenny home, that is."

"Of course," Harriet said.

Tom pulled his phone from his pocket and began dialing the tow truck as Harriet led Jenny and her aunt to her car. They drove to Jenny's house in silence.

"Do you want to come in for a cup of tea?" Jenny asked when Harriet pulled into the driveway.

"I'd love a cup, if you're not too tired," Aunt Beth said. Harriet nodded in agreement, following her aunt's lead.

"I'd appreciate the company." Jenny ushered them inside. "Go ahead and sit in the den, and I'll bring the tea," she added and disappeared down a hallway to the back of the house.

Harriet took off her jacket then helped Beth out of hers, laying them across the arm of the chintz-covered sofa.

"Harriet, I'm sorry I didn't tell you the complete truth this morning," Jenny began fifteen minutes later as she set a tray laden with a teapot and three cups along with a sugar bowl and small pitcher of milk on the coffee table in front of the sofa. "I was taken by surprise when my brother showed up, and I guess I'm embarrassed by him.

"It's not just how he looks, although that's gotten more bizarre each time I see him. It's the way he's chosen to live his life. When he worked at all, it was usually as a gofer for some minor league drug dealer. Now I think he has some disability scam going, so we're all supporting him and paying for his 'medical' marijuana."

"Oh, honey," Aunt Beth soothed. "That's none of your doing."

"Still, like I said, it's embarrassing. He showed up today, and he had yet another get-rich-quick scheme, and all he needed was ten thousand dollars. I guess he thinks we're made of money and have wads of it sitting around the house waiting for someone like him to ask for it. I tried to explain to him that, even if I did want to help him, which I don't, no one has that kind of cash laying around."

"Did he say what the scheme was?" Harriet asked.

"No, but then, I didn't give him a chance. I told him I didn't want to know."

Beth reached over and patted Jenny's hand.

"Don't worry about it," she said. "No one is responsible for how their kinfolk act, and if he's that troubled, you did right by refusing to help him."

"How'd things go at the show today?" Harriet asked, changing the subject.

"No one wants to come close to my quilt. I'm not sure why the committee still wants me to be there. I barely got to take a break, too. Sharon was afraid to stand on the stage by it, so she would only talk to people from the aisle in front of the stage."

"Did you talk to Marjory?" Harriet asked.

"She came by and could see no one was stopping. I think Sharon might have said something to her as well."

"What did Marjory say?" Beth asked and took another sip of her tea.

"She was going to talk to the Amish group and see if they would be willing to take over my platform and let me have theirs, but I haven't heard what they said yet."

Beth turned the conversation to the perils of preparing food in an outdoor food cart, successfully distracting Jenny for the next half-hour.

"We should get going and let you get comfortable," she said when they'd exhausted the topic. "I hope you can go to bed early and get some rest."

Harriet got up and handed Aunt Beth her coat before leading the way to the front door.

Chapter 16

"How ow tired are you?" Harriet asked her aunt when they were back in the car.

"I'd like to get back to Brownie. Why? What did you have in mind?"

"I want to see what Lauren has dug up on Jenny's brother, and I'd rather talk it over in person."

"Well, I gave Penny a key so she could walk Brownie in the evening when Rod's off-duty, just in case something came up. Let me check in with her."

"While you do that, I'll call Lauren and see if she's available."

✂ - - - ✂ - - - ✂

"Lauren said she can meet us at the Steaming Cup," Harriet reported when Aunt Beth finished telling her neighbor about the goings on at the festival.

"Penny said she's just taken Brownie out for a quick potty break, so we're good to go. I didn't know the Cup stayed open that late."

"Lauren says it does, and she spends a lot of hours on her computer with her coffee cup in hand. I think she knows every late-night spot in town."

"I'm usually in my jammies by now, so I wouldn't know."

"I can take you home, if it's too late for you."

"I think I can bear up," Aunt Beth said with a grin.

Harriet parked next to Lauren's car in the lot and led her aunt into the coffeehouse. Lauren was sitting in a large upholstered chair near the door.

"Where's your computer?" Harriet asked.

"I finished my work and was about to leave when you called. I figured you two would like cushy chairs, so I moved over here. Get your drinks, and let's talk."

"Hot chocolate?" Harriet asked, and when her aunt nodded, she went to the counter to order. Beth sat in a purple chair with a matching ottoman and put her feet up. Her ankles looked swollen, and Harriet made a mental note to ask about it when they were alone.

"So, Bobby Cosgrove lives in the St. Martin de Porres Shelter on Alaskan Way in Seattle," Lauren reported when Harriet had delivered her aunt's chocolate and settled in a chair with her own cup. "My sources tell me the shelter specializes in homeless men over the age of fifty. They, of course, wouldn't tell me anything about him other than to verify his address when I pretended to be a prospective employer.

"So far, I can't find anything about him on the Internet. Either Bobby Cosgrove isn't his real name, or it's possible, if he's been long-term homeless, that he's just never done anything that leaves a trail out in the ether. I'll keep digging, though."

"We learned he's Jenny's brother," Harriet reported. She described the tire-slashing incident.

"Wait a minute," Lauren said, holding her hand up for emphasis.

Harriet had been about to take a sip of her chocolate but stopped.

"What time did this happen?"

"We're not sure. Tom and I came out of the movie at eight-thirty. Jenny was at her car with its shredded tires."

"Bobby didn't do it."

"But we don't know when it happened," Harriet said. "Most of the parking lot emptied at five when the exhibit hall closed. He could have slashed the tires any time after that."

"Wasn't Bobby," Lauren insisted.

"How can you be so sure?" Aunt Beth asked.

"My guys had so much fun tracking him down they went into overdrive. They decided to follow him and see if they could find out where he's staying locally. Before you say anything, they didn't tell me until he went to ground. They've had eyes on him all night.

"He hung around Annie's after we left, hitchhiked to the Catholic church, where they were serving dinner for the hungry or homeless and then he got a ride to Fogg Park, presumably to stay in the homeless camp. He was last seen walking into the woods in that direction. My watcher drove around the perimeter then took up a post just beyond the access road into the park. He hasn't moved."

"Then who slashed Jenny's tires?" Beth asked.

"Don't ask me," Lauren replied. "All I know is, it wasn't Bobby."

"Detective Morse said it wasn't likely a sniper would also be a tire-slasher. She said the shooter would likely have taken a second chance to shoot."

"Sounds logical, but clearly, Bobby didn't slash her tires, so who did?" Lauren asked.

"That's the question," Aunt Beth said thoughtfully. "Jenny made a good case for why it should be her brother. I guess it's within his character."

"I just wonder if Jenny is telling us the whole story yet," Harriet said.

"Well, we aren't going to solve this tonight," Aunt Beth said. "And if Jenny is holding something back, I'm sure she has a good reason.

"You ladies going to the prom tomorrow night?" Lauren asked.

"No," Harriet said at the same time her aunt said, "Yes."

"Really?" Harriet asked, turning to look at Aunt Beth.

"Don't sound so surprised. Jorge asked me, and I said yes."

"I'd have guessed you'd be going with one of your many beaux," Lauren said to Harriet.

"Aiden and I had planned on going, but after the other night, that's not going to happen. Tom would probably go if I wanted, but my outfit matches Aiden's, and somehow that doesn't seem right, so I'm going to sit this one out."

"What about you?" Aunt Beth asked Lauren.

"I'm going to be leading an antiwar protest at the entrance. Before you get on my case—the festival committee asked me to organize it. They thought it would add authenticity to the event. I don't know if I'm insulted or flattered that they assumed I wouldn't be going to the prom, but as a concession, they're letting us protest inside the entrance so we don't freeze to death, so I figured, what the hey, I wasn't going to go, and this way I get to see everyone's costumes."

"This could be useful," Harriet said and leaned back in her chair.

"What? You want to join our protest?"

"I believe I do. I think it will be the perfect excuse to keep an eye on things."

"Need I remind you that Foggy Point has a police force, and you're not on it?" Aunt Beth said.

"You're starting to sound like Detective Morse," Harriet chided. "Besides, I'm not going to do anything but keep my eyes open."

"I've heard that one before," Aunt Beth said and drained the last of the chocolate from her cup. She stood up. "I'm going to need my beauty rest if I'm going to be ready for the big dance.

"Let me know if you hear anything interesting from your surveillance team," Harriet said as she also stood up and zipped her coat.

"Will do, chief," Lauren said with a mock salute.

"Do you know who else is going to the prom?" Harriet asked as she and her aunt walked to the car.

Aunt Beth filled Harriet in on the Loose Threads prom plans on the ride to her cottage on the Strait of Juan de Fuca. A chill wind swept in from the water as she got out of the car and hurried to her door. Everyone talked about the "Summer of Love" when they were discussing the nineteen-sixties, Harriet mused as she drove away, but there must have been winters, too, weren't there?

✂ - - - ✂ - - - ✂

Harriet's headlights illuminated a dark figure sitting on the steps to her studio as she drove up her driveway, past the studio, and into her garage. She got out, dropping her purse and coat in the kitchen as she hurried to the studio. She unlocked the door.

It was Aiden. His cheeks and nose were bright red, and his fingers were like ice as she grabbed him by the hand and pulled him inside.

"Are you trying to kill yourself? It's freezing out there."

He stood inside the door, rubbing his arms with his hands.

"Come into the kitchen and let me make you something hot to drink. Then you can tell me why you're trying to commit suicide by hypothermia on my porch steps."

He followed her without saying anything.

Harriet put a paper filter in her single-cup filter holder and set it over a large mug. She scooped coffee into the filter and put the water kettle on to boil. Scooter was bouncing around Aiden's feet as she worked. He picked the little dog up and examined the nearly healed wound on his back.

"He's almost better," he said with approval.

"I'm going to take him out real quick. If your water boils, pour it, okay?"

She didn't wait for a reply. She crossed the kitchen and pulled Scooter's sweater and leash from the broom closet and put them on him before carrying him outside.

Aiden was sitting hunched over his cup of coffee at the kitchen table when she returned. She put a small scoop of food in Scooter's dish and a larger scoop of Fred's hypoallergenic cat food in his dish then turned to the man at her table.

"Okay, why are you here?"

"I don't know. We need to talk, I guess."

"You *guess?*" She moved closer. "I think you said all that needs to be said the other night. Oh, that's right, you didn't say anything, because you weren't there. That said everything that needed to be said."

"I'm so sorry for that. You have no idea. Let me make it up to you."

"You know, that might have meant something a couple of nights ago, but now is a little too late for a simple sorry."

"You can't mean that."

"Yes, I can. I do."

"You have to let me make it up to you," he repeated. He ran his hands through his silky black hair.

"No matter how many times you say it, it's not about making up for our missed dinner—and we both know it."

"Then tell me what it's about."

"Aiden," Harriet took his hand in both of hers. "We've had this discussion…more than once. It's really quite simple. You want a relationship, but you're not available."

"What do you mean?" he challenged. "You think I'm seeing someone else?"

"Of course not. But that doesn't mean you're available. We keep talking about this over and over again, but in the end nothing changes."

"It's my sister, isn't it?"

"Do you think?", Her frustration was clear in her voice. "This is what I mean. The fact that you have to ask says it all. A relationship is two people, not three."

"But everyone has family. You have your aunt. I would never stand in your way if your aunt needed you."

"My aunt would never try to keep me from being with you or anyone else."

"What's that supposed to mean? Have I been replaced already?"

"No! The point is, I don't believe your sister hates me, not really. She hates sharing you with *anyone*. She'll do this no matter who you're seeing."

"But she's my sister. What am I supposed to do? Our parents are dead. I'm all she's got."

"See, that's the trouble. You're *not* all she has. She has another brother, and a husband and two children who need her."

"Her husband left her. That's why she did what she did. And she and Marcel don't get along."

Harriet took in a deep breath and let it out slowly.

"Nothing's changed, so why are you here?"

"I want to fix things. How can we make this better? There must be some way to make it work. Tell me. I'll do anything."

"Don't say things you don't mean. I'm not willing to be part of a triangle. You want two women in your life, and she will never accept that even if I could."

"It's not her decision," he protested, but Harriet could see from his face that even he knew it wasn't true.

"Look, I don't want to fight with you, and I don't like ultimatums. Having said that, I also can't allow you to treat me the way you did the other night."

He started to protest, but Harriet let go of his hands and put her fingers against his lips.

"Let me finish," she said. "I know you believe your sister was having an authentic emergency. But even if she was, you didn't call me. Not that night, not the next day. Not at all. Once she..." Harriet grasped for words that wouldn't be offensive to him. "...did what she did, I ceased to exist for you.

"And *that* is the problem. That's the part of all this that you refuse to take responsibility for. Even now, you walked through the woods and sat on my steps freezing so she wouldn't know you'd come here, didn't you? You're afraid of what she'll do or say if she knows you're talking to me."

Aiden's chin dropped to his chest.

"What am I supposed to do?" he said, his voice thick with emotion.

"Grow up" comes to mind, Harriet thought, but instead of giving voice to it, she moved around to his side of the table and pulled him up. He wrapped his arms around her and rested his chin on the top of her head.

"Only you can figure this out, Aiden. I can't, and Michelle certainly won't."

He bent his head down and grazed her lips with his. When she didn't protest, he deepened the kiss. She threaded her hands under his shirt and stroked his back.

"This has never been our problem," she said when their lips finally parted.

He hugged her, swaying slightly as he held her.

"I've missed this," he said. "Us. You." He breathed in deeply. "I love the way your hair smells." He held her silently. "Maybe we could run away somewhere," he murmured into her hair.

Harriet leaned back and looked into his face to be sure he didn't seriously believe that was a viable solution.

"Let me give you a ride home," she said and turned away from him. "I promise I'll drop you at the end of your road so your sister doesn't know where you were."

"When can I see you again," he asked.

Harriet stopped and turned back to him.

"I'm not going to play the other woman, sneaking around behind your sister's back. You've got some decisions to make, and I've
got my hands full with this festival and everything."

"Has something else happened? Everyone's been talking about
the murder, but it sounds like they suspect her husband."

She told him about the tire-slashing.

"You should have called me," he said automatically.

"So you could ask Michelle's permission to come out? I don't
think so."

"I want to see you again."

"I want to see you, too. But not until the festival's over. We can talk,
but, Aiden, there won't be any point to it unless something changes."

"I guess that's all I can ask," he said and shrugged into his coat.

"I wish you would talk to someone about your sister, someone
who isn't me. There must be a family counselor in Foggy Point, or
maybe you could see Pastor Hafer."

He stood in silence, his lips clamped tight. She sighed and put
her coat on, picked up her purse and keys and led the way to the
garage.

Chapter 17

*H*arriet got up early the next morning and went straight to her studio. Connie had found a box of granny-style dresses made with small print floral cotton fabrics stored in her attic. She'd distributed them among her friends; but since she was shorter than anyone else in the Loose Threads, the dresses didn't reach the ankle length they were intended to be but ended mid-calf.

Harriet dug through her stash and found a similar piece of fabric in a coordinating print. She pulled out the hem on the dress and used her fabric to make a border, covering the seam with a piece of flat lace that was left over from another project. She held it up when she'd finished.

"Well, boys," she said to her two pets, "it'll have to do."

Scooter wagged his tail, but Fred had no opinion.

An hour later, she was showered, had eaten and was wearing her handiwork. She'd put gel in her short dark hair and blown it dry, fluffing it into her facsimile of an afro. She'd pulled on a pair of running tights under the dress and added hiking boots to finish the look.

"You boys behave yourselves," she said to the dog and cat. "I'm going to be a little late, but Uncle Rod is going to come by twice just to be sure you're okay."

With that, she picked up her purse, stitching bag and coat and headed for the garage.

Jenny was standing by her quilt when Harriet came into the exhibit hall; she had done a more extensive makeover on her granny dress. In addition to adding wine-colored velveteen around the bottom, she'd sewn a velveteen panel up the front of both the skirt and bodice, trimming it with strips of small flat lace.

"Far out," Harriet said.

"Groovy, isn't it?" she said dryly.

Harriet smiled.

"Thank you for last night," Jenny said. "I don't know what I was thinking, not calling nine-one-one right away."

"I'm sure you were in shock," Harriet said. "I hope it isn't too much of a hassle."

"Actually, I've got my car back already. The tire store opens up at six am. They put on new tires and even delivered it before eight o'clock."

"At least that was nice, I just wish we knew who did it."

"It has to have been my brother. It's the sort of thing he'd do."

It definitely wasn't her brother, but Harriet couldn't tell her that without confessing that Lauren's friends were following him.

"Are you going to the prom tonight?" she asked.

"No. Since it's Friday, the committee decided we should keep the quilt show open until the dance is over. My group is already down a person, and Sharon really wanted to go to the prom. She's dating again for the first time since her husband died, so she needs to go. How about you? Have you and Aiden patched things up yet?"

"You say that like it's a foregone conclusion."

"Isn't it?"

"I'm not sure. His sister is a powerful influence. We talked about it again last night, but we never get anywhere. She doesn't like me—or any other female, really—and she's making him choose between us, with lots of dramatic gestures thrown in. He doesn't want to have to decide, so here we are. I've suggested he talk to a professional about it, but so far he's been resistant to that idea."

"What about Tom?"

"It doesn't seem fair to get more involved with him while things are still up in the air with Aiden. He's so easy to be with I don't want to take advantage of him."

"If you like him, and he's easy to be with, maybe there's a message there." Jenny smiled at her. "He's good-looking enough."

"Maybe," Harriet said.

"So, if you're not going to the prom, what are you doing?"

"I'll be helping Lauren protest the war in front of the entrance."

"Really? Aren't you going to freeze to death in that dress?"

"I have a Vietnam-era army coat I found at the surplus store. But since the event is sanctioned by the festival committee, we will be inside the main entry doors in the foyer."

"Is there any chance you could swing by and give me a potty break partway through? I hate to ask, but I think the rest of the Threads are all going to the prom. It doesn't seem right to take them from the dance, and the committee volunteers are stretched thin because they have so many events going on tonight."

"I'd be happy to help. I'm sure I'll need a break from sitting down myself. We may be indoors, but it'll still be a hard tile floor we're sitting on."

"I've got a pillow I use for my back in the car. I can bring it in when I go to lunch. You're welcome to sit on it for your protest."

"Thanks, that'll be great. I better get on to my booth. I'll talk to you later."

"I'll be right here," Jenny said.

Harriet kept busy all morning with potential customers and even took two orders to stitch queen-sized tops. She was just finishing with a woman who had made her lay out every stitch sample she'd brought and then looked through both of her photo albums of past projects before announcing that she'd have to think about it before making a decision.

"You have my permission to send Diane Frank packing if she comes back," Aunt Beth said. "She pulls that nonsense every time we have a booth at any sort of show."

"And never once has it resulted in an order," Mavis added.

Harriet hadn't seen the two women come into the opposite end of the booth while she was tending to Diane.

"What are you two up to?"

Mavis held up a brown paper bag.

"Jorge made taco salads for today's special. I hope you don't mind, but we got three of them and thought we'd have lunch with you," she said.

"That's great," Harriet said. "Let me make a space on the table here." She spent a moment packing her samples into plastic storage boxes and stowing them under one of her tables.

"Have you heard anything more from Lauren?" Aunt Beth asked.

"I haven't seen her."

"Beth told me what Lauren found out last night," Mavis said around a bite of salad, but she was interrupted before she could add her own thoughts on the matter by the wiry little man they had assumed was Colm Byrne's manager.

"I brought you ladies the extra backstage passes we talked about," he said with an expression that landed halfway between a charming smile and a lecherous leer. "These are good for the dance tonight and the big concert on Saturday night." He handed four large yellow cards and their lanyards to Aunt Beth and Mavis.

"By the way, we haven't been formally introduced," he said to Harriet, "but they call me Skeeter. Your aunt and her friend helped us out when the refrigerator in our food truck went belly-up yesterday. Will four be enough?" he asked. "Colm wants you to be able to bring all your friends after you saved our bacon, literally,"

"Don't forget you already gave us three, the other day."

He smiled, and Harriet saw he was missing two bottom teeth. Apparently, only the onstage talent had to look beautiful.

"Four should be plenty," Harriet said. "Our friend missed the impromptu concert, but I'm sure she'd love to come."

Skeeter separated two more passes and began untangling their lanyards.

"Yes," Mavis said. "She'll be the one in the Afro wig."

Skeeter dropped the passes and their lanyards. Harriet looked at her aunt as he bent down to pick them up. He yanked a pass out of the mess, thrust it into Mavis's hand and turned abruptly and walked away.

"Well, that was bit strange," Harriet commented.

"I'm sure a lot is strange in that little man's life," Aunt Beth said and turned back to her salad.

"Did you notice that he has the same tattoo Jenny's brother has?" Harriet asked. "That stylized peace symbol. They both have them as part of other images, but it's the same tattoo."

"Oh, honey, everyone had peace symbols on everything back in those days. And that elongated variation was quite common," Mavis said. "It's a sign of the times, you might say."

"We better get going," Aunt Beth said when everyone had finished their lunch. "We promised Marjory we'd help with the prom decorations."

"See you later," Harriet said. "I'll be the one with the 'Make Love Not War' sign."

Aunt Beth glared at her over the top of her glasses but didn't say anything.

"Love you, too," Harriet said as they walked away.

✂- - - ✂- - - ✂

Lauren came by as Harriet was closing up for the day. The nature of her business meant she didn't have to deal with a cashbox at the show, so shutting her booth down for the day consisted of putting her samples under the table and getting her purse and coat out. This time, she pulled her army jacket from a bag and put it on and picked up the pillow Jenny had brought during her lunch break.

"I'm as ready as I'm going to be," she announced.

Lauren was dressed in hip-hugging wide bell bottoms that had been embroidered with antiwar slogans, and an embroidered Mexican peasant blouse over a fitted navy blue long-sleeved T-shirt. She wore round-lensed granny-style eyeglasses to complete the look.

"Where did you get the pants?" Harriet asked.

"I hate to admit it, but I found them two years ago at a thrift store in Seattle. They were too classic to pass up. What's with the pillow?"

"Jenny had it in her car. She thought I might need it, especially if we have to sit the whole time. Will we be getting up to march, or will this be more of a sit-in?"

"I think we'll mostly sit there. Marjory wants us to get up and march when the mayor and the Chamber of Commerce president arrive. We do have to chant off and on, though."

"So, what are our chants?"

"Most of them aren't anything that can be said in polite company, so we'll use 'Hey-Hey, LBJ, how many kids did you kill today,' 'Hell, no, we won't go,' and 'Draft beer not boys.'"

"Those are the tame ones? What happened to 'make love not war,' and 'give peace a chance?'"

"The first one is a slogan for a sign, not a chant, and the second is a song by John Lennon—again, not a chant."

"Okay, whatever you say," Harriet said. "Lead the way."

Lauren's group looked more like computer geeks from the two thousands than protesters from the nineteen-sixties, but to their credit, there were a lot of them, and they all carried signs with appropriate slogans.

"You sit on this side," Lauren directed Harriet when they'd all gathered in the foyer of the exhibit hall. "I'll sit on the other side. When I get up, you make sure everyone between us does the same. Marjory will call on my cell when the mayor and the president are about to arrive."

"Sounds easy enough," Harriet said, and it was. The march went off without a hitch an hour later. The mayor and his faux-police escort had clearly been prepped ahead of time. Both Harriet and Lauren were "arrested" and restrained with toy handcuffs.

"They didn't tell me we were going to be arrested," Lauren said when they'd been freed and were returning to their floor space inside the entrance.

"At least it gave us a chance to get up and move around a little," Harriet said and returned to her spot on the other side of the group.

"Can I talk to you a minute?" said a soft male voice from over her left shoulder. "Outside," the man added.

Harriet turned and was surprised to see Bobby Cosgrove crouched behind her. He stood up and went outside.

"I'll be right back," she said to Lauren and followed him. "What do you want?" she asked when the door had closed.

Bobby glanced around nervously before speaking.

"I need you to take a message to Jenny."

"If you're asking her for more money, I'm not helping you."

"You think you know everything, but you don't know anything. This was never about money. Not like you think, anyway."

"I saw you in the parking lot."

"You saw Jenny trying to push money on me. I tried to tell her I wasn't there to ask for money but she wouldn't listen. I was there to warn her. She's in danger."

"You haven't seen her in years. Why all the concern now?"

"I've stayed away from her for her own good. I been laying low, but they found her anyway."

"So, you're not homeless because of your habit?" Harriet said and turned as if to go back inside.

"I'm clean. I haven't used for over a year," Bobby said, straining to see into the shadows as he spoke.

"You reeked of marijuana at the coffeehouse the other day."

"That don't mean I was using. I had to talk to some guys who were smoking, but not me. Not anymore."

"If Jenny's in trouble, why can't you talk to her or, better yet, talk to the police?"

"You saw what happened when I tried to talk to her. She won't listen. I can't say I blame her. I wouldn't believe me. I've let her down more times than I can count."

"So, how do I know you're being straight with me now? Maybe you're still lying, trying a more sophisticated con on her."

Bobby stopped his nervous searching of the shadows and put his hands out in front of him.

"Sophisticated con. Me? Really?"

"I guess not. How about this? I'll go talk to Jenny. She's working late. I told her I'd give her a break. Let me go do that, and when she comes back, I'll see if she's willing to give you another chance to talk. You can stay across the aisle. I'll signal you if it's okay to approach her."

"What if she says no?"

"Have a little faith. I can be pretty persuasive. If she doesn't agree, we'll go to plan B."

"Plan B?"

"I'll call the Loose Threads."

"What the heck are the Loose Threads?"

"It's our quilting group. They're her best friends. If she's in danger, they'll make sure she'll talk to you. Let me go tell my friend what's going on. Meet me at the back of the exhibit hall in the aisle to the right in about five minutes."

Bobby agreed and disappeared into the night.

"What was that all about?" Lauren asked when Harriet had returned.

"That was Jenny's brother. It was weird. He said I'd misinterpreted what I saw in the parking lot. He claims he was trying to warn Jenny that she was in danger, but she wouldn't listen to him. He wants me to make her to talk to him."

"Are you going to do it?"

"He was pretty convincing."

"He's a drug user," Lauren countered.

"He claims he's clean. He says he met with some guys who were smoking, but that he wasn't."

"This ought to be good. Jenny's gonna go ballistic. I'll be waiting here with bated breath to hear what happens."

Harriet got up and went through the second set of doors and into the exhibit hall. A few people wandered the aisles, looking at the quilts and other exhibits. She noticed one woman wearing a well-cut navy blue wool suit with a large leather hobo bag slung over her shoulder pacing back and forth an aisle away from Jenny's stage. She must have just gotten off work, Harriet mused. You didn't see many expensive business suits at quilt shows, or even in Foggy Point in general.

"Hey, Jenny," she called when she reached her friend's display. "Ready for a break?" She tried to force a cheerful tone into her voice. If Jenny noticed, she didn't say anything.

"Boy, am I," she said. "I thought it was hard standing and answering questions all day, but it's excruciating standing here with almost no one in the hall. I'm going to run out to the restroom and then dash by the food court, if that's okay. It shouldn't take more than five or ten minutes."

"No problem, I'll be right here."

Harriet looked around. She didn't see suit lady or anyone else. She studied Jenny's quilt and was glad her friend had chosen the blue and mauve tones that were also used in the sixties rather than the more popular gold, orange and green.

It seemed like an eternity before Bobby came to the stage.

"Did you talk to her?" he asked.

"No, she's still on her break. She should be back any minute. She'll probably come back down the main aisle. Wait over there." She pointed to her left. "If you stand one booth in and watch through that display, you can see me wave at you without being noticed."

Fifteen minutes had passed when Harriet finally saw Jenny coming down the main aisle toward her. What occurred next happened so fast, she wasn't sure afterward what the actual sequence was.

She saw the woman in the suit looking at something in a booth, her back to Jenny's stage, saw her glance to the side as Jenny approached. One row over, Bobby apparently saw Jenny and decided to jump the gun, stepping out into the main aisle.

"I'm going to put my purse away," Jenny had said, and ducked behind the black curtain on the stage. At the same time, a stout gray-haired women accompanied by a younger version of herself approached the stage and asked Harriet to show them the back of Jenny's quilt.

Harriet pulled a white cotton glove from her pocket, put it on and picked up the edge of the quilt. As she folded it back, stepping behind it so the women could see the careful stitches, she saw blue-suit woman whirl and, at the same time, pull a large plastic bottle from her bag. She ripped off the top then flung the contents toward Harriet. Bobby turned and tackled the woman pulling the bottle from her hand and throwing it away down the aisle.

Harriet screamed as burning liquid splashed over her arm; her lower body was protected by the edge of Jenny's quilt. The fabric around her hand turned brown and began to disintegrate.

"Harriet, what happened?" Jenny cried as she appeared through the curtains.

The pain was so intense Harriet couldn't answer. She dropped the quilt edge and waved her arm back and forth, trying to escape the searing burn.

"Do you have any water?" the older woman who had been looking at Jenny's quilt asked.

Jenny disappeared through the curtains briefly and returned with two plastic bottles of water.

"I'm a nurse," the woman said and uncapped the first bottle, pouring the water over Harriet's arm. "We need more," she ordered. "and a first-aid kit."

"Pour some on the quilt," Harriet said in a strained voice.

Jenny went behind the curtains again. The vendor across the aisle brought two more bottles and set them down beside the nurse, who was pouring the second bottle over Harriet's arm. Jenny returned with more, uncapping one and pouring water over the brown spot on her quilt then pulling it down from its hanger. She folded it up and stuffed it behind the curtain then returned to Harriet's side.

"I'm Dorothy," the nurse said. "This is my daughter Jessica." She looked at her daughter. "Honey, call nine-one-one."

"Is that necessary?" Harriet gasped through clenched teeth.

"I'm afraid so," Dorothy said as she continued flushing Harriet's arm with bottled water. "We don't know what was in that liquid. It clearly included an acid, but who knows what else was with it. You need to be checked out. And someone will want to analyze the remains in the bottle to be sure there aren't any surprises."

To avoid seeing her arm, Harriet scanned the area around her. The woman in the blue suit was being held by two men she didn't recognize. Bobby was nowhere to be seen.

"Who is she?" she asked.

"Who knows?" Jenny replied frantically, her cell phone held to her ear. "I'm trying to call your aunt, but she's not answering."

"She probably doesn't have her phone with her."

Jenny turned as if to go.

"Don't go get her. Leave the ladies to their dance. Lauren is at the protest in the foyer to the dance hall. Tell her to bring her car out front. She can drive me to the hospital after the paramedics look at my arm."

"They're going to want to transport you," Jenny protested.

"And I'm not paying for an ambulance ride when I don't need to."

Jenny looked at Dorothy for help. The nurse shrugged.

"Her arm is burned, but if there was something really nasty in the mix she'd be reacting by now, and it's true—they can't force her."

The same team of paramedics that had responded to the shooting came up, ending the discussion. The quilter-nurse identified herself and gave a concise description of the event as one EMT began taking Harriet's vitals and the other opened a bottle of Milk of Magnesia, dumping it into a long-armed latex glove before slipping the glove over Harriet's burned hand and arm. When the injury was covered, he taped the glove in place.

"What's the white stuff for?" Harriet asked.

"Milk of Magnesia will neutralize hydrofluoric acid, if that's what she used," the paramedic said with a nod at blue-suit-woman. "She's incoherent, but my partner heard her say something about rotting bones, so we figured we'd better be safe than sorry.

"Hydrofluoric acid is used in the electronics industry, so it's pretty readily available here in the Northwest. It's nasty stuff. You don't feel the burn immediately, but it penetrates to the bone and destroys everything along the way. Clearly, it was mixed with something else that burned immediately—maybe sulfuric or hydrochloric acid, or even both."

Harriet felt the blood leave her face as she listened to the description. The second paramedic inserted a needle into her unaffected hand and began a saline drip.

"I think you'd better reconsider taking that ambulance ride," he said when he'd finished.

"Why am I not surprised to see you?" Office Nguyen said as he approached.

Harriet started to protest, but Dorothy shushed her.

"I saw the whole thing," she said. "She was standing there on the stage, showing the quilt to me and my daughter, and that woman came up and threw a bottle of acid on her. Without provocation, I might add."

Officer Nguyen raised his eyebrows but didn't say anything.

"That woman in the blue suit is who you need to be talking to," Dorothy continued, pointing at the her. She was sitting quietly, talking to herself in a continuous litany that made sense to no one but her.

Nguyen walked over to where two men still held the acid thrower. He said something into the radio on his shoulder then went behind the woman and handcuffed her.

"What have you gotten yourself into now?" Lauren demanded as she pushed through the growing crowd, kneeling beside Harriet when she arrived. "Are you okay? What happened?" She was more rattled than Harriet had ever seen her.

"That woman over there threw acid on my arm," she said. "Luckily, I had just turned the edge up on the quilt and stepped behind it as she threw, so she only got my arm."

"Where's your aunt?"

"She's at the prom still, and I told Jenny not to bother her or the rest of the Threads. Will you come with me to the hospital?"

"Your aunt is going to flip—you do know that, right?"

"She's going to be upset in any case, so she might as well enjoy the dance. Before you come to the hospital, go look at Jenny's quilt where the acid burned it." Jenny was now talking to Officer Nguyen. "It's behind the curtain. Hurry, before she gets done."

"Aren't you just the bossy one?" Lauren said, but she got up and went behind the curtain. She hadn't returned before the paramedics loaded Harriet onto a gurney and pushed her out to the waiting ambulance.

Chapter 18

"Harriet, what are you doing here?" Aiden asked as she was wheeled into a curtained slot in the emergency room.

"I could ask you the same thing," she replied. "I didn't think this hospital handled animals."

"Michelle is here."

"My mistake."

"She's got food poisoning," he said in an empty voice. "She's very sick."

"I'm sorry to hear that," Harriet said without feeling. "Are Carla and Wendy okay?"

"Fortunately, they went out to dinner with Terry tonight, and I had to work late."

"I hope it wasn't something Carla made."

"You don't even care about my sister, do you? She's in there having her stomach pumped, and all you care about is that it's not Carla's fault."

"Excuse me for caring about my friend."

"Why are *you* here, anyway? What's wrong with your arm?" As if he had only just noticed she was lying on a gurney with her arm wrapped in ice packs.

"You need to wait outside, sir," a dark-haired nurse said as she came through the curtained entrance to the cubicle. She gently tried to guide Aiden out. He pulled his arm away from her grasp.

"I'm not leaving until you tell me what happened to Ms. Truman." He returned to her bedside. "Are you okay?"

Harriet felt a flutter in her stomach in spite of her pain as his ice-blue eyes searched her face.

"Are you family?" The nurse raised one eyebrow, and she kept her gaze on him as she checked her patient's pulse. Finally, she looked at her watch.

"What happened?" Aiden asked.

"I had an accident," Harriet finally said. "Not that it's any of your concern."

He started to protest, but a different nurse stuck her head into Harriet's space.

"There you are, Dr. Jalbert. Your sister is asking for you."

He hesitated, resting his hand on Harriet's leg.

"I'm fine, really," she said. "You better go, your sister needs you."

A muscle in Aiden's jaw twitched. He hesitated, looked at Harriet, then turned and followed his sister's nurse.

Harriet's nurse reached into a cabinet and pulled out two white paper-covered packages. She set one down and opened the other, revealing a sterile syringe.

"This will be a little pinch," she said.

"My arm is on fire. Do you really think I'm going to feel your needle?"

"I suppose not, but it's what they teach us to say. It seems like a better thing to say than 'I know you're in pain, but let me add a little more,' don't you think?"

"I guess," Harriet said and only then realized the nurse had efficiently drawn two syringes of blood while she was talking.

"These will go to the lab just to be sure there wasn't anything nasty in whatever was splashed on your arm. They'll check to see if you absorbed anything into your bloodstream."

"We recovered enough liquid from the bottle to test," Detective Morse said as she came through the curtain.

"Great, so I didn't need the blood test?"

"I'm sure they need to test your blood in any case, but we sent the bottle and liquid to the forensic lab for analysis."

"I suppose you're going to yell at me for being involved in yet another crime," Harriet said and leaned her head back on her pillow.

"Actually, no. From all accounts, you were an innocent victim in this little drama. And the perp seems pretty upset that she got you and not whoever she intended to attack. Given the rather specific location, and the events of the last few days, I'm going to assume Jenny was her intended target."

"Did she say she was trying to hit Jenny?" Harriet asked.

"She's talked nonstop since we took her into custody, but none of it makes sense. She hasn't mentioned Jenny by name, but it's clear she was the target. I talked to the nurse who helped you and her daughter, but now I'd like to hear what you saw."

Harriet described the blue-suited woman and the sequence of events that led to her being burned.

"Did you see or hear anything else that might shed some light on this incident?"

Harriet thought about Bobby and the story he'd told her but then rejected the idea of telling Morse before she'd had a chance to talk to Jenny. *She* should be the one to tell Morse about her brother, if she thought it was relevant, not Harriet.

"There was an incident of bleach being thrown on a show quilt a few years ago in Houston," Harriet said. "It turned out to be a case of a sore loser in a civil lawsuit. Maybe this is something like that."

"Maybe, but that would imply a relationship between Jenny and the perp."

"Unless the woman got the wrong quilt altogether. Everyone involved in this show is in costume. Lots of people are wearing Afro wigs and big sunglasses with granny dresses."

"Hopefully, the woman will calm down and tell us what this is all about. She wasn't carrying any ID, so we don't know who she is or why she might have done this. So far, she's yelling something about her father. Does that mean anything to you?"

"Not at all. I've never seen that woman before in my life."

A tall man in green scrubs with a stethoscope around his neck came into the curtained room.

"I'm afraid you're going to have to leave, Detective," he said.

"I hope you feel better soon," Morse said with a smile that didn't reach her eyes. "I'll check back with you tomorrow."

"I'm Doctor Mitchell," the new arrival told Harriet, "and I'm going to take a look at that burn. If that's okay with you."

"Sure," Harriet said. She wasn't sure what he'd expected her to say. *Did people in this situation refuse treatment?* she wondered.

The nurse—Mary Gonzales, according to her name tag—pulled a bundle wrapped in blue cloth from a cabinet and unfolded it next to her arm. It contained a pair of bandage scissors and several pairs of tweezers, along with a plastic tray. Mary removed the ice packs, and Dr. Mitchell moved Harriet's arm onto the cloth and began cutting away the glove. Harriet turned her face away and studied the curtain on the opposite side of her cubicle. Whatever else they were going to do to her arm wasn't anything she wanted to see. She took a deep breath and closed her eyes.

Someone must have slipped pain medication into her IV while her eyes were closed, because when she opened them again, her arm was wrapped in a new dressing, and Lauren was sitting in a chair at her bedside.

"How long have I been asleep?" she asked, her voice hoarse.

"Shhh." Lauren held her forefinger to her lips. "Listen," she whispered.

Harriet could hear two voices coming from one of the cubicles farther down her row.

"That was one of the strangest cases of food poisoning I've ever seen," a woman said.

Harriet looked at Lauren.

"She sure recovered quickly," a deeper female voice commented.

"Yeah, just in time to avoid the stomach pump."

"She made a real point of the fact that Dr. Jalbert's housekeeper made the soup she'd eaten."

"Funny how no one else got sick."

"Hard to imagine how vegetable beef soup poisoned even one person. Especially since it was served hot, according to the patient."

"If you ask me, she was faking," deep voice replied. "It's a shame people like that are willing to waste our time and resources when

120

there's a waiting room full of sick or hurt people who really do need care."

"It takes all kinds, I guess," the first woman said.

Harriet and Lauren heard the crinkling of paper and the sound of a broom. Michelle and Aiden must have gone.

"You've been out at least an hour. I passed Aiden and that witch he calls a sister as I came in. I assume that conversation was about her," Lauren said. "She was screeching about Carla trying to kill her."

"Oh, my gosh! Michelle is trying to get Carla fired," Harriet said.

"Seems like," Lauren replied. "I think we need to call your aunt now. I mean, it's great to let her and Jorge have their moment at the prom and all, but she needs to be here with you. Your nurse was just in here a while ago asking if you'd had a tetanus shot recently. I told her I didn't have a clue. If your aunt was here, she'd know."

"She doesn't have her cell phone with her."

"Robin has hers—she never goes anywhere without it. Connie, too. She'll have hers in Rod's coat pocket."

"Let's wait until you take me home. As soon as they figure out that I don't need a tetanus shot, I should be good to go. My arm is bandaged, so I assume they're through with it."

"I asked while you were napping. They want to wait until the test results from the liquid in the bottle are back. They want to be sure the crazy lady didn't add anything poisonous besides the acids."

"Did they give any idea how long that would take?"

"Not really," Lauren told her. "If you're going to lay there and whine, I'll go see if I can find anyone who can tell us anything. If they don't say you're leaving in the next thirty minutes, I'm calling Robin. The prom is going to be ending in an hour or so, and your aunt is going to be looking for you. She knew you were going to be protesting, right?"

Harriet nodded and closed her eyes. The next thing she knew, Dr. Mitchell was at her bedside holding a clipboard full of papers.

"Your blood test looks okay so far. You should see your regular doctor tomorrow and have your dressing changed. Have you had a tetanus shot recently?"

"Sadly, yes," Harriet replied. The nurse was looking it up on a tablet. "I was hit on the head and had to have a couple of stitches. They gave me one then."

"The nurses told me you're a bit of a regular here," Dr. Mitchell said. "Anything you can do about that?"

"I was an innocent bystander tonight. My friend may have been the target, but I was just watching her station while she took a break."

"Maybe you need new friends."

He proceeded to recite a litany of cautions, care instructions and medication instructions and finished by handing her a printout of prescriptions for pain pills and burn ointment for some smaller splash spots away from the main injury.

"You get to leave," Lauren said as she came through the curtained doorway. She stopped when she saw the doctor. "Oh, sorry," she said and moved to the other side of Harriet's bed.

"As your friend said, you get to leave," Dr. Mitchell said with a smile. "Since you're a frequent flyer, I'm sure they have your insurance information, but if anything has changed, take care of it on your way out. Don't get up until someone comes and gets you with a wheelchair."

"*Now* can we call your aunt?" Lauren asked as soon as the doctor was gone.

"I guess I can't avoid it any longer."

Lauren had her cell phone out and was dialing Robin before Harriet had stopped speaking.

Chapter 19

*L*auren pulled into Harriet's driveway and parked as close to the studio door as she could. Harriet recognized Connie's car along with her aunt's silver Beetle, Robin's minivan and the older model Mercedes Aiden let Carla drive.

"How was the prom?" she asked as she came through the door, a sheepish smile on her face.

"What were you thinking, not letting anyone call us?" Aunt Beth demanded.

"Let the girl sit down," Mavis scolded. She must have come with Aunt Beth, Harriet thought. Likewise, DeAnn was sitting beside Robin. With the exception of Jenny—and Sarah, whom they hadn't seen in weeks—all of the Loose Threads were present. Harriet assumed the monitor receiver in Carla's left hand meant Wendy was asleep somewhere out of earshot.

She sat down in one of the swivel chairs that had been pushed up to her cutting table. Lauren went through the kitchen door, returning a minute later with a throw pillow from the living room sofa. She put it on the table beside Harriet.

"Elevate," she said.

Harriet put her arm on the pillow and settled herself.

"So, what happened?" Aunt Beth asked, unable to keep the stern look off her face.

"I was an innocent bystander," Harriet protested, and then related the whole story one more time.

"No one seems to know who the crazy lady is," Lauren added when Harriet was finished. "They actually brought her to the hospital instead of the jail because she was acting so crazy. I heard one of the nurses say they had to sedate her and would be sending her to the psych ward."

"We need to talk to Jenny," Harriet said. "Not only about why the acid thrower would want to attack her, if, indeed, that was the intention but also, I didn't get a chance to tell her that her brother wanted to talk to her. He came to me and claimed he isn't using drugs anymore, and that he needed to warn Jenny about something. He said she was in danger."

"Do you think he was talking about the woman who threw the acid?" Mavis asked.

"I've been thinking about that," Harriet said thoughtfully. "He was lurking around waiting for me to convince Jenny to talk to him. The woman was also wandering the aisles. If I saw her, he must have, and if he knew she was the danger, why wouldn't he have stopped her?"

"Maybe he was afraid of what she was going to do," Aunt Beth suggested.

"But he was the one who tackled the woman and threw her bottle of acid out of reach. Then he just disappeared. If he knew she was the danger, why did he wait until she threw the liquid?"

"Maybe he misjudged the level of danger," Robin suggested.

"But he said Jenny was in danger. He said he'd laid low, but they'd found her anyway. Somehow, that doesn't seem to match with one crazy woman."

"What did the doctor say about your arm?" Connie asked. "Is it terribly painful?"

"They didn't really tell me much," Harriet said.

"Actually, they had a lot to say," Lauren told them. "Harriet's too drugged with pain medicine to remember it all." She pulled a piece of paper from her pocket, unfolded it and handed it to Aunt Beth. "She's supposed to keep it level or slightly elevated, and she's supposed to call her doctor tomorrow and have the dressing changed. And she's supposed to take antibiotics just in case, and pain meds, and they said her own doctor could tell her about plastic surgery in the future.

"The police are testing the brew from the bottle to see what-all was in it. They're pretty sure it was both hydrofluoric acid and something like sulfuric acid. They want to be sure they got the hydrofluoric stopped. I guess it heads for your bones when it can."

"So, there you go," Harriet said. "To answer your other question, it *is* tender but the pain meds are keeping it in check. Can we talk about Jenny, please?"

"I'm not sure what else there is to say about Jenny until she comes and tells us what's going on," Robin said. "Then we can find out what, if any, trouble she's in."

Robin hadn't actively practiced law since her children had started school, but she kept her license current just for these occasions.

"I bet acid lady will turn out to be our tire slasher," Lauren said.

"We need to find Jenny's brother," Harriet said. "Not to minimize the damage of the tire-slashing or the acid-throwing, but Bobby seemed way more worried than one crazy person would warrant."

"Honey, you're starting to repeat yourself," Mavis said.

"Sorry," Harriet said. "Here's a new topic for you. Aiden was in the ER. Any guesses as to why he was there? And, Carla, you don't get to play."

"Michelle is trying to get Aiden to fire me," Carla blurted out before anyone could make a guess. "She said my soup poisoned her, and she made Aiden take her to the emergency room. Aiden left me a message on my phone, and Terry brought me home but they'd already left for the hospital."

"Oh, honey, that's terrible," Connie said.

"You can't get food poisoning from hot soup," Mavis stated. "Not if you brought it to a boil."

"Terry searched Michelle's room, and he found two empty bottles of syrup of ipecac," Carla said.

"So, she poisoned herself?" DeAnn asked, frowning.

"No one else had any of the soup, because Aiden worked late, and Terry took Wendy and I out to dinner, but Terry thinks she waited until Aiden was home and then drank a dose to make sure she produced the right effect at the right time."

"And she blamed Carla," Robin said in a clipped tone.

"Apparently," Harriet said.

"That's really bad," DeAnn said.

"What a psycho," Lauren said.

Mavis looked at Beth and then Connie.

"We may need to stage an intervention here," she said. "Interfering with Harriet and Aiden is bad enough, but trying to get Carla fired and ruining her reputation in the process is not acceptable."

"First things first," Beth said. "We need to get Jenny out of trouble before something worse happens. Then we can worry about Aiden and his sister."

"Honey, if it's getting too uncomfortable, you and Wendy can stay with Rod and me," Connie said. "You know we have plenty of room, and everything is baby-proofed."

Carla rolled the baby monitor receiver back and forth from one hand to the other, indecision etched on her face.

"I'll go back tonight and see how things are," she said and blushed. "Terry offered to talk to Aiden, but I want to give Aiden a chance to do the right thing."

"If Michelle is that out-of-control, maybe you should consider Connie's offer," Harriet said.

"My two rooms have locks on the doors. I'll keep Wendy in my rooms instead of the nursery. And Terry gave me a can of pepper spray if all else fails."

"Keep your cell phone on and with you at all times," Aunt Beth instructed.

The sound of a car pulling into the driveway silenced everyone. A moment later, there was a knock on the door and Jenny entered.

"Hi," she said with a wan smile.

"Here, sit down," Mavis said and brought her a wheeled workroom chair.

"Can I get you some tea?" Connie asked.

"That sounds wonderful," Jenny answered as she took off her coat and sat down. She turned to Harriet. "I'm so sorry. I know that woman thought it was me standing there by my quilt. I have no idea why she wanted to hurt me, but I was her target."

"You didn't throw the acid," Harriet said. "And you couldn't have guessed it was going to happen."

"What did the police say?" Robin asked.

"They wanted to know if I know who she is—I don't—and told me her name is Patty. They weren't able to get a last name or any other information from her. She was avenging something, they think, but they can't be sure because she was ranting so much. They had to sedate her just to remove her from the exhibit hall."

"That's very strange," Aunt Beth said. "Have you ever known a Patty? Maybe when you were in school?"

"Of course I've known people named Pat or Patty through the years, but no one who bore me any ill will, and I would recognize them on sight. There was a Patty in the commune, but she was African American, so it couldn't possibly be her."

"I wonder what her last name is." Connie mused. "That might tell us something."

"It was hard to tell how old she was," Harriet said. "She was definitely older than me, but I don't think she was fifty yet."

"So, we can rule out her being a classmate," Mavis said.

"Can I get anyone some tea?" DeAnn asked. Several people agreed, and she disappeared into the kitchen.

"I'm going to go check Wendy," Carla said, even though the baby monitor indicated the toddler was asleep and breathing evenly.

"Can I get you anything?" Aunt Beth asked Harriet.

"No, I'm as good as I'm going to get for right now."

The remaining Loose Threads looked at each other as the crunch of gravel indicated another car had driven into Harriet's driveway.

"Who could that be?" Mavis wondered. "We're all here."

A light knock sounded on the door, and Robin got up to see who was on the porch; her facial expression indicated it was someone she knew.

"Come in, Detective," she said and stood aside so Jane Morse could come into the room. "What brings you out this late on such a cold night?"

"Let's not be coy, Ms. McLeod."

"Which of my clients are you here to question, then."

"Can we drop the formalities?" Morse asked.

"Are we off the record?" Robin countered.

"For now."

Robin looked at the ladies sitting in a circle.

"My advice to everyone is that 'off the record' only exists on television, and therefore, you shouldn't say anything without counsel present. I'm available to anyone who feels the need to unburden themselves in the presence of our esteemed colleague. Hand me a dollar before you speak so we're covered."

"I'm not here to accuse anyone of anything," Jane Morse said. "I wanted to see how Harriet was doing, and I took a chance and drove by. I saw all the cars and figured you wouldn't mind if I stopped."

"Thank you," Harriet said.

"I'm guessing you've all been doing what the police are doing—trying to figure out who the real target was," Morse said.

DeAnn and Carla returned with a tray of steaming teacups with containers of milk, lemon, and honey and other sweeteners, passing them around then offering a cup to Jane.

"None of us who saw the woman recognized her," Harriet said. "And both Jenny and I have known Pattys in the past, but we would recognize them, so we're drawing a blank."

"What if I tell you her full name is Patty Sullivan?" Morse asked.

Harriet shook her head.

"Doesn't help." She looked at Jenny.

The blood had left Jenny's face, and she looked like she might faint.

"Put your head between your knees," Connie ordered.

Lauren quietly slipped the laptop from her messenger bag and turned it on.

"I'd like to speak to my client alone before you question her," Robin said.

"It's okay," Jenny said as she slowly sat up again. She looked at Robin and took a deep breath. "I know—or knew—someone named Sullivan. I mean, I didn't know him, I knew *of* him. He was a policeman who was killed a long time ago during the commission of a robbery. My brother Bobby was involved in the incident, although he was not the shooter nor was he a bank robber; he spent two years in jail for it."

"How long ago are we talking?" Morse asked in a quiet voice.

"Oh, gosh," Jenny said and looked at the ceiling. "Bobby wasn't quite twenty, so that would have been...nineteen sixty-eight. Forty-four years ago, maybe."

Lauren's fingers flew over the keys as they talked.

"A James Sullivan was killed in the line of duty during a robbery of the Bank of Washington in Lynnwood, Washington. He left behind three small children, including a one-year-old named Patty Sue," she reported.

"I thought you grew up in a commune," Harriet said.

"I did," Jenny said. "We did, but Bobby left when he was eighteen. He got involved in drugs while he was still in Minnesota, and they asked him to leave."

"I thought everyone used drugs in the sixties," Lauren said.

"They did," Jenny said. "And it was the professors' fault Bobby got into it. They all smoked pot and let the kids over eighteen join them. Bobby began dealing and was good at it—too good. He was attracting too much attention; and not only from the police. He was climbing the ranks of the local drug organization. That didn't fit with the peace-and-love message of the commune, although I'm not sure where they thought their own illegal drugs were coming from. At any rate, they told Bobby he had to find a new job or move, and so he left."

"That explains why Patty might want to throw acid on your *brother*," Morse said.

"I don't know what else to tell you," Jenny said. "I found out about it when Bobby wrote to me from jail."

"Maybe Patty was doing the 'eye for an eye' brand of justice. She lost her father, maybe she wanted Bobby's sister to suffer." Mavis suggested.

"How did she even know about Bobby's sister?" Aunt Beth asked.

"Hello—the Internet," Lauren said. "That's why she waited so long, too. She had to wait until the information became accessible."

"That's a theory," Detective Morse said. "But it doesn't feel right. Why now? Forty-four years later."

"Mental illness can come on at any age, can't it?" Harriet asked.

"Yes, it can, but how would she know how to find Jenny, or the relationship to her brother. I know she could find basic information, but most mentally-ill people aren't that organized.

"And I agree basic information about people can be found on the Internet, but that doesn't tell you their daily schedule or what kind of car they drive. I'll be surprised if Patty doesn't turn out to be the tire-slasher, so she had to know which car was Jenny's."

"She could have asked around town," Harriet suggested. "Or found out her address and then followed her."

"Most people don't have the skill to follow someone without being detected for long enough to learn what you'd need to know," Morse said.

Lauren and Harriet looked at each other but didn't say anything.

"What about Bobby?" Harriet asked Jenny.

"We haven't spoken to each other in years. He showed up in town asking for money, I refused, and he left. I don't know if he's still in town."

Harriet shared a look with Lauren again.

"If he's here, we'll find him," Morse said. She stood up. "You probably need to rest. I really did stop by to see how you're doing. And thanks for the tea," she added.

Mavis got up and helped the detective into her coat.

"Let us know if you find out why this happened to Harriet, will you?" she asked.

"I'll do my best to find out, and I'll share what I can."

"That's all we ask," Beth said and joined Mavis at the door. They watched until Detective Morse was out the door and into her car.

"Jenny, I talked to your brother today, and he says he wasn't asking you for money. He says he was trying to warn you about something," Harriet said. "Given what happened, I'm wondering if he was going to warn you about Patty the acid thrower or something else entirely. You were there—you have to have noticed that he was the first one to tackle the woman. He was the one who got the acid bottle from her and threw it out of reach. Then he took off."

"And I'm wondering why you're not being truthful about it," Aunt Beth said firmly. "Maybe if you'd told us about your brother and maybe even talked to him, Harriet wouldn't be scarred for life."

Harriet thought Aunt Beth laid it on a little thick but was glad she was pressing Jenny to come clean.

"I just don't want anything to do with him," Jenny said, the color draining from her face. "He's been nothing but trouble all our lives." She turned to Harriet. "I'm really sorry about all this."

"He told me he's getting his life together. He said he's off drugs. He said he's been lying low, trying to leave you alone, but he had to make contact now for your own good." Harriet said. "Don't you think you need to hear him out?"

"How am I supposed to find him?" Jenny asked with a sigh.

"He might be at the Fogg Park campground," Lauren offered. "Or maybe he's still hanging around the festival grounds."

"Fine. If you can find him, I'll talk to him. I don't want to open that chapter of my life after all these years, but if it will help make sure that woman isn't set loose to hurt anyone else, I'll try."

Harriet sat up straighter in her chair.

"Don't even think you're going along with whoever is going to look for Jenny's brother," Aunt Beth informed her. "And just for the record, I think now is a time for us to call Jane. She should be the one talking to him. Or at least be there when it takes place."

Jenny's shoulders drooped.

"I may not welcome my brother and all his drama back into my life, but if he's truly gotten his life straightened out, like Harriet says, then I don't want to mess that up for him by having the police pick him up, even if it is just for questioning. Once they check his record, they'll assume he's guilty of something."

"Do we have to go looking for him tonight?" Mavis wondered "Patty's in custody, and it's not likely she was working with anyone else. Let's all get a good night's sleep, and then Jenny can find her brother and see what he was trying to warn her about."

"That sounds like a good idea to me," Beth said.

"Will everyone be safe?" Connie asked. She looked at Jenny. "Why don't you stay in my guest room? I think we'd all feel better if you weren't alone."

"I have to admit I'm a little nervous about staying alone at my place," Jenny confessed. "My husband isn't going to be home for another week."

"I'll call Rod and tell him to be ready to go to your house with us," Connie said and pulled her cell phone from her purse.

"I can cover your booth for part of the day tomorrow," DeAnn offered Harriet. "Kissa goes to baby playtime at the church in the morning—her therapist told us we should help her spend time with other babies. Since we don't know what her life was like before we adopted her, she thought socialization with a group of other babies was in order as a precaution."

"Precaution against what?" Connie demanded.

"Nothing specific. She mentioned listening to the other babies talking and learning to share and interact in a group."

"She's a baby," Connie said. "Young children don't develop an awareness of other children until three years at least."

"I figured it wouldn't hurt her to go," DeAnn said. "She seems to like playing around the other kids. So, I'm available in the morning if you want."

"I can find a sub for the raffle booth in the afternoon," Mavis said.

"I have to check with my client and see if they've finished their system test yet. If they haven't, I could do time in the booth," Lauren said.

"Harriet," Carla said, "if you don't mind Wendy coming along, I could help you tomorrow."

"I would love to see Wendy, and I'd appreciate having a little help. I'm not supposed to move my arm, and I could use a ride to the doctor, if you don't mind, since I have to have the burn checked and redressed. I'm not supposed to drive when I take the medication they gave me."

"Carla can take Scooter out for you, too," Aunt Beth said. "And I'm going to go get Brownie, and we're going to both spend the night with you."

"That's not necessary—" Harriet tried to protest.

"Don't argue with me. We're not letting you spend the night alone."

Harriet knew by the tone of her voice there would be no changing her mind.

"Jenny, if you don't mind, I'd like to go with you when you talk to your brother," Robin said. "He told Harriet he's off drugs, but we're just taking his word for it. Even if he is, with everything that's happened, I don't think you should go anywhere alone until we figure out what's going on."

"I think that's a good idea," Aunt Beth agreed. She stood up and wrestled her plump frame into her coat.

"You'll get no argument from me," Jenny said. "I may not want anything to do with my brother, but I'm not a complete fool. Since we don't know what's going on, I think we all should be careful."

The group nodded their agreement and, one by one, finished their tea and carried their mugs to the kitchen before putting on their coats and gathering their purses.

"I'll wait with Harriet until you get back," Lauren said to Aunt Beth.

"Thank you, honey, I'd appreciate it. I won't be long."

"Take your time, Carter is spending some quality time with my neighbor, the little rat. She's been knitting him sweaters, so he feels obligated to go watch movies with her on Saturday nights."

"Of course he does," Mavis said. Harriet couldn't tell if she was joking or not, so she didn't say anything.

The group finished their goodbyes and left.

<hr />

"Did you learn anything from Jenny's quilt?" Harriet asked Lauren when the rest of the group had dispersed. "It felt weird when I turned it to show the back to that nurse, like there was something stiff in the batting."

"There is. The acid turned whatever it is black where it penetrated the backing. It felt like paper of some sort. It wasn't solid like a big piece of cardboard or anything like that. The way the quilt folded and bent, it had to have been smallish pieces of paper or posterboard."

"What do you think it was?"

"I only got a quick look and feel. It's not like I got to open a seam or put it under a microscope or anything."

"Throw me a bone here; make a guess as to what it could be."

"Given how old it is, it could be computer punch cards, index cards, or depending how it was packaged, it could even be money."

"Why on earth would Jenny have money or cards of some sort inside her quilt?" Harriet asked, more to herself than to her friend.

"That would be the question, now, wouldn't it?"

"Unfortunately, I think it means Jenny still isn't telling us everything she knows about what's happening," Harriet said.

"We could get out the spotlight and rubber hose and force her to tell us," Lauren said with a grin.

"Short of torture, I'm afraid we have to wait until she's ready to tell us what she knows. And judging by her recent behavior, I'm not holding my breath on that."

"I've got to dig out my *Star Trek* costume when I get home," Lauren said, changing the subject. "In some circles, the most important event of the nineteen-sixties was the three-year flight of the starship *Enterprise*."

"Gosh, was it really only three years?"

"It was," Lauren replied. "Seems like it should have been longer, given the following it still has, but the original TV series was just three seasons. Of course, there were the movies and the spin-off series, but for the purists it was only three glorious years."

Harriet didn't know what to say to that, so she remained silent.

"Does your arm hurt?" Lauren asked.

"The medication is taking the edge off, but I can still feel the fire."

"Do you want an ice pack or anything?"

"No, I just want to go to bed. Besides, if I have any hope of going to the concert tomorrow night, I have to convince my aunt it's not as bad as she thinks, which means no ice pack or other display of discomfort."

"Aren't you just the tough one?"

"Would you want to miss a chance to go backstage at a Colm Byrne concert?"

"He's not my style, but if you like that sort of thing, I guess not."

"One of your merry band of protesters told me the band is going to play covers of a sampling of popular songs from the decade."

"That might be interesting." Lauren allowed. "Or it could be hideous," she added. "If they're like most tribute bands."

"Have you looked up what songs made the top ten for the decade?" Harriet asked, knowing Lauren's love of data.

"As a matter of fact, I did look up the top one hundred songs. Somehow, I can't see Colm Byrne doing Aretha Franklin or Marvin Gaye. Likewise, Simon and Garfunkel had a range between the two of them that most people can't imitate. 'Louie, Louie' has been played by every high school band every year since the Kingsmen recorded it, so they can probably do that one."

She continued her analysis of the songs and her opinion as to the likelihood of Colm Byrne being able to cover them adequately until Aunt Beth returned.

"If you don't need anything else, I'm out of here," Lauren announced when she came back in from taking Scooter for his last walk of the night.

"Thanks for all your help," Harriet said and yawned.

"Try not to get in any more trouble until tomorrow," Lauren admonished as she gathered her bag and left.

"Let's get you to bed," Aunt Beth said when she'd taken her coat off and stowed her overnight bag in her bedroom. She followed Harriet upstairs carrying Brownie under her arm, Fred and Scooter following behind them.

Chapter 20

Carla brought a bag of doughnuts with her when she and Wendy arrived the following morning. She set the toddler on the kitchen floor with a brightly colored toy piano keyboard then went to the stove to make tea.

She put three cups on the table then put four doughnuts on a plate, emptying the bag, and set the plate in front of Harriet, who was sitting in her customary spot.

"How thoughtful," Aunt Beth said as she came into the kitchen. "I'm afraid I'm going to have to take mine to go." She took her cup to the sink and poured the hot tea into a travel mug, picked a plain doughnut up in a napkin, and left, shouting a quick goodbye when she reached the door.

Carla broke another plain doughnut into thirds and handed a piece to Wendy. When Wendy was settled, she went to the diaper bag and pulled a second white sack from under the toddler's diapers. She silently unloaded two apple fritters, three jelly doughnuts and a cinnamon twist, putting each on the plate, and returned the remaining plain doughnuts to the bag.

"Well, well, aren't you—" Harriet started.

"Sneaky was what you were going to say," Carla said with a small smile, her cheeks pinking as she spoke. "With everything going on at Aiden's, I needed this."

"Whatever the reason, I appreciate the extra sugar and fat today."

"How's your arm?" Carla asked.

"I'll live, but it's not fun. It feels hot this morning. Enough about me, though. Anything new with Michelle?"

"Aiden hasn't kicked her out or anything, but I can tell he's getting tired of all her drama. She's called him home from work twice for an imaginary crisis, and that's in addition to the food poisoning last night."

"I hope he figures it out, for all of our sakes."

"Do you miss him?"

"Ah…" Harriet started.

A knock sounded on the studio door, saving her from having to answer, and Carla went to answer it, returning after a moment with Tom Bainbridge. Scooter wagged his tail but didn't get out of his fleece-lined dog bed.

"You were the talk of the festival last night," he said. "I thought I'd come by and see what happened and how you're doing." He pulled a small gold foil-wrapped box from his pocket. "Here, this should make it feel better," he added and handed her the box.

Harriet took the box and, recognizing it, held it to her nose.

"Mmmmm, chocolate." She smiled as she took a deep breath.

"Let me help you," Tom said and slid the gold ribbon from the box, then lifted the top, revealing a half-dozen plump truffles. His hand brushed hers as he completed the motion, sending a jolt of electricity through her that had nothing to do with pain or her burn.

"Do you feel well enough to come to the concert tonight?" he asked, the concern plain in his voice.

"I do, unless the doctor forbids it."

"Is it okay if I lay Wendy on a bed upstairs to change her?" Carla asked, scooping up the toddler and taking a clean diaper and a travel pack of baby wipes as she spoke.

"Sure," Harriet said, not fooled by her friend's move to give her and Tom a little privacy.

"How are you really?" he asked when Carla was out of earshot. He pulled a chair beside Harriet's and sat down.

"I won't really know until I see my doctor this morning. My arm is sore, but I think at least part of it is from the scrubbing they gave it as opposed to the burn itself. They said something about abrading away the damaged tissue to help the skin graft they expect I'll need."

"Sounds awful," Tom said in the whispery voice he used only when they were alone. He leaned in and put his arm carefully around her shoulders, pulling her gently to him. She laid her head on his shoulder, her heart thudding in her chest.

"The sad part is, I was just in the wrong place at the wrong time. I mean, I'm glad it was me instead of Jenny if someone had to be hurt, but I would rather have had neither one of us be a target."

"You're lucky it was only your arm. From what I heard from the other vendors, the lady had a pretty big jug of acid with her."

"It was just a large water bottle, but I *was* fortunate—someone asked to see the back of the quilt just as acid lady was beginning her attack. I had pulled the corner up to show the back just as she threw the liquid. The quilt was wrapped around me, protecting most of my body."

"Why on earth would someone want to harm Jenny, of all people?"

Harriet was quiet.

"What do you know?" Tom asked.

"Nothing for sure. We just think Jenny isn't being forthcoming about her past. Lauren looked the attacker up on the Internet, and it seems that Jenny's brother was involved in an incident that ended with the woman's father being killed. Jenny's brother didn't kill him, but he was jailed for two years for his involvement."

"So, why come after Jenny? Why not her brother?"

"That's why we think there's more to the story than Jenny is telling."

"Clearly," Tom said and snuggled Harriet more tightly to him. He took his forefinger and tilted her chin up then laid a gentle kiss on her lips. She didn't protest, so he deepened the kiss, only ending when they heard the artificially loud sound of Carla's voice as she reached the top of the stairs.

"Thanks, I needed that," Harriet whispered as Tom scooted his chair back to its normal place at the table.

"Can I bring you ladies anything?" he asked, getting up. He walked over to Scooter's basket and scratched the little dog behind the ears. "You take care of your mother for once," he said to the dog.

"We're good. We have to go to the doctor in a little bit, so we can stop at the store then, if we need to." Harriet said.

"I hate to leave you like this, but I've got to go tend my booth. I've got a group of ladies from the school coming in today to do macrame demonstrations, and I've got to help them set up."

"I'm glad you stopped by," Harriet said.

"I can see myself out," Tom said and then made his way out through the studio.

Harriet picked up a jelly doughnut and took a bite.

"Things are looking up," she said.

Carla's face turned pink again, and she busied herself with Wendy's hair clip.

✂- - - ✂- - - ✂

"How do you feel?" Carla asked when Harriet came back into the waiting room after seeing her doctor. Harriet sat down beside her. Wendy was playing with a wooden train set that sat on a child-size table in the corner; Carla set a timer on her phone and told Wendy she had five more minutes and then they would be leaving.

"It was no picnic having it cleaned and dressed, but he put this elastic sleeve over this gelatin-like dressing and the combination of gel and pressure actually feels good. He also said I have to get a different antibiotic. In spite of all the precautions, it has a spot of infection."

"Do you want to go anywhere on your way home?" Carla asked.

"I was hoping to stop by the festival and check on my booth. I don't expect DeAnn to have any trouble, but I'd like to make sure everything is going smoothly."

"I figured you wouldn't want to sit home all day. I'm guessing you can't stitch with that thing on your arm," Carla said, pointing at the bulky over-wrap on Harriet's arm.

"Yeah, he says I only have to wear this for a few days, luckily."

A few minutes later, Carla's phone chimed, and she scooped her protesting child up in her arms, slinging the diaper bag over her opposite shoulder. Harriet led the way out of the office and to the parking lot.

✂- - - ✂- - - ✂

"Isn't that Colm Byrne?" Carla asked and pointed to a small man walking toward the exhibit hall as she unbuckled Wendy from her carseat.

"Looks like it. I wonder where he's been that he's coming back this early in the morning—and carrying a guitar case."

"I thought he and his band were staying in a tour bus behind the auditorium."

"Someone said he was from this area—he has some connection to Jerry Weber. Maybe he spent the night with the Webers. He probably brings his guitar wherever he goes so he can play for his host."

He caught sight of them and turned toward them.

"Good morning, ladies," he said when he reached them.

Carla eased Wendy back into her carseat.

"Did Skeeter bring you ladies the extra backstage passes for your group?" Byrne asked. "I saw you getting out of your car," he explained to Harriet as he stopped. "I heard you'd been injured last night. Are you okay?" He nodded toward the white bandage on her arm.

"I'm fine, or I will be in a few days."

"Do you know who did this to you? I was having a few brews with an old friend last night so I didn't hear there'd been an accident until this morning. Skeeter didn't mention any names, though. I hope the festival committee has hired additional security."

"The police think it was a case of mistaken identity. I don't know who the woman is, and I haven't heard anything about increasing security. It was late when I got done at the hospital, and I went straight home. Since the woman who threw the acid seemed kinda crazy, I'm assuming she was acting alone, but no one's told me that."

"I suppose it would be locking the barn after the horse is stolen, but I'm going to bring in some private security guards for the rest of our stay," Colm said in his lilting accent. "I'd be happy to provide coverage for you, too." he added. "It's the least I can do, given your injury."

"It wasn't your fault I ran into a crazy," Harriet said.

"When someone like me comes to town it tends to draw the crazies in. It's part of the business. I'm sure you know how many celebrities have been killed by overzealous fans. I can't help but think that if I wasn't headlining your event, maybe your acid lady would have stayed home."

"I'm sure you do draw your share of weirdos, but this time it doesn't seem like it's about you."

"My offer stands. I have a security firm on retainer, so it's really not a problem to add one more assignment to the roster."

"Thanks, but I don't think it will be necessary."

"I hope you're well enough to attend the show tonight. And if you're up to it, maybe you'd like to join me for a late dinner."

"I wouldn't miss the concert, but dinner? I'm not sure how I'll feel by then."

"You would tell me if you were spoken for, wouldn't you?" he asked. "I wouldn't want to step on any toes, but I would certainly enjoy the company of an attractive lass like yourself."

"Can I take a rain check?" Harriet asked.

"Until then," he said and nodded first to Harriet, then Carla before heading to the auditorium.

"Maybe you should take him up on the offer of security," Carla said when Colm was out of earshot.

"No one's after me. I was just in the way. Jenny's the one in trouble, but until she comes clean and tells us what's really going on, we don't know how much. Acid lady may be the extent of it."

"But you don't think so, do you?" Carla asked.

"I don't. She's supposed to go talk to her brother with Robin, but it will remain to be seen if she does. He came to me for help; maybe I can convince him to tell me what's going on. And even if she does talk to him, I'd like to see if their stories match."

"Maybe your aunt is right, and we should stay out of police business."

"*Jenny's* right—Bobby isn't going to talk to the police, and in her misguided attempt to protect him, neither is she."

"You are going to rest at least part of the day, aren't you? I mean, you aren't going to make me lie to Beth, are you?"

"Carla," Harriet said, "I would never ask you to lie for me."

Carla blushed a fierce red.

"Leaving things out is the same as lying," she insisted.

"Don't worry. We'll check in with DeAnn, see if we can catch up with Bobby, and then I'll go home without argument."

"Do you promise?"

"You're getting tough," Harriet said with a smile then headed toward the south vendor area.

"What are you doing here?" DeAnn asked when they arrived at the booth

"I just wanted to check and see that everything is okay," Harriet said. "Diane Frank was difficult the other day, and I expect she'll be back before this event is over."

"I figured you were here to find out if Robin and Jenny had spoken to Bobby yet."

"I did want to make sure you were doing okay here, but you're right, I'm curious as to what, if anything's, been said."

"Robin said they looked for him at Fogg Park, but the other homeless people said he hadn't been there the previous night. They tried the warming shelter at the Methodist church and the food line at the Catholic church without luck and then took a swing past the coffee shops in town, but still nothing."

"Where are they now?" Harriet asked.

"Robin called an hour ago and said the police wanted to talk to Jenny again about acid lady. They were going to drive by Jenny's so she could change into her costume before coming back here, but so far I haven't seen either one of them."

"I was going to be surprised if Jenny actually followed through and talked to her brother, and I should have guessed the police would want to talk to her after last night."

"Speaking of last night, shouldn't you be at home resting?"

"We're on our way home from the doctor. Don't tell my aunt we were here." Harriet glanced at Carla. "Unless she asks, that is."

"Do you have food at home for me to make you lunch?" Carla asked as they walked back to the car. "Or do I need to swing by the store and pick something up?"

"I have stuff," Harriet said. "But I would like to make one more brief stop."

Carla sighed.

"I hope your aunt doesn't come by to check on you while we're still out."

"This will only take a minute. I'm going to call Lauren and find out if her guys know where Bobby is. If they do, we'll go have a chat with him."

"Who are her guys?"

"Long story, but the short version is, her personal geek squad is playing private surveillance."

"Detective Morse isn't going to like that," Carla said.

"Only if she finds out," Harriet said with a laugh. "Don't worry, it will be fine. Lauren's people aren't interfering with the police. They're just watching and reporting back to Lauren."

Carla sighed—something she'd been doing a lot of lately.

"If this is too much for you, I can see if Lauren can pick me up. I know she's curious about what's going on."

"I'm sorry. It's not that I'm not curious," Carla said. "It's all the drama going on at Aiden's. I'm afraid I'm going to have to quit my job." Tears filled her dark blue eyes.

"I knew it was bad, but I didn't think it would come to this. Do you need a place to stay? I know Connie would be happy to have you, too."

"I don't want to leave Aiden. He's not handling things very well, and I know my being there helps, but I don't want Wendy to grow up thinking it's okay to let people abuse you. And make no mistake—living with Michelle is daily abuse."

"We can go home," Harriet said. "I'm being selfish."

Carla used the heels of her hands to wipe her eyes.

"I'm sorry. I shouldn't be complaining to you when you're not well. The distraction is probably just what I need. If we sit around your house too long, I'll just worry about what to do. Besides, look." She pointed at Wendy, who had fallen asleep in her car seat while they were talking. "She's been missing a lot of naps lately." She helped Harriet into the passenger seat. "It'll be better if we let Wendy sleep for a while. I can sit in the car with her if Lauren tells you where Jenny's brother is."

"Are you sure? We can wait and see what Robin says. She'll make Jenny talk to her brother eventually."

"No, let's do this thing," Carla said and started her car.

Chapter 21

*H*arriet fumbled one-handed in her purse, trying to locate her phone.

"Here, let me do that," Carla said, and put the car into park. She reached into Harriet's bag and came out with the phone. "Is she in your favorites list?"

Harriet nodded, and Carla swiped the touch screen open then pressed it twice and handed the phone to her.

"Lauren?" she said. "Do you know where Bobby is?"

"Not sure."

"What's that mean?"

"The two guys on watch said he showed up at Jenny's last night. She wasn't home because, of course, she was at your house. He went around to the back, and they haven't seen him since. They don't know if he made them and went on out through her back yard, or if he's still in the house.

"Jenny came by and went out a few minutes later with an overnight bag. If she talked to him, it didn't take long. Just to be sure, the rest of the watchers checked out all the other locations they've seen him at, but no luck. Their best guess is that he's still inside."

"That's weird."

"Well, there you go. This whole thing has been weird, if you ask me."

"I talked to DeAnn on the way home from my doctor appointment, and she says Jenny and Robin looked for Bobby with no luck."

"Did they check Jenny's house?"

"Not that DeAnn said. She said they checked the homeless camp and the churches."

"My guys just observed, they didn't approach the house. Maybe you should try that. If you're out and not resting like you're supposed to anyway. I'd go, but I'm finishing up some work so I can do your booth this afternoon."

"I do appreciate that," Harriet said. "Carla and I can at least go by and try the doorbell."

"Let me know what you find out," Lauren said. "I'll call the watchers and let them know you're coming."

"Thanks for everything," Harriet said and pressed the off-button. "We need to go to Jenny's." She told her what Lauren had said.

"Wouldn't Jenny know her brother was at her house last night when she and Connie went there?" Carla asked.

"That would be a reasonable assumption, but I'm pretty sure Jenny isn't telling the truth about what's going on, so she might not have told Robin that she already knew where he was, even though they were looking for him."

"I'm not sure if I hope he's there or not," Carla said.

"Yeah, I know, I hate to think Jenny is lying to all of us to this degree."

✂ - - - ✂ - - - ✂

Jenny lived in an older subdivision of well-tended homes and tidy gardens. Harriet noticed a gray Prius halfway down the block and assumed it was Lauren's guys.

"Let me go to the door," Carla said. "You can stay with Wendy. If he answers, you can take over. If he doesn't, then we won't have jostled your arm around for nothing."

Harriet wanted to protest, but her arm *was* starting to hurt, and she couldn't think of a good reason not to let Carla go.

Carla stood on the sidewalk and looked up and down the street before walking up to Jenny's door. Harriet couldn't see the doorbell from her position, but she saw Carla reach out toward the door, pause then drop her arm, waiting a few beats before repeating the process. There was no response. Carla came back to the car and got in.

"I'm going to go around back," Harriet said. "Jenny has those French doors to her patio, and she usually leaves the blinds open. I just want to be sure Bobby isn't inside sipping coffee and waiting for us to leave."

Carla's shoulders slumped.

"I'll go," she said. "For all the same reasons it wasn't a good idea for you to go to the front door."

"You're starting to sound a little bit like Lauren," Harriet said with a smile.

Carla's face turned pink.

"That doesn't mean I'm wrong, though," she said quietly.

"Okay, fine," Harriet said. "Look in the French doors, and then see if you can look in the two sets of bedroom windows you can reach from the patio. If we're lucky, he's in one of them and left the curtains and blinds open."

Carla walked back up Jenny's path then turned left, cutting across the yard and disappearing around the side of the house. She returned a few minutes later, almost running and looking back over her shoulder. She slid into the driver's seat and pulled her phone from her purse.

"What's wrong?" Harriet asked, but Carla didn't answer. She pressed the face of her phone three times.

"I just found a dead body," she said.

✂ - - - ✂ - - - ✂

They stayed in the car, Wendy asleep in her car-seat, in front of Jenny's house until the police arrived. A knock on the driver's-side window startled them.

"I can't even say it again," Jane Morse said to Harriet when Carla rolled down the window. "Has there been a crime in this town since you've been back that you haven't been involved in?"

Harriet got out of the car. She shrugged then winced in pain when it moved her burned arm too much.

147

"We were helping Jenny look for her brother. She was going to try to find him, but you-all were talking to her, so Carla and I thought we'd help by checking to see if he was here."

"She came to the station thirty minutes ago. How is it she wouldn't know her brother is staying at her house?" Morse asked.

"*Jenny* isn't staying at her house right now," Carla offered.

"Her husband is out of town," Harriet added. "We suggested she not stay home alone, since the trouble at the festival seems to be targeted on her."

"That's the first sensible thing I've heard today," Morse admonished. "If she'd been home, she might be lying there beside her brother with a bullet in her head."

"Jenny was estranged from her brother," Harriet said. "He came to me at the festival and said he was trying to warn her about something, but she wouldn't talk to him. He asked me to help him convince her to listen. That's what I was doing when that woman threw acid on me. And before you ask, no, he didn't tell me what kind of trouble he was going to warn her about."

Morse made a note in her notepad.

"Is there anything else you've failed to tell me about this whole mess?"

"No," Harriet said, pausing to think first.

"You're sure? This information would have been useful last night when I came by your house. We might have been able to save this man."

"That's not fair." I was on heavy-duty pain medication."

"I'm sorry, you're right," Morse said. "I'm just frustrated, and I'm taking it out on you." She looked down. "Someone killed Pam Gilbert, and until this morning, we were liking the ex-husband for it. Now we have a second victim shot in the same manner. There's no obvious connection between Pam and Bobbie."

"Except Jenny," Harriet said. "They both knew Jenny."

"They did. And then there's the slashed tire incident. Other than it having happened to Jenny, it doesn't fit with either murder."

"Don't forget this," Harriet said and raised her bandaged arm.

"Your incident *really* doesn't fit," Morse said. "That poor woman is so out of touch, it's hard to imagine her being part of any coordinated effort."

"Doesn't it seem like one coincidence too many?" Harriet asked.

"Normally, I'd say yes, but in this case, the woman is so sick I'm not seeing it."

Wendy started moving around in her seat, and Carla opened the door then looked back at Harriet.

"I think we need to go home," Harriet said to Morse. "I'm supposed to be resting."

"Good idea. Go home and stay there until your arm is better."

"I was only out today to have my bandage changed."

"And yet, here you are," Morse said with a shake of her head. "Convince your friend not to come back here. We told her, but that doesn't seem to mean anything to you Loose Threads."

Harriet started to protest, but Carla came to stand beside her.

"Let me help you get in the car," she said and guided Harriet away from Detective Morse.

Chapter 22

*H*arriet woke from the nap Carla had insisted she take and found Carla gone and that Mavis had replaced her. Scooter was on his fleece mat beside the older woman; her own dog Curley was asleep in her lap.

"Oh, good, you're awake. I thought I was going to have to wake you, and I was afraid I'd hurt your arm."

"Are we late? Did I sleep too long?" Harriet asked as she rubbed her eyes with her good hand. She had agreed to go upstairs to her TV room and was propped up on the sofa with her arm resting on a pillow across her chest.

"No, we've still got a few hours before we have to go. You were moaning in your sleep. Does your arm hurt?"

"I was dreaming. There was a mountain lion on a narrow ledge looking over a sandstorm. And a scary-looking clown was climbing up the sheer cliff toward the cat."

"That's a weird one." Mavis said.

"During the dream, I was terrified. My heart felt like it was going to burst out of my chest."

"Your dreams are supposed to mean something if you know how to interpret them."

"Do you know what this one means?"

Mavis made a derisive noise.

"I don't believe in that nonsense," she said.

Harriet laughed.

"Why did you tell me they meant something, then?"

"You young people seem to believe."

"I'm not sure I follow your logic, but maybe Lauren can look it up for me."

"Are you hungry? I made a couple of grilled cheese sandwiches and heated some tomato soup."

"That sounds good," Harriet said. "I can come down to the kitchen."

"As long as you can get upstairs again—if you're going to change into a sixties outfit, that is."

"We have to wear costumes to the kitchen?" Harriet asked with a smile.

"To the concert, Miss Smarty Pants, but I suppose if it hurts your arm too much we could make excuses for you."

"My arm hurts, but it's a burn, not an amputation or paralysis or something serious."

"I was just giving you an out," Mavis said. "Excuse me for trying to take care of you."

"Sorry, I didn't mean to be critical."

✂ - - - ✂ - - - ✂

It was full dark when Harriet and Mavis met Carla and Lauren in front of the auditorium; this time of the year it usually happened around five-thirty and then only if it wasn't cloudy.

"Where's Jenny?" Harriet asked.

"Robin called and said Jenny didn't want to come at the last minute, so she insisted she come to her house. Connie and Rod are babysitting Wendy so Carla can enjoy herself. Robin's husband brought their passes to Connie's so Carla could bring them to the concert in case anyone needed them."

Carla reached into her jacket pocket and pulled the passes out.

"I was going to have a sitter come to Aiden's, but with Michelle there, I didn't want to risk it," Carla said.

"That's a smart decision," Harriet said. "Has anyone talked to Aunt Beth? Is she coming?"

"I think she's going to help Jorge with food," Mavis said. "They've set up tables in the lobby and are going to sell light snacks and

151

drinks during the intermission. Beth figures they'll be able to hear the concert from there."

"Has anyone heard from DeAnn?" Harriet asked.

"She called when you were resting and said she needed to spend some time with her kids."

The door to the auditorium opened, and Colm Byrne's assistant came out.

"You ladies ready for your tour?" Skeeter asked. "Do we need to wait for more people?"

"No," Harriet said. "Jenny decided not to come, and our friend Robin is staying with her. And another lady had to be with her kids tonight."

"Jenny not a Colm Byrne fan?" he asked. It was clear he couldn't believe that could be true of anyone.

"It's not that," Harriet answered. "She just had something else to do."

"Well, they're going to miss a good show," Skeeter said. "Shall we go in?" He didn't wait for an answer, just went to the nearest set of doors and held one open.

Burly black-T-shirted men were in evidence inside the door and outside of each doorway they passed. As promised, Colm Byrne had increased the security.

Harriet was wearing bell-bottom jeans and a Mexican peasant blouse. She'd discovered that, after her visit to the doctor, her bandage was too big to comfortably wear a long-sleeved shirt over it. She layered two tank tops under the short-sleeved blouse and put on a knitted poncho Mavis had brought along when she'd come to sit with her. Harriet wasn't quite sure if Mavis had gotten it at a secondhand store last week or if she'd had it in her closet since the nineteen-sixties, but she was thankful.

Skeeter instructed the women to put the lanyards around their necks and turn the passes so the front was visible. He checked to see that everyone had complied.

"We have strict security procedures in place because of what's going on here," he said and, turning, led them to a door beside the stage. "You need to stay together at all times, and don't wander off into any area I've not taken you to.

"We have a green room where performers hang out when they're not performing—we usually have a local band from whatever city we're in to open for us. They play before Colm and then midway between sets." He made a noise that Harriet guessed was supposed to be a chuckle. "He's not as young as he once was. He doesn't perform two hours straight anymore like he used to.

"For this event we ran open auditions for folk artists and other types of tribute bands. We have a Peter, Paul and Mary tribute band, a Four Tops band, a trio that plays Simon and Garfunkle music and a really good Stevie Wonder impersonator."

True to his word, the room was green, and it was full of people dressed to look like the singer or band they were supposed to be.

"Are you one of the Tops or Stevie Wonder?" Harriet asked a man with coffee-colored skin and shoulder-length dreadlocks.

"Both," he said with a laugh. "I come out first with the Four Tops and then again two sets later in a different outfit as Stevie Wonder."

"Are there a lot of sixties festivals?"

"No. We do a few, but mostly we do cruise ships. But never with a big name like Colm Byrne."

"Cruising all the time must be fun," Mavis said.

"It's a living," the man said with a smile.

The Threads spoke to the other performers, and then Skeeter ushered them to the backstage dining room. Comfy chairs were placed around small tables throughout the space, with a loaded buffet table along the back wall. Two men in white aprons stood behind the buffet, ready to carve meat for the guests. They were both covered in tattoos, including, Harriet noticed, a stylized peace symbol.

One man had a full head of shoulder-length white hair pulled into a low ponytail. He was big, with biceps that strained the rolled up sleeves of his denim work shirt. The second man also sported a tail, but in his case the top of his head was nearly bald and his hair was a dirty gray color. He was thin but muscular.

"Don't look like your typical food service people, do they?" Lauren muttered as she headed toward their table.

Harriet had to hurry to catch up.

"Do you cook the food yourselves?" she asked white-hair.

"Do I look like Julia Child?" he shot back.

"My friend meant to say, no, we don't," said the gray-haired man. "Can we cut some meat for you?"

The big man gave his partner a dirty look but didn't say anything.

Lauren asked for roast beef and then moved on down the table. Harriet chose pork roast, which the white-haired man was serving.

"Which one of you was wearing the Afro wig yesterday?" he asked as he sliced her meat.

"None of us, actually," Harriet replied. "Why?"

White Hair narrowed his eyes and glared at her.

"I thought I recognized her. We went to high school together."

Harriet added fruit to her plate and joined Lauren at one of the small tables.

"That was weird," she said. "The big guy just asked me where Jenny was. He said they went to high school together."

"If I'm not mistaken, those are prison tattoos on their arms. And those teardrops by their eyes represent people they've murdered."

Mavis filled her plate and pulled a chair up to Lauren and Harriet's table.

"What are you two whispering about?" she asked.

"The big guy that's slicing pork asked me where Jenny was. He said he went to high school with her."

"Well, that sounds fishy, given she was schooled in the commune."

"He asked me about Jenny, too," Carla said. She'd just joined them. "He asked me if I knew the lady who had been wearing the afro."

"What did you say?" Harriet asked.

"I told him I didn't know who he was talking about, and that lots of people were wearing afro wigs at this event."

"Good girl," Harriet said.

Several of the singers brought their plates to the next table and sat down, ending the conversation.

✂ - - - ✂ - - - ✂

Twenty minutes passed before Skeeter came back to escort them to their next backstage activity.

"You ladies ready to meet the man?" he asked.

"I have a question," Harriet said. "Who are those two guys carving the meat? They don't seem like your usual food service workers."

"And they were asking a lot of questions," Mavis added.

Skeeter glared at the two men then turned back to Harriet.

"Since Colm's made it big he's tried to hire people who couldn't get a job otherwise. I'm sure you wouldn't be surprised to find out these two have done time. They usually do more physical labor, but our regular cook got hurt, so the kitchen helpers had to step in, and we had to move those two up. I thought they could handle it, but I guess not."

He glanced at his watch.

"We better move. Colm will meet you in his dressing room. But we've got to swing back by the front entrance to gather up some folks who won backstage visits in a radio contest."

The newcomers wore red passes with the radio station's call letters around their necks, apparently denoting their lesser status. When they returned backstage, Colm Byrne and his band members sat at a table in the main passageway. The radio station bunch was ushered to the table while Skeeter sent the Threads into what turned out to be Colm's dressing room.

A large bowl of fresh fruit sat in the middle of a table on one wall. To the left of the fruit, bottles of water stuck out of a large tin wash bucket that was half-full of crushed ice. To the right, a ceramic bowl was filled with dark chocolate truffles.

"Make yourself at home," Skeeter said and shut the door as he left.

Harriet immediately made a move toward the truffle bowl.

"You don't have to ask me twice when it comes to chocolate."

She selected a truffle with a pink dot of hard frosting on its top. Mavis joined her and selected one with a sprinkle of large salt crystals.

"Somehow I thought they'd have beer and chips for snacks," she said.

"When they were younger, they probably did eat like that," Lauren said. "I read an article on the Internet that said the groups that survived the sixties and still are active have learned to live a healthier life. Ozzy Osbourne travels with a personal trainer!"

"Wow," Carla said.

"Are you ladies enjoying your tour?" Colm Byrne asked as he joined them

"We definitely like the chocolates," Harriet said.

Colm went to the bowl and selected a truffle.

"Our nutritionist only lets us have them on performance days."

"We were just talking about how healthy your snacks are," Lauren said.

"We've been in the game a long time," he said with a smile. "We have to use every trick in the book to keep up with the younger guns." He stepped over to an electric kettle sitting on his dressing table and began preparing a cup of peppermint tea laced with honey. "I hope I can trust you ladies not to let out my secret weapon." He held up his teacup.

"Our lips are sealed," Mavis said.

"When I met you ladies the other day, I thought there were more of you. Are some of your group not fans?" Colm asked.

"Some people had better things to do," Lauren said.

"Ouch," he said with a smile.

"What my friend meant to say is that some of our group had obligations in other areas of the festival," Harriet said. "My aunt, for one, will be helping serve food during your intermission."

"How did the festival end up landing a big act like yours for our little event?" Lauren asked sweetly.

"We like to get back to our roots once in a while. We used to play small festivals in Ireland when we were starting out. We had some time off a couple of months ago and saw the notice that you were looking for a band. It sounded fun, so I called my buddy Jerry to see if we could get in."

"Did you meet Jerry in Ireland?" Harriet asked.

"That I did," Colm said. "That I did."

"Everyone is happy to have a big name like you. We'll probably get a lot of out-of-town people tonight," Mavis said.

"I had them save front-row seats for you for the performance. The radio people will be behind you. Skeeter will come get you in a few minutes. We'll have a couple of sets by the local bands before I come out. I hope you enjoy the show."

"Thank you so much," Carla said, blushing furiously.

"Are you the young lady who's never been to a show before?"

Carla was so starstruck all she could do was nod her head. Colm opened a drawer in his dressing table and pulled out a colorful scarf.

"These are my trademark," he said and handed it to Carla.

"Thank you so much," she stammered and carefully took the scarf from his hands.

Mavis wound it around Carla's neck, crossing it into a loose knot at her throat. Carla thanked Colm again, and then Skeeter came into the room and led them to the front row of the auditorium. The seats were roped off, including the ones that would have been Robin's and Jenny's.

"I'm going to the restroom one last time," Harriet said.

"Take Lauren with you, and when you get back, Carla and I will go," Mavis instructed.

✂ - - - ✂ - - - ✂

Harriet was standing outside the restroom door waiting for Lauren when Tom approached her.

"Hey," he said. "You here for the concert?"

"Not only am I here, I have front-row seats."

"Did the organizers feel sorry for you?" he asked with a smile.

"No, we actually had these tickets before I got hurt."

"Did you charm Mister Byrne out of them?"

"Actually, we performed a service for him—and not the one you're thinking of. His stage manager asked us to sit and listen while they adjusted the sound and lights for the smaller venue."

"That's lucky. I paid twenty-five dollars for my ticket at the vendor's rate, and I'm halfway back."

"Come sit with us," Harriet said.

"How can I do that? I heard it's a sellout."

"Jenny and Robin decided to stay home at the last minute. We have their passes."

"In that case, I'd be happy to join you," Tom said and smiled at her.

They waited for Lauren then went back to their seats, guarding purses while Mavis and Carla had their turn powdering their noses. Then the show began.

The first act was the Simon and Garfunkle tribute trio, consisting of two men and a woman. The men were deft guitarists, and with the woman to cover the higher ranges, they were able to sing credible versions of "Sounds of Silence," "Scarborough Fair," and "Bridge Over Troubled Water." The Four Tops send-up group sang "I Can't Help Myself," which was the song most people knew of as "Sugar Pie Honey Bunch," and finished with "Reach Out, I'll be There."

The background band played a musical interlude while the stage was reset, and then the man himself walked out on stage, guitar in hand.

Colm played a medley of songs, starting with the ballad "Roses are Red (My Love)," an old Bobby Vinton song, and several others from the early sixties. Harriet couldn't have told anyone what else he played. Mavis and Carla were clapping and, in Mavis's case, singing along. Lauren had her smartphone concealed by her leg and was looking something up. Tom seemed to be listening, but Harriet was mentally reviewing what had been going on for the last few days.

The police were treating the shooting, the tire-slashing, her acid attack and Bobby's killing as if they were four coincidental but separate incidents, but it didn't seem likely to Harriet. Their festival was too small to have so many unless they were related. And Jenny seemed to be at the center of it all.

Before she realized it, Tom had taken her hand and was urging her to her feet.

"It's intermission," he whispered into her ear. "You were a million miles away—want to tell me where?"

"Not here," she murmured.

"We're going to the restrooms and then maybe check out the food," Harriet told Carla and Mavis.

"We're going to go find a band T-shirt for Carla," Mavis said. "After all, she needs something to commemorate her first-ever rock concert." She beamed at her.

"I'm going to the bathroom with them," Lauren said, gesturing toward Harriet and Tom. Mavis glared at her but didn't say anything.

Tom led Harriet and Lauren out of their row and into the main aisle.

"I presume we aren't really going to the restrooms," he said when they were far enough from Mavis and Carla they wouldn't be heard.

"No, we are not," Harriet said.

"I knew it," Lauren said. "Are we going backstage?"

"No. I think with all the extra security Colm has in place, we wouldn't get very far. We're going to see if Jenny's quilt is still at her display. If it is, we're going to see if we can figure out what's inside it besides batting."

"I thought they closed the exhibit during the concert," Lauren said.

"They did, but only for the general public. Those of us with vendor badges can get in," Harriet informed her.

"What about those of us without a badge?" Tom asked.

"I'll wave this," Harriet lifted her bandaged arm. "I'll tell them I need you to carry something for me. We can grab something from my booth if we need to."

"Time's a-wasting, kids," Lauren said and then led the way out of the auditorium and toward the exhibit hall.

The attendant opened the exhibit hall door and waved them in, barely glancing at Harriet's proffered badge. They started down the main aisle, but Harriet stopped, putting a finger to her lips. She waved them down a side aisle then stopped to listen. She could hear muffled voices at the back of the hall.

They made their way slowly toward Jenny's stage, stopping at every aisle to look and listen before advancing. The quilts hanging in almost every vendor booth limited their visibility.

"Look, Jonquil, we just want our money," a deep male voice said.

"I don't know what you're talking about," Jenny said, "and I don't know who Jonquil is. Is this some sort of joke?"

"Don't give me that," the man said. "You and Paisley are the only ones who got away."

They heard the sound of scuffling, and then a woman screamed.

Harriet rushed down the aisle, followed by Tom, stopping abruptly when they reached Jenny's stage. Lauren cut down the last side row and disappeared. The two cooks from the buffet were restraining Jenny and Robin.

"What do you think you're doing?" Harriet yelled at them. "Let them go."

"I suppose you're going to make me," the white-haired guy said.

Tom came up behind Harriet.

"Oh, are you the muscle for the ladies?" White Hair said.

"Let them go," Harriet repeated.

The smaller man looked at his partner. He was clearly not prepared for an audience.

In that moment both men looked at each other at the same time, Lauren came out from behind the black curtain where Jenny's quilt had hung. She jumped from the raised stage, kicking the big guy in the back of his knees as she landed. Before the gray-haired man could move, Tom did a sweeping karate kick that knocked him to the floor. Lauren hit White Hair with a punch to the kidney, dropping him to the floor.

Harriet grabbed a roll of pre-made quilt binding from the vendor booth across from Jenny's display. She tossed it with her good hand to Lauren, who promptly tied her man's hands behind his back. Tom was sitting on the back of his guy, pinning the man's wrist in the small of his own back.

"Everyone good?" Harriet asked.

Robin nodded and turned around so they could see she was on her cell phone. Jenny was nowhere to be seen.

Robin finished her call and put her phone down.

"I called nine-one-one," she announced.

"Where's Jenny?" Harriet asked.

"I don't know. I started dialing the police as soon as I was free. Thank you, Lauren and Tom," she added.

"When did you learn those moves?" Harriet asked them.

"I've been taking martial arts classes since I was in grade school. Mom insisted," Tom said.

"I took a women's self-defense class when Avanell passed away. My class decided to keep going," Lauren said.

"It's a good thing," Harriet said.

"I called Detective Morse, too," Robin advised.

"Where do we think Jenny went?" Lauren asked.

"Not far, I hope," Robin said. "We came here together, and she drove. We intended to get her quilt—she hung it up today with a

160

piece of fabric basted over the damage, and wanted to appliqué a more permanent cover for the burned area."

"You can ride home with me," Harriet offered.

"Thanks."

Detective Morse arrived at the same time as the patrol cars. She directed two officers Harriet had never seen before to cuff the men and take them to the jail on charges of assaulting Robin and Jenny. When the reading of rights was done and the officers and the two cooks were gone, she turned to Harriet, Robin, Lauren and Tom.

"Somebody better start talking before I start arresting people for obstruction of justice," she said.

"Hey, I *called* you," Robin protested.

"That's a step in the right direction, counselor. Now, how about the rest of you tell me everything you know. And by the way, where is Jenny? If I understand what went on here, she was one of the people being assaulted."

"She ran out during the scuffle," Harriet said, "We truly don't know what's going on, except that we keep finding ourselves in the middle of whatever this is, and not in a good way."

"The other thing we know, and I'm thinking this should already be obvious to you, is that Jenny is the connecting thread in all this," Lauren said.

Harriet glared at her.

"I'm not trying to throw her under the bus, but let's get real. Pamela Gilbert gets shot standing on Jenny's stage, Jenny's tires get slashed, and Harriet gets acid thrown at her while holding Jenny's quilt. Then Jenny's brother gets killed. Now, Jenny and Robin get grabbed by a couple of ex-cons, and Jenny doesn't hang around to report it. Anyone with half a brain can see that Jenny is the common denominator here."

"How do you know the two men we just arrested are ex-cons?" Morse asked.

"There's only one place you can get tattoos like those, and it's in prison. I mean, come on—teardrops? Spider webs on their elbows? They're classic prison ink."

"Colm Byrne's stage manager told us he liked to give a hand up to ex-cons," Harriet added.

"How does Jenny connect to a pair of ex-cons?" Morse asked.

"We have no idea," Harriet said. "We've been trying to get her to tell us what's going on, but so far she's told us very little."

"So tell me what she's told you," Morse said.

"She told us she grew up in a commune," Lauren said. "Big whoop."

"I presume you checked it out," Morse asked.

"I did, but I didn't find much. The commune exists and is known locally for its truck farming. Oh, and it's in Minnesota—Georgeville, to be exact."

"We couldn't see how that mattered," Harriet said. "Except for the fact she's been lying to us for years—by omission, but a lie, nonetheless."

"Someone needs to go tell Mavis and Carla why we didn't return after intermission, or they're goin-g to be sending out a search party," Tom said.

Detective Morse looked at her notepad.

"Do you have anything else to add?" she asked Tom.

"Not really," he said. "I was just tagging along with Harriet and Lauren when we found the thugs holding Jenny and Robin hostage."

"Do you have any idea where Jenny went?"

"Not a clue."

"You can go, but the rest of you stay." She waited until he was gone. "What's the story with Jenny?" she demanded of the Loose Threads. "Why was she here tonight, and where is she now? The hall is closed to the public. And how did she get here?"

"She was spending the evening with me," Robin explained. "At the last minute, she decided not to go to the concert, so I volunteered to stay home with her. Her husband is off on a hunting trip in Africa, and with everything that's going on, we all agreed she shouldn't be home, given what happened at her house. And we can't be sure she wasn't the intended target. We really don't know where she is. You know I'd tell you if I knew."

"I don't know, either," Harriet said. "I didn't expect to see Jenny here tonight. She was planning to skip the concert."

"What she said," Lauren chimed in.

"Any idea where she'd go?" Morse asked the trio.

They all shook their heads no.

"Maybe she's waiting out front," Lauren suggested.

"My guess is she'll show up at one of our houses," Harriet said.

"I want to hear from you the minute she turns up. And that goes for the rest of the Loose Threads, too," Morse cautioned. "I'm going to go see what our two ex-cons have to say for themselves. Please, stay out of trouble." With that, she turned and left.

"What now, chief?" Lauren asked Harriet.

"First we need to see if the quilt is here, and if it is, take it home with us. Then, we need to find Jenny."

Robin put her fingers in her ears.

"I can't hear this part," she said and stepped away from Lauren and Harriet.

"Can your people find Jenny?" Harriet asked Lauren in a quiet voice.

"Probably, let me check." She tapped out a quick text message and sent it. "Someone should get back to me in a few minutes."

Harriet stepped up on the small stage and pulled aside the black curtain. Jenny had taken her quilt off display and put another of her on the hanging rod. The damaged quilt was folded up and stowed in a pillowcase.

"It's here," she said.

"Get out of the way, cripple," Lauren said. "You're not supposed to be using your bad arm."

"I'll take the quilt," Robin said. "I don't have a ticket for the concert, and I'm pretty sure I don't have a ride home, either. I'll wait out in the lobby until the show's over."

"We have a spare badge," Lauren said. She held out her keys. "You can put the quilt in my car and then come back in. We're in the front row, center. With the lighting effects, you can slip in without being noticed."

Robin took the keys and pass and left the hall; Harriet and Lauren returned to the auditorium.

✂- - - ✂- - - ✂

It seemed to Harriet they had been in the exhibit hall for hours, but in reality, the concert had barely started again when she and Lauren returned.

"We were beginning to wonder where you'd gotten to," Mavis said, leaning over Carla "I'll tell you about it when this is over," Harriet said loud enough so Mavis could hear over the noise of the music.

The black man Harriet had spoken to in the green room earlier came out in his Stevie Wonder persona to start the second half of the concert. He began with "A Place in the Sun" followed by "Tears of a Clown." By the third song, Harriet was no longer listening. She'd slipped her phone from her pocket and was silently tapping a group text to the Threads.

Meet at my house after the concert.

Aunt Beth answered immediately, asking if everything was okay. Harriet answered that it was, but that they all needed to talk.

She looked up again, and Colm Byrne had taken the stage. He sang a medley of hits from the era, starting with "Like a Rolling Stone" and on through the "Ballad of the Green Berets" by Sgt. Barry Sadler, whoever he was, and then several Beatles songs.

"Are we done yet?" Lauren texted to Harriet.

Harriet just rolled her eyes then looked back to the stage. Colm had transitioned to some of his own most popular hits. If the truth were told, Harriet was with Lauren—she was ready to be done with the concert and on to talking with the Threads.

Colm sang for another thirty minutes and finally took his bow, and after one encore, the audience let him go. Harriet, Mavis, Lauren and Carla waited politely for the crowd in the aisle to ease then stood up and gathered their purses and coats.

"Would you ladies like to join Colm in the back?" Skeeter asked. He'd been waiting for them to exit their row. He looked at Tom.

"I've got to go. Will you ladies be okay?" Tom asked, looking at Harriet.

Harriet and Lauren looked at each other and then at Mavis.

"We can come for a few minutes," Mavis told Skeeter. "I have a little dog I have to take out, so we can't stay long."

"Will I see you tomorrow?" Harriet asked Tom.

"If you wish," he said with a crooked smile. He leaned in and gave her a quick kiss, then turned and went up the aisle.

Skeeter led them to the door at the base of the stage and once again into the labyrinthine backstage area, guiding them to a room they hadn't seen in their previous visit. Everything in this room was intended to soothe, from the pastel wall drapes and overstuffed furniture to the table full of soothing drinks and warming oven full of heated towels for the singer to wrap around his neck.

"That was great," Harriet said, hoping she had conveyed an enthusiasm she didn't feel. "I especially liked the part at the end where you did your own music." That part was true anyway, The man could sing.

"I was going to get a CD, but the booth we went to had sold out," Carla said, her cheeks flaming.

"I'm sorry, that shouldn't happen. We carry a lot of inventory in the truck, but the sales crew sometimes underestimates what the demand will be. Once the intermission starts, there isn't time to restock."

"I can buy it at the store," Carla said.

"Would you like something to drink?" Colm asked.

Harriet and Lauren accepted tea with honey, but Mavis and Carla declined.

"Is your friend Jerry here tonight?" Harriet asked.

"No, he doesn't like loud music. I went to his house and played some of my new stuff on my acoustic guitar the other night."

"Oh, yeah, you were coming from there the other morning when we saw you in the parking lot."

"Ah, yeah, we were up late, so I spent the night on his couch."

"Thank you for treating us so special," Mavis said, "But I really do need to get home to take care of my dog. She's a recent rescue, so she needs more TLC than the average pet."

Harriet and Lauren set their cups down in unison and turned toward the door.

"I'm glad to be of service," Byrne said. "I understand that, in addition to aiding us in our setup tests, you ladies rescued us when our freezer broke."

"Anyone would have done the same," Mavis said. "Now, we really do have to leave."

She led the group out the door and into the now-quiet auditorium.

"Is Curly having problems?" Harriet asked Mavis.

"No, I just couldn't see the point of wasting time heaping more praise on that man."

"Didn't you like the concert?" Carla asked.

"It was fine, as these things go, but I'd rather find out why Harriet is texting us all for a meeting this late at night."

"We need to find Robin," Harriet said. "She was supposed to join us."

"I thought she was home with Jenny," Mavis said.

"It's a long story."

"Jenny and Robin came to get Jenny's quilt," Lauren said. "We found them at the quilt stage fighting with those two cooks. We subdued the villains, called Jane Morse, Jenny took off and now we're all meeting at Harriet house," she finished with a deep breath.

Harriet tapped on the face of her phone, spoke quickly into it and hung up.

"Robin's outside. She went out to make some calls and said by the time she was done, it was too late to come back in unobtrusively," she reported.

"Let's get this show on the road," Mavis said. "I really do have to take Curly out eventually."

Carla and Lauren were both on their phones.

"Grandpa Rod is okay with keeping Wendy, and Connie said she'd meet us at Harriet's." Carla reported.

"Jenny has been located," Lauren said cryptically. "We can swing by the Steaming Cup and pick her up, if you want," she told Harriet.

With their meeting plan in place, they went to their cars to carry out their assignments before driving to Harriet's.

Chapter 23

"Honey, you need to sit down with your arm up on a pillow while you've got these few minutes before everyone gets here," Mavis said. "I'll get some of those cookies from the freezer and set them to thawing in a warm oven and get the kettles heating; then I can take his nibs there out for a quick walk." She nodded at Scooter.

Harriet thought about protesting, but the fact was it felt like her blood vessels were trying to make a break for it. Mavis settled her in one of the wing chairs in the studio and disappeared back into the kitchen.

A soft tapping sounded on the outside door.

"Come in," Harriet called.

The door opened, and Aiden stepped in.

"Hi," he said softly. "I just stopped by to see how you were doing. I came by earlier, but you weren't here." He took his jacket off and sat down on one of the wheeled chairs.

"I was out."

"With Tom?"

"I think that's none of your business."

"Must have been pretty important if you risked letting your burn get infected going out in public."

"My doctor hasn't put any restrictions on my activities."

"He probably assumed you'd use common sense."

"Does your sister know you came to check up on me?" Harriet asked, changing the subject.

Aiden's face reddened, but his silence was all the answer she needed.

"Can we not go there," he said finally.

"I'm just curious as to why you're here. Your sister's never going to let you see me. You know that, I know that, so what are we doing?"

"I just wanted to see how you are. I care about you."

"I know you care about me—just not enough to have an open, honest relationship. You might be willing to treat me like some kind of illicit affair, but I'm sorry—that's not good enough. I don't need or want your sister's approval, but apparently that means more to you than us being a couple does. When you're ready to cut your sister out of our relationship, come back and see me. Until then, it's none of your business where I go or who I go there with."

"Are you willing to wait until I get things straightened out?"

"See, that's exactly what I'm talking about," Harriet said. She moved her arm as she spoke, and winced at the pain the movement caused. She drew in her breath. "I can't see you, but I'm not supposed to see anyone else. Your sister not only controls your life, but you want me to agree to let her control mine, too. Well, hear me loud and clear—that's not going to happen."

Mavis came through the door from the kitchen.

"You leave Harriet alone," she scolded. "She needs her rest, and I could hear you two from the kitchen, and the door was closed. And Harriet's right. If you're not willing to take that sister of yours to task, then just stay away from here. Can't you see that Harriet's injured? She's supposed to be resting, not being badgered by someone who claims to be her friend."

"I *am* her friend," Aiden protested, hurt apparent in his voice.

"Then start acting like it and leave Harriet alone so she can rest. Now go, before your sister notices you're gone and comes looking for you. The last thing we need is that witch showing up here." Mavis pointed to the door.

Aiden got up, put his jacket on and, with an angry scowl at Harriet, left.

Harriet was dozing in her chair when Connie arrived. She woke to discover Mavis had carried the carafes full of hot water and coffee, as well as the tea bags, sugar, milk and a plate full of warm cookies, into the studio and set them on a kitchen towel on her cutting table.

"Robin was just pulling in," Connie reported. "How are we going to approach this?"

"I think we need to lock the door and demand the truth from Jenny," Harriet said. "You can tell she's holding something back, and my feeling is that I wouldn't be sitting here with my arm wrapped like a mummy if she'd come clean from the start."

Aunt Beth came in with Robin and took her coat off, laying it over one of the work chairs.

"Can someone fill me in on what this is about?" she asked.

Harriet quickly told her aunt what had transpired during the break in the concert.

"I guess you're lucky Tom and Lauren were there," Beth said when she had finished.

"Geez," DeAnn said. "I leave you guys alone for one evening, and you find more trouble."

"It was Jenny and Robin who had the problem," Harriet said. "I was on the rescue team."

"With that arm?"

"Lauren and Tom actually did the saving. I was the witness, and we called Detective Morse right away."

"That must have been Robin," DeAnn said.

"If you want to split hairs, yes," Harriet said.

"You should come fix your tea or coffee and get some cookies," Mavis said. "Jenny is going to be here any minute."

"We hope," Harriet said.

✂- - - ✂- - - ✂

Ten more minutes passed before Lauren came through the door, holding Jenny by the elbow. Robin took Jenny's coat, and Connie handed her a cup of tea and a sugar cookie.

"Here, eat and drink a little and get warmed up before we get started," she said.

Harriet took a long look at Jenny. A strand of silver-gray hair fell over her left eye. No longer dressed in nineteen-sixties clothes, her silk blouse was wrinkled, and her wool slacks were becoming baggy around her knees. She'd never seen her friend go out in public in such disarray.

The room quieted as everyone settled in with their drinks and cookies, and the quilters looked around the circle of chairs, exchanging glances. Lauren pulled her chair up beside Harriet's.

"This isn't going to get any easier if we keep stalling," Mavis said and looked at Jenny. "We need an explanation, and we need it to be the truth this time."

"I don't know what you want me to say," Jenny said.

"That's simply not true," Mavis said. "We've been very patient, trying to let you work through whatever it is that's happening in your life without us intruding, but it's clear to everyone you've not been truthful, and as a result, your friends are paying the price."

"Harriet is sitting here with a burned arm, and if it wasn't for Lauren and Tom, it sounds like you and Robin could have been hurt," Aunt Beth said.

"Not to mention your dead brother," Lauren muttered, so only Harriet could hear her.

"We don't know if Harriet's burn was because of Jenny," Connie protested. "That crazy lady would have come no matter what Jenny did or didn't do,"

"I don't believe that," Mavis said, "and neither will you, if you think about it."

"Can we get on with it?" Lauren asked and yawned. "Some of us have work tomorrow."

"I'm sorry all of you have been dragged into my problems." Jenny hung her head, staring at the wheels of her chair. "As I told you," she began carefully, "my brother has always been a problem. He got involved with the wrong people and that led to his selling drugs." She paused.

"Go on," Mavis directed. "Get it off your chest. You'll feel better."

170

"Bobby was supplying drugs to a group of young political idealists in the late sixties. They decided to make a statement by bombing a Selective Service registration office. Bobby didn't have any political ambitions, but he went along with whatever they did because the more paranoid they became, the more drugs and LSD they used. Needless to say, this didn't lead to clarity of thought.

"Something went wrong, and the participants were caught. The police figured out Bobby was a fringe player. He had no real knowledge of the crime, and he only had a small amount of marijuana in his pocket, so they let him off with a couple of years for drug possession. The other people who were involved got more serious time."

"Can we fast-forward to the part where people are coming after you?" Lauren asked.

"And I'd like to know what Bobby was trying to warn you about, and why you didn't want to listen to him," Harriet added.

"I told you," Jenny said. "He's nothing but trouble. You can't believe a word he says."

"I talked to him several times, and you know what? I did believe him. He was afraid, and he was trying to help you, and look what he got for it. He's dead," Harriet said. "And while we're talking about it, I don't believe you don't know the woman who threw acid on me.

"And last time you tried to sell this story, your brother was a bank robber, not a political protester. Which was it?"

"Both," Jenny said, her voice getting louder. "That's what I'm trying to tell you."

Mavis added hot water to Jenny's teacup. Jenny dunked her used teabag up and down. Harriet looked at Jenny, waiting for an explanation.

"The group of young people who were planning the break-in at the Selective Service office quickly realized that they knew nothing about how to successfully break in to anything without being caught. A guy named Cosmic had an uncle who was a bank robber. The uncle was barely older than Cosmic, but he was just out of jail for the second time for robbery, and he was willing to help if the group would supply him with drugs at no cost."

She took a sip of tea and let out a big sigh.

"It's hard to explain what times were like back then. Everyone had at least one friend who'd been killed in Vietnam. Guys graduated high school and went to Vietnam, and you were lucky if you ever saw them again. And if you did, they weren't the same person you went to prom with or played basketball with. No one wanted that to happen to them."

"Back to the bank robbers," Lauren prompted.

"Cosmic's uncle drove by the Selective Service Office and made a fateful discovery. There was a branch of the Bank of Washington right next door. They shared an interior wall. Suddenly, there was more than a few drugs as a payoff for risking another jail sentence.

"Cosmic's uncle said he needed to involve a friend, and eventually told Cosmic and his group that while they were stealing the computer punch cards, he and his friend were going to blow through the wall and rob the bank."

"And everyone agreed to that?" Harriet asked.

"Daily use of marijuana along with the occasional tab of LSD did not leave the group with great critical thinking skills, no matter how passionate their anti-Selective Service sentiments were," Jenny countered.

"Can we skip to the end?" Lauren asked.

"The result was, there must have been a silent alarm or something. Bobby never knew what went wrong. He just said that while everyone was still inside, the police arrived. Cosmic's uncle and his friend had gone in armed. A shootout of some sort ensued, and a policeman was shot and killed. Several of the other players were also shot. Bobby didn't carry a gun, and he didn't think Cosmic or the other idealists did, either. I think I told you, Bobby wasn't really involved. He was in the getaway car, in the back seat, and he got rid of most of the drugs when he heard sirens."

"So, how does this relate to someone trying to hurt you?" Harriet asked.

"I don't know. I mean, the police were tipped about the Selective Service break-in, but they weren't expecting the robbery. Since Bobby didn't know about the robbery plan, he was the one everyone suspected of being the snitch. I guess killing Bobby wasn't enough revenge for them."

"And where were you during all this?" Harriet asked.

"At the commune," she said. "I was too young and naive to see who my brother really was at that point. He used to call me every Sunday, but this time he called me on a Wednesday."

"How did you end up living on the commune, anyway?" Harriet asked.

"I don't really know," Jenny said and paused a moment, her eyes distant. "Let me explain. My parents were not your traditional *Ozzie and Harriet*, *Leave it to Beaver* sort of folks. They lived in a variety of small group situations. My dad left at some point—I don't know why or where he went. He just wasn't there one day.

"Eventually, we ended up at the commune, and we saw less and less of my mother, and then *she* was gone. When Bobby got in trouble for drugs, he was gone, too. By that time, I was attached to other, more stable parental figures, so it wasn't traumatic, but like I said, Bobby did call every week until that Wednesday.

"After that he'd call or send postcards from all over the place, but they got fewer and farther between, and then they stopped. When I was older, Maggie May, the woman I consider to be my mother, told me about Bobby and his involvement in the drug world."

"I suppose those two men who grabbed us tonight were the bank robbers," Robin said.

"I assume so," Jenny said. "Like I said, I was in the commune when Bobby called to tell me what happened."

"That must have been terrible," Connie said.

"It was bad for Bobby, but I led a somewhat sheltered life in the commune. We didn't have television, and limited radio. We heard news of the war, of course. People passed through and spent time with us, and they brought news of the outside, but mostly we lived off the land and enjoyed nature."

No one knew what to say after that.

"I better go get Wendy," Carla said, breaking the silence.

"Oh, honey, why don't you take a night off from Aiden's and spend the night with us. You won't have to wake that baby, and you can get a good night's sleep. You can go back to the snake pit early in the morning, and Michelle won't even know you were gone."

"Thanks," Carla said. "I've been sleeping with one eye open since she moved in. Even with my door locked."

Connie patted her arm, and they got their coats and bags and left. DeAnn left with Robin and Jenny right afterwards; Robin's car was in the parking lot of the Steaming Cup where Jenny had left it when Lauren intercepted her. Jenny's own car was at Robin's house.

"I can come over in the morning," Mavis said to Harriet. "What time do you need to get your arm dressed?"

"I don't need to see the doctor, so they said I could come anytime before noon. I just need to call and give them a few minutes to get the room ready."

"I'll be here at nine."

"Jorge has to cater a breakfast at the festival, so I told him I'd man the booth for him while he's setting up the buffet," Aunt Beth said.

"I have an eight o'clock video call with a client, but I'm free after that," Lauren said.

"I need to go take down my booth in the afternoon," Harriet said.

"I guess we know what I'll be doing, then," Lauren said with a dramatic eye roll.

"We'll all help, and it won't take any time at all," Mavis said. "And Harriet can sit and watch."

"Isn't that always her job?" Lauren muttered, starting for the kitchen as if to put her teacup away. Mavis pretended to swat at her then gave her a stern look.

Harriet noticed it was not, in fact, Lauren's own cup, Connie had picked up and put in the kitchen earlier. She was pretty sure it was a decorative mug from a long-arm quilting convention she'd attended earlier in the year. It was clear Lauren had something on her mind. Something she didn't want to share with the rest of the Loose Threads.

"You can come out now," Harriet called to her when she was sure the last car save Lauren's had left her driveway.

Chapter 24

G uess what we still have?" Lauren asked and held her keys up, jingling them as she did.

"Your car?" Harriet guessed.

"Geez, those pain meds are dulling your brain. Good thing you've got me here to do the thinking."

"I'm tired. Can you just tell me what you're talking about without all the commentary on my brain power?"

"You're no fun." Lauren put her keys in her pocket. "With all the excitement at the concert, guess where Jenny's quilt is?"

Harriet sat up straighter in her chair, finally catching some of Lauren's enthusiasm.

"The back seat of your car?"

"Give the girl a prize. I'll be right back."

Lauren slipped into her jacket and went outside, returning a moment later with a pillowcase-covered bundle; Harriet was standing by her large cutting table. She'd cleared the surface so they could spread the quilt out flat.

"Let's put it face-down," she suggested. "The bulk of the acid hit the back side corner."

They bent over the quilt corner to examine the burned area.

"Hold on," Harriet said. "I've got curved tweezers by my serger." she added referring to the special sewing machine that was used to produce encased edge seams. It was intricate work, and most people used tweezers to help guide the thread through the series of hooks and loops leading to the double needles.

She returned to the table and carefully grasped the blackened, burned edge of the quilt backing, lifting and pulling it to the side.

"That looks weird." Lauren pointed to the layer of batting exposed by the burned fabric.

Harriet picked at the fuzzy remains of batting with the tweezer tips.

"I don't think this was regular batting before it was burned. It's way too thin."

"What's that underneath the fuzz?" Lauren went to Harriet's storage shelf on the back wall for a tabletop Ott light. Harriet plugged it into a power strip mounted under the edge of the cutting table's top. Lauren flicked the switch, and the bright, natural light illuminated the quilt corner.

"Is that newspaper?" she asked as Harriet gently probed under the batting.

Harriet poked harder, finally penetrating what indeed turned out to be newsprint. She grabbed an edge and pulled, and an inch-square piece of the paper tore loose.

"What does it say?" Lauren asked as Harriet held it under the light.

"It's from the *St. Cloud Times* newspaper dated January fifteenth, nineteen-sixty-seven."

"Where's St. Cloud?"

Harriet turned the square of paper over and read the printing on the reverse side.

"Looks like Minnesota. This is talking about something in Minneapolis."

"Isn't that where Jenny's commune was?"

"That's what she claimed, but I'm not sure I believe anything she says at this point." She turned back to the quilt and poked into the burn hole again. "Hold this," she told Lauren, pointing to the corner of the quilt. She poked and prodded and finally came out with another piece of paper. This one was green and did not require a high-powered light to identify.

"Is that what I think it is?" Lauren asked.

"If you're thinking large denomination money, yes. I think it's a piece of a one hundred-dollar bill."

"Whoa."

"Jenny's been holding out on us. She clearly knows more about the bank robbery than she's admitted."

"Like the part where she was there?" Lauren asked.

"Yeah, for starters. For all we know, she could have been the mastermind."

Harriet spun the quilt until the opposite corner was in front of her. She took a pair of bandage scissors from a holder on her tool shelf, carefully created a hole then a slit along the seam of the first border. With the tweezers, she peeled back the layers of batting and newspaper and exposed more hundred-dollar bills. At the same time, Lauren crumpled another spot in her hands, listening for the crunch of paper.

"It feels like the whole quilt is filled with money," she said.

"No wonder Jenny was so paranoid about this quilt."

"So, now what are we going to do?"

"That's a good question," Harriet replied. "We should call Detective Morse, but I feel like we should let Jenny have a chance to do the right thing first."

"Maybe we should call Robin," Lauren suggested.

"Once we do that, she'll be required to report it, whether Jenny knows about it or not."

"We could call your aunt, or Mavis."

Before Harriet could express an opinion about that idea, her phone rang. She went to her work desk and answered.

"That was Tom," she reported after she'd hung up. "He was just checking to make sure nothing else had happened. He also wanted to know if we'd gotten anything resembling an explanation for the attack by the kitchen crew. I said no. I didn't want to go into the whole 'they're probably the bank robbers Jenny worked with when she robbed a bank forty some years ago.'"

"Probably a good idea."

Harriet felt a small twang of guilt. Tom had been nothing but helpful, but with this latest revelation, and Jenny's new version of her past life, she just hadn't had the energy to recount it all.

"I guess we probably shouldn't tear her quilt apart," Lauren said with a disappointed sigh.

"Not without Robin or Detective Morse or Jenny or someone else weighing in on the matter."

"I better go," Lauren said. "I've got an early start tomorrow."

Harriet started to reply but then froze.

"Did you hear that?"

"What?"

Harriet held her finger to her lips. From outside came the sound of a car door.

Lauren quickly grabbed the quilt and the pillowcase and disappeared into the kitchen. Someone knocked on the door. Harriet got up and looked through the side pane of the bow window.

Colm Byrne stood on her porch holding a large shopping bag. She opened the door.

"I hope it's not too late to come calling," he said. "I drove by and saw your lights on and a car in the driveway, so I hoped you'd still be awake.

"Come in," she said and stepped aside to let him in.

"I know your young friend was hoping to get a CD earlier, and I was hoping you might want a CD set for yourself." He held the bag up. "Here are sets for both of you, along with tour T-shirts and souvenir scarves." He pulled the items from the bag and laid them on the seat of one of the wing chairs.

"This is way too generous," Harriet protested.

"I was hoping we could cash in that rain check from the other day," he said.

"Now?" Her voice was a little too loud.

"No, no. I thought maybe we could go to dinner tomorrow night. We have to leave town in a few days, and I was hoping, if dinner went well, you'd see me again before that happened."

Before Harriet could answer, Lauren came back from the kitchen.

"That sounds like a great idea," she said. "I happen to know Harriet is free tomorrow night. She had to cancel all her plans because of her arm."

"Speaking of my arm, if you two don't mind, I'm getting a little tired."

"Yeah, when you see the doctor tomorrow morning, he's going to know you haven't been staying home with it elevated like he told you to do."

"I'm sorry if that's my fault," Colm said, trying to appear sheepish but not succeeding.

"It's fine," Harriet assured him. "I wouldn't have missed your concert for anything."

"I hope I didn't disappoint."

"It was wonderful," she said. "Especially when you did all the old songs before you did your own. It showed a lot of versatility."

"Well, thank you," he said. "My mother used to make me play whatever was popular on American radio at the time. It's finally paying off."

Lauren picked up her coat and swung her messenger bag over her shoulder. She stared at Colm.

"I'll take my leave, too," he said with obvious reluctance. "I'm glad you were still up and look forward to seeing you tomorrow night." With that, he turned and went out the door.

"Thanks for accepting an invitation for me," Harriet complained when he was gone.

"Are you telling me you were going to turn down a date with Colm Byrne?" Lauren asked.

"Don't you think I have enough men in my life?"

"Yeah, but this isn't like that. This is just dinner with a rock star and maybe one more date, and then he's out of here to start his 'Irish Spring' tour. I saw it on his web page."

"You looked him up on his web page? *You* should go out on a date with him."

"He didn't ask me, groupie. Besides, it will make a great picture for your MyFace page."

"My MyFace page?" Harriet asked. "I don't have a MyFace, YourFace or AnyoneElse'sFace page."

"Seriously?" Lauren asked, shock plain on her face. "How can you expect to grow your business without using social media?"

"I don't know, I guess I'll just muddle through the old-fashioned way—word of mouth."

"Geez, do I have to do everything? When this whole festival business is over, I'll come over and set you up basic pages on the popular apps. We should join you to some of the e-quilting groups, too."

"Whatever," Harriet said.

"I'll call you tomorrow to see what the plan is for tearing your booth down. Do you need help getting into your jammies?"

"No, I can handle it."

"Good, I hate that sort of thing," Lauren said as she turned and went out the door.

Chapter 25

Harriet awoke with a shout the next morning as Scooter jumped onto her bandaged arm. He immediately cowered at the bottom corner of the bed as she sat up and leaned against her headboard.

"Come here, little guy." She managed to coax him back to her lap. "Mommy's not mad at you," she said in a higher than normal voice. "Mommy's arm is hurt, just like your back. I know you didn't mean anything."

"Who are you talking to?" Mavis called up the stairs.

"Scooter," she called back and then noticed the aroma of bacon. "We need to go down and see what your auntie Mavis is making," she said to Scooter.

She carefully set him aside and got out of bed. Dressing was a bit tricky with her arm, so she eased it into an old flannel bathrobe her aunt had left behind then picked up her dog and went downstairs.

"Don't tell your aunt what I cooked you," Mavis said as soon as Harriet came into sight.

"What are you making me?"

"I've got some buttermilk waffles in the oven, bacon and scrambled eggs and some homemade sourdough toast."

"Bless you," Harriet said. "I'm sure I need this to heal my arm."

"My thinking exactly." Mavis extracted a bottle of maple syrup from a pan of hot water and wiped it dry with a dishcloth before putting it on the kitchen table, where she'd set two places. "I put food down for both your pets, too, so you sit down and tell me whether you want tea or coffee or something else."

Harriet chose tea, and Mavis fixed two cups then sat down on the opposite side of the table. She made small talk while they ate. She reminisced about quilting in the sixties and swore she had only made one polyester quilt during that time.

"I mostly did what I've always done," she said. "Traditional patterns, stitched by hand. There weren't any new designs or designers that I remember."

"Okay, I'm done," Harriet said when she'd eaten some of everything Mavis had cooked for her. "Can we talk about Jenny now? I know you were trying to avoid controversy while I was eating, but I'm through, and it was delicious, and I've got some things to tell you."

"Let me top off our tea, and then I'm ready to listen."

"After you-all left last night, Lauren remembered that she had Jenny's quilt in her car." Harriet paused to sip her tea. Mavis leaned forward in her seat. "I'd noticed there was something weird about the quilt where the acid had splashed it. I think Lauren had, too, so we brought it in and poked at the spot where the acid had eaten the fabric away."

"And?"

"And, first, the batting wasn't regular batting. There was a little bit of something fuzzy that was much thinner than the batting we use. Then there was newspaper—from the nineteen-sixties. And finally, there was money—a lot of money."

"How much are we talking?" Mavis looked intently at her.

"Hard to tell. The piece of bill I pulled out looked like it was a hundred. We opened a seam on the opposite corner, and there were more. I can't even guess how much is in there, but it looks like it's multiple layers of bills."

"That would be a little over fifty thousand dollars per layer." Mavis and Harriet had been so focused on their discussion neither one had noticed Lauren come in. "My client had some crisis that didn't involve me, so they rescheduled my eight o'clock. I thought I'd drop by and see what was happening here."

"Have you eaten?" Mavis asked. "We just finished, and I've got plenty left."

"In that case, I'd love some."

Once again, Mavis wouldn't let them talk about anything stressful while Lauren was eating.

"So, I take it Harriet told you what we found last night," Lauren said when she'd finished.

"Is there more?" Mavis asked.

"Nothing but speculation after we found the money."

"The money has to be related to the robbery, don't you think?" Harriet asked.

"It's hard to see how it could be any other way," Lauren agreed. "Especially with the newspaper scrap dated nineteen-sixty-seven."

Harriet paused, deep in thought.

"Uh-oh," Lauren said. "Harriet's about to have a big idea."

"What if Jenny is one of the bank robbers?" she said.

"Oh, honey, that's not possible," Mavis said.

"Think about it," Harriet insisted. "It's become pretty obvious that Jenny's been keeping secrets for a long time. What's to say she's telling the truth now? No doubt some of what she's saying is true, but I'll bet there are still some big holes in her story."

"This has possibilities," Lauren said.

"She could be one of the robbers," Harriet persisted. "That would give those two goons that jumped her and Robin a motive, especially if she has all the money and not just her share. Do we know how much was taken in the robbery?"

"I don't think the article I saw said, but I can look it up," Lauren said.

"Maybe she was the mastermind," Harriet suggested.

"I still can't believe that," Mavis said. "A person doesn't change that completely, and your aunt and I have known Jenny for a lot of years."

"Maybe she got caught up in something she couldn't control," Harriet suggested.

"On the other hand," Lauren said, "she could be a psychopath. They're always much-beloved members of their community, aren't they?"

"Even if she was part of the robbery, that doesn't explain the shooting or her brother being killed," Harriet said, scooping Scooter up onto her lap.

"She wasn't with us when Pamela was shot. We were outside waiting for her to get out of the bathroom, and when her tires were slashed, everyone came up after the fact, didn't they?" Lauren pointed out. "And where was she when her brother was killed?"

"She and Robin were looking for Bobby earlier in the morning, but we'll have to ask Robin if they were together the whole time until we found him," Harriet said.

"You can speculate all you want, but I'm reserving judgment until we know the facts," Mavis said stubbornly. "I'm going to clear these dishes up, and then we better get you to the doctor."

"I'll take the dogs out," Lauren volunteered. "Carter is out in the car on his microwave heating pad," she said. "I assume Curley is around here somewhere?"

"She's in her cage in the front room. She'd have eaten Scooter's breakfast otherwise."

Lauren opened Harriet's coat closet and got out Scooter's leash, and then picked him up from Harriet's lap before disappearing into the living room to gather up Mavis's dog.

"Do you really think Jenny could have been involved in all of this?" Mavis asked Harriet when Lauren was outside with the dogs.

"Anything's possible," Harriet said. "But I'm with you—there must be something more to this story. I definitely can't see Jenny killing Pamela, but Lauren's right. Every time you hear them interview neighbors of killers, they always describe them as normal citizens and profess to be shocked."

"Can you get dressed by yourself?" Mavis asked, ending the discussion.

"I'll manage," Harriet said as she stood up and headed for the stairs.

✂ - - ✂ - - ✂

Lauren was sitting at the kitchen table tapping the keys of her laptop when Harriet came back downstairs. Mavis was wiping the countertops while the dishwasher did its job.

"My client is still busy with their problem," Lauren announced as she snapped the lid of the computer closed.

"Would you like to come along with Harriet and me," Mavis asked.

"Sure, why not. I can't really do anything else until my client either fixes their problem or reschedules."

"You can keep me company in the waiting room."

"You're delusional if you think I was going to try to go in with Harriet while the doctor digs around on her arm."

✂- - - ✂- - - ✂

Mavis and Lauren were laughing when Harriet came back into the waiting room.

"What did the nurse say?" Mavis asked.

"Not much," Harriet said a little too nonchalantly.

"She could tell you've been overdoing it, couldn't she."

"She might have mentioned something about resting more," Harriet said. "Along with the healing being nonexistent, but that's mostly because of the infection."

"Oh, honey, I knew you were doing too much."

"Would it help if I promised to take it easier now that the festival is coming to an end?"

"It would help…if you'll do it," Mavis replied.

"In the spirit of resting Harriet's arm, is anyone up for a trip to the Steaming Cup before we take her home?" Lauren asked.

"That sounds like a fine idea," Mavis said. "If Harriet's up to it," she added.

"I'm not an invalid," Harriet muttered. "And I could use a cookie after my visit with Nurse Ratched."

"If it were true about you not being an invalid, your doctor wouldn't be telling you your arm isn't healing," Mavis said.

✂- - - ✂- - - ✂

Harriet and Mavis were sitting across the table from Lauren, their cups of hot cocoa nearly emptied, when Harriet's cell phone started ringing. Mavis picked it up off the table and answered.

"This is Harriet's phone, how may I help you?" she said. Then: "Slow down, honey." She turned to Harriet and Lauren. "Carla says Wendy is missing." She turned back to the phone. "Hang up and dial nine-one-one. We'll be right there."

She ended the call and handed Harriet her phone, digging in her purse for her keys as she did.

"You two get on your phones and call the rest of the Threads," she ordered. "And then call Detective Morse."

She hurried them to her car and drove as fast as the speed limit allowed straight to Aiden's house.

Chapter 26

Harriet and Lauren were out of the car before Mavis had turned off the engine.

"What's happening?" Harriet asked as they approached Officer Nguyen, who was standing in Aiden's kitchen questioning Carla. Tears streamed down the young woman's face, and she was pacing a small pattern in front of the policeman.

"Harriet, tell him! We need to be looking for Wendy, not standing around talking."

"Miss, we need to get the information about your child so we can put out an Amber Alert," Officer Nguyen said.

"You think she's been kidnapped?" Carla shrieked and then began crying.

"We'll look for Wendy while you answer Officer Nguyen's questions," Harriet told her.

"This is a crime scene," Nguyen said.

Carla fainted as soon as the words were out of his mouth.

Lauren turned and went out of the kitchen and up the stairs. Mavis crouched beside Carla, who was already waking, slipped her arms out of her jacket and laid it over her.

"Can you tell us what happened?" Harriet said in a quiet voice.

Officer Nguyen glared at her but didn't stop Carla from speaking.

"I put Wendy down for her morning nap a little early, since she's been up later than usual the last few nights. I turned on the monitor and was sorting her laundry in the sitting room part of our rooms when Michelle called me on my cell phone to tell me to come get her sheets and wash them.

"I went to her room, stripped her bed and put her sheets in the wash. When I came back to my rooms, I went in to check on Wendy and she was gone." She started crying again.

"Has she gotten out of her crib before?" Harriet asked.

"Never," Carla said. "And I should have heard her, whatever happened. And I didn't put the chair beside the crib. I would never have done that."

A policeman Harriet remembered from the storm came into the kitchen.

"Mary and I searched all the rooms on the second floor, and Glen searched the basement, but nothing so far."

"What's going on?" Michelle asked, as she entered the kitchen carrying an empty coffee cup.

"You tell us," Harriet said. "You're the one who lives here."

"Miss Salter called us to report her child missing," Nguyen said. "Can you tell us where you've been for the last half-hour?"

"Didn't Carla tell you?" She turned and stared at the sobbing woman. "I called her to get my sheets in the wash. She didn't have the brat with her when she came to my room. She took the sheets and went down to the laundry, and I went up to the third floor to work on my mom's old computer where it's quiet. And no, I didn't see the kid or its supposed kidnapper."

As Michelle spoke, more people came into the kitchen. She edged her way toward the servant's stairs that led upstairs.

Connie came to Carla and scooped her into her arms, pulling the young woman into a hug.

"I'm sure there's an explanation for all this," Michelle said. "The kid is probably somewhere right under our noses. Now, if you don't mind—"

"Where is she, Michelle?" Harriet interrupted.

"How dare you even suggest I know where that noisy little brat is? Now, if you'll all excuse me, I've got work to do. I'll be upstairs in the office."

"You and Carla were here, right? You on the third floor, Carla in the basement—with the monitor on. Even when the alarm isn't armed, a beep sounds if any of the exterior doors are opened. There's a panel with a speaker on each floor. Did either of you hear the door chime?" Harriet asked.

Carla shook her head no.

"Of course not," Michelle said. "I would have come down immediately if I'd heard it."

"So," Harriet said, "if no one came into the house, someone had to already be in the house, or it had to be one of you two."

"Excuse me," Officer Nguyen said to Harriet. "We can take it from here. If you want to be helpful, sit in the living room with Miss Salter while we continue searching the house. And you," he said to Michelle, "stay right here."

Michelle looked toward the stairs again and sighed, but she didn't move.

Connie had made tea and was passing cups around to the people assembled in Aiden's living room when Carla's boyfriend Terry arrived. Terry Jansen was a Navy Seal currently attached to a special investigations unit based at Naval Base Kitsap. He had the sort of job that kept him out of town a good deal of the time, and when he was in town, he couldn't talk about where he'd been or what he'd been doing. Carla was a good match for him, Harriet mused. Growing up with an abusive, drug-addicted mother, the girl had learned not to ask too many questions.

He strode across the living room and crouched in front of Carla, who was sitting on the sofa between Connie and Mavis.

"Baby, I'm so sorry," he said, cupping her face in his hands.

"Find her," Carla choked out, barely containing her tears.

"Where's Michelle?" he demanded.

"I think she's in the kitchen," Harriet said. "Officer Nguyen told her to stay put, but who knows if she did."

Terry stood up abruptly and stormed into the kitchen. Harriet jumped up and followed before anyone could stop her.

"Where's Wendy?" Terry demanded, crossing the room and getting into Michelle's face.

"I don't know," Michelle protested.

He grabbed her, twisted her arm behind her back and pulled it between her shoulder blades, then slammed her into the closed kitchen door.

"Try again," he hissed.

"You're hurting me," she cried.

"I'm not doing anything compared to what's coming if you don't tell me where Wendy is—right now."

"Upstairs," she choked out.

Lauren came down the servant's stair into the kitchen, pausing a few steps from the bottom.

"Where upstairs?" Terry demanded and pulled her arm up higher.

"In the bedroom," she said in a strained voice. "There's a door at the back of the closet. It leads to a secret room my mom had put in for us kids."

Lauren ran upstairs, followed closely by Terry and Harriet. Terry crossed the landing and went up another flight of stairs that led to Aiden's mother's office and the spare bedroom on the third floor. He swung the door to the bedroom open, and they could hear the muffled sound of Wendy crying. A moment later, he'd crossed the room, crawled into the closet and emerged with Wendy, who was smiling now she was in Terry's arms.

"That man attacked me," Michelle screeched when Terry came into sight of the group assembled in the kitchen. A group that now included Aiden.

"What did you do to my sister?" Aiden demanded, glaring at the other man.

"Your *sister* stashed Wendy in a dark hidden closet on the third floor. If I hadn't interrogated her, that baby would still be up there alone and scared while the police were busy sending out Amber Alerts and setting up search teams. Don't you think you should be asking your sister what she did to an innocent child?"

"She wasn't hurt," Michelle yelled. "She was asleep when I put her in the closet. It was just going to be for a little while. Just until everyone noticed her missing, then I was going to go find her—but *he*…" She pointed at Officer Nguyen. "*He* wouldn't let me go find her. I was supposed to be the one to find her. Not him." She thrust her finger at Terry.

Aiden slumped against the kitchen counter.

"You kidnapped Wendy just so you could play hero? You terri-fied Carla, wasted police resources, and interrupted everyone here's workday so you could get attention for yourself when you found the baby?"

"You always talk about Harriet did this and Harriet did that, and she's always the hero of the story. I just wanted you to talk about me like that."

"You are sick," Aiden said in disgust.

"Let's hope that's true," Detective Morse said, emerging from the back of the group in the kitchen. "Because, Michelle Jalbert, you are under arrest for the kidnapping of Wendy Salter…"

Morse continued the litany of charges and rights, then put hand-cuffs on Michelle and turned her over to Officer Nguyen.

"Is that necessary?" Aiden demanded.

"You should be thanking me," Morse said. "But you seem to have drunk the same Kool-Aid as your delusional sister. In case you haven't noticed, this is the third time in a week the police, firemen, paramedics and emergency medical personnel of this town have had to waste precious time and resources because your sister has staged an emergency. This time she's taken it too far."

"But she'll lose her license to practice law," Aiden said. "Carla, you're not going to press charges, are you?"

Carla looked up from Wendy, a panicked look on her face.

"She has no choice," Morse interrupted. "And Dr. Jalbert, losing her license is the least of your sister's problems. She has been cry-ing out for help. Maybe now she'll get it. And by the way, you're very lucky she didn't accidentally kill herself or anyone else." Morse looked pointedly at Carla and Wendy. "If I could charge you as an accessory for not stopping her, I would."

"What was I supposed to do?" Aiden argued. "She attempted suicide, and she assured me she was going to see a therapist—and she really was sick to her stomach. I thought she did have food poi-soning."

"I hope you're better with sick dogs than you are with sick peo-ple," Morse said and turned her back on him.

"You should call an attorney for your sister," Harriet said, and watched as he disappeared in the direction of his office.

"Go pack a bag," Terry said. "You're not staying here."

"That's not necessary," Aiden protested. "Michelle won't even be here."

"That will remain to be seen," Terry said.

"You and Wendy can stay at our house for a while," Connie said. "At least come until we find out what will happen to Michelle. Then, if she's gone, you can decide if you want to come back here or not."

Carla nodded silently and went upstairs, Wendy clutched to her chest the whole time.

Chapter 27

*H*arriet and Lauren left the kitchen and went into the living room where the rest of the Loose Threads had gathered. Detective Morse joined them a minute later after instructing the remaining police officers as to their final tasks and reports.

"I'm glad you're all here," she told them.

"That's a first," Lauren said.

"With everything that's going on, I think you deserve to know something."

"And what would that be?" Robin asked, assuming her lawyer demeanor.

"You know those men who assaulted you and Jenny Logan?"

"Hard to forget," Robin said.

"They made bail rather quickly."

"How quickly?"

"They didn't even spend one night in jail. In other words, they have friends with deep pockets, the kind of pockets that can get a judge out of bed in the middle of the night to process them."

"Do you know who paid the bail money?" Harriet asked.

"We don't," Morse said. "The check was written on a corporate account for what's probably a shell company. We don't have the manpower to look any deeper, out of curiosity. These guys were arrested for simple assault."

"So, what are you telling us?" Harriet asked. "Are Robin and Jenny in danger?"

"You tell me. None of you seem to know why they attacked you in the first place. Those two ex-cons weren't sharing, and you-all are equally silent, so I don't know what to tell you about how much danger any of you are in. All I know is they attacked you once, and they got out real quick. If I were you-all, I'd keep my doors locked and not go anywhere alone or where there aren't a lot of other people."

"That's sort of vague," Lauren said. "But, hey, thanks. We weren't going to figure that one out."

Morse whirled on her.

"Do you have any idea how frustrating it is trying to work with you ladies?" she said, her face flushing. "We've had two murders, and you're once again in the middle of it, and once again, you have information you're unwilling to share. How am I supposed to keep you safe?"

Harriet started to speak.

"Don't even start with that 'we can take care of ourselves' routine." She looked at Harriet. "You've been lucky so far. You could have been killed several times this last year."

Aunt Beth cleared her throat.

"I can see how you would feel we've been less than forthcoming, but this time, we truly don't know what's going on."

Detective Morse took a deep breath and ran her hands through her short blond hair.

"I'm surprised Jenny Logan isn't with you here," she said. "Do any of you know where she is?"

The quilters looked at each other.

"With the excitement over Wendy, I didn't notice she wasn't here," Mavis said, giving voice to what Harriet and the others were thinking.

"Who saw her last?" Harriet asked.

The women looked at each other, and one-by-one, each indicated they hadn't seen her. Harriet pulled her phone out and dialed Jenny's number.

"Her phone went straight to voicemail," she reported. She and Lauren shared a look.

"Here's a perfect example," Detective Morse said.

"We were just asking ourselves last night if Jenny had a previous relationship with the ex-cons," Lauren said.

"Diós mio," Connie said. "Jenny would never consort with those two...thugs."

DeAnn said she couldn't believe it, either.

"You might think differently if you knew what we know," Harriet said.

"Way to spill it," Lauren said.

"Spill what?" Morse asked. She looked at Harriet then Lauren then Harriet again. "If you think I won't arrest you for obstruction, you better think again."

"This is Jenny's story to tell, and we haven't been able to ask her about what we found," Harriet said. "There may be a perfectly reasonable explanation that has nothing to do with anything that's happening in Foggy Point this week."

"Let's let me be the judge," Morse said.

"Harriet, if you know anything about what's going on, you tell her right now," Aunt Beth ordered. Harriet suspected the real reason her aunt was so adamant was that she was upset Harriet hadn't told her first, but there hadn't been time.

"Last night, after everyone else left my house, Lauren and I realized Jenny's quilt was in Lauren's car. Jenny's been acting so weird about her quilt..."

"Define *weird*," Morse said.

"She stepped past Pamela Gilbert's body to check on her quilt," Lauren said. "And she checked on her quilt while other people poured water on Harriet's flaming arm."

"Okay, that's weird. Continue," Morse said. "You got the quilt out of the car, I presume."

"So, we spread the quilt out and started examining the burned part and..—"

"For crying out loud," Lauren blurted. "We found a bunch of money."

"Define *bunch*," the detective asked.

"We didn't take it out and count it," Harriet said. "We didn't think we should destroy Jenny's quilt until we'd talked to her."

"It looks like the whole quilt is involved, and it's several layers thick. My best guess would be fifty thousand per layer, if all the layers go all the way to the edges," Lauren said.

"I guess we know why the bank robbers were after Jenny," Morse said. "You thought she was going to be able to explain away several hundred thousand dollars? Really?"

"Things aren't always what they seem," Harriet shot back.

"Let me hear it," Morse said. "What else are you not telling me?"

"We're not real sure after that," Mavis said. "Jenny told us she'd grown up in a commune, and that her brother had been kicked out for dealing drugs. Then she told us some of his friends had broken into a Selective Service office."

"After that, when we tried to get her to tell us more, she said her brother was involved in a bank robbery," DeAnn said.

"Then it was both," Connie added.

"We're pretty sure some of that is true, but we all agreed she wasn't telling us the whole truth," Harriet said.

Carla came in with Wendy, ending the discussion.

"Sorry to interrupt," she said. "Terry is loading our bags and Wendy's teddy bear and blankie," she said.

Connie stood up.

"Time for me to go, then," she said. "Let us know if you find Jenny."

Chapter 28

*L*auren looked at her watch.

"We need to get you home," she told Harriet. "Or really, we need to get *me* home. I need check in with my client."

"I'm ready." Harriet looked around at the groups of people clustered around Carla, Wendy and Terry, making prolonged goodbyes to Carla and professing their thanks to Terry for producing such a swift resolution to the incident.

"We just need to find Mavis, and we're out of here."

Beth and Mavis were standing by the door into the dining room, deep in discussion. Lauren gestured to Mavis when the older woman looked up.

"You two ready to go?" Mavis said when she joined them.

"Lauren needs to check with her client," Harriet said. "I think we're done here anyway."

"Beth said she can use Jorge's truck to bring your booth stuff home. DeAnn is going to take the quilts down and pack the samples." Harriet started to protest but Mavis cut her off. "Don't even start. Your arm isn't healing well, and the sooner you get some rest, the sooner that will change."

✂ - - - ✂ - - - ✂

"Those of us who are available at the moment are going to search for Jenny," Mavis reported when the trio had settled in the car and she'd driven back to the main road.

"What do you think will happen to Michelle?" Harriet asked.

"Robin's the one we need to ask, but my uneducated guess would be that she'll be going to some sort of mental facility. What happens after that, I don't know. Her life as a high-powered lawyer is over, I imagine."

"Even though Aiden's been a total jerk, I still feel sorry for him."

Lauren had been typing on her smartphone.

"I have to go to my house and start a test run of my clients program," she said. "Shall I come back to make sure Harriet rests? It sounds like they aren't going to need my help with the booth."

"I promise I'll take a nap," Harriet said. "You don't need to babysit me."

"Yeah, that's why I'll be over in a couple of hours."

✄ - - - ✄ - - - ✄

Harriet woke up from her nap on the TV room sofa with two fur-covered bodies clamped to her—one fuzzy and perched on the crest of her hip with a claw lightly hooked into her jeans for balance, the other short-haired and wedged into the bend of her knees.

"Well, boys, that would have been a little more restful without your help."

She moved her companions, got up and went downstairs to feed them. Fred didn't really need food again until nighttime, but she was trying to fatten Scooter up and Fred wouldn't let the dog eat if he didn't get something, too.

She tried to distract herself looking at the latest issue of *The Quilter* magazine, but she couldn't concentrate. Her thoughts kept bouncing between Jenny and what she really knew about the murders, and Aiden and how he was dealing with the arrest of his sister. She finally dug her cell phone from her pocket and dialed.

"Carla?"

"Hi, Harriet, what's up?"

"I was checking to see how you're all doing."

"We're good. Wendy's taking a real nap, and I can finally relax with that witch in jail where she belongs."

"Have you heard from Aiden?"

She heard rustling, and then Carla sighed.

"He called, but I let it go to voicemail. I'm just not ready to talk to him yet. I know it's not his fault, but I'm angry that he could be so stupid and that it ended hurting Wendy. I'm taking her to a counselor on Monday just to be sure she's okay."

Harriet thought that sounded a bit extreme, since Wendy had pretty much slept through the whole incident, but since she wasn't a mother, she kept her opinion to herself.

"Has Aiden's brother Marcel been to the house that you know of?"

"Not since Michelle came," Carla said. "The kids called him when they first got there, after their mother went to the hospital. I think he's the one that told them to call their father."

"Do you need anything?"

"We're good. Terry is still here, and Connie and Grandpa Rod are hovering."

"Let me know if that changes."

"The only thing we need is for Michelle to never come back," Carla said. "But I guess she's always going to be Aiden's sister."

"Yeah, that's the kicker, isn't it?" Harriet agreed and rang off.

She looked at the clock on the microwave; she'd slept an hour. Lauren probably wouldn't be back for at least another hour. She phoned Marcel Jalbert.

Marcel answered on the first ring. Harriet asked if she could talk to him in person, and he agreed as long as she made it brief. He was working on a business plan at his home office, he said, and he needed to keep at it. Before Michelle came to Aiden's, he'd told her his brother was planning to reorganize and reopen the vitamin factory that had been their mother's.

"Thanks for agreeing to talk to me," she said when Marcel opened the front door to his neat townhouse. She had made the drive to the Miller Hill neighborhood with her arm in a sling and steering one-handed, but the speed limit was low enough to not present a problem.

She could hear voices coming from another room, but they weren't loud enough for her to identify. Marcel took her coat and hung it on a coat tree in the entry then led her to his upstairs office and offered her a chair opposite his at his desk.

The entryway, stairwell and Marcel's office were all painted a soft celadon green, the wood trim was dark but modern, not the traditional style of Harriet's own home. Classical music played quietly in the background.

"Are you aware your sister was arrested for kidnapping this morning?" she asked without preamble.

Marcel was silent for a moment. His face resembled Aiden's, but his features were coarser, and his skin bore the residual scars of acne that had been professionally treated—probably with lasers or at least serious sandpaper. His eyes were blue, but not the nearly white color of his brother's. Marcel's were more of a robin's egg.

"I hadn't heard that, but I'm not surprised. She clearly has some sort of mental defect. She's been troubled her whole life. I learned a long time ago that I can't fix what's wrong with her, but I *can* protect my family and myself by staying as far away from her as I can."

"I wish Aiden would realize that," Harriet said.

"The whole family protected Michelle all her life. My parents could have educated half the kids in this town for the money they spent on therapists, special schools and new-age treatments, but none of it made even a small dent in her problems. As I understand it, there is no effective treatment for narcissism and histrionic personality disorder. All you can do is stay far enough away to avoid being caught up in their web.

"And, if you were wondering, I'm not hiring her a lawyer, or aiding in her defense in any way. I hope Aiden will follow my lead for once."

"I wish he would take that attitude. He tells me I don't understand because I'm an only child. To me, it seems like she's using him."

"Trust your instincts. She's sick, and she's played on his vulnerabilities. Now that she'll be out of the picture for a while, I'll see what I can do to convince him to cut her loose. I assume that's what you're here for."

Harriet felt her face turn hot.

"I don't know if he talks to you about us, but it seems like everyone in town knows he and I have been having trouble in our relationship."

"Cookie did mention she'd heard something about him standing you up at that new restaurant at Smuggler's Cove."

Cookie was Marcel's wife, and Harriet suspected she had told Marcel every detail, but she appreciated that he downplayed it.

"We seem to do fine when Michelle's not around, but I don't exist when she's here."

"He's a big boy, but she's a pro. She has no conscience when it comes to manipulation. He was vulnerable when our mom died right after he came back to the States after his research in Uganda. He hadn't had a chance to make new friends or reconnect with old ones, and you two were just starting to date. Michelle jumped in with both feet. After he got over her trying to steal the house out from under him, she wormed her way back into his life somehow."

"I'm sorry to take up so much time when you're busy," Harriet said and started to get up.

"Sit down," He said. "I can take another few minutes. You want something to drink?" He opened the door to a small refrigerator containing several types of soda as well as bottled tea and water. Harriet pointed to a Diet Coke, and he wiped it with a napkin he took from a holder on the credenza behind his desk and handed it to her.

"Thanks," she said, then opened it and took a sip.

"I've suggested he talk to a counselor or therapist, but my ideas have fallen on deaf ears. I can try again—as I said, now that she's going to be out of the picture for a while there may be hope. I'll try to be a better brother, too. I've been so busy trying to get things in place to open the vitamin factory again that I haven't made enough effort to connect with Aiden."

"I've suggested a counselor, but he won't listen to me, either."

"Don't give up on him yet," Marcel said. "But he's stubborn, and if he refuses to cut her loose, you may have to weigh your options. I admit I didn't get it myself at first, and Cookie's been a great help in keeping my eyes wide open where Michelle's concerned."

"Thanks for listening to me," Harriet said. "And now, I really will leave you to your planning."

"Come say hi to Cookie before you go." He led her back downstairs. "Look who's here, Cookie," he said as they walked into the kitchen.

Two women were sitting on stools at the center island.

"Harriet? What are you doing here? Did you follow me?" Jenny shrieked.

Chapter 29

J enny?" Harriet said at almost the same time. "What are you doing here? People are looking for you. And no, I didn't follow you. I came here to talk to Marcel about Aiden."

"I'm sorry." Jenny's shoulders sagged. "All this stuff the last few days has got me on edge."

"Can you stay and have some coffee or tea?" Cookie asked. "Jenny was just telling me you were attacked with acid. Are you okay?"

"I need to get home. I'm supposed to be resting," Harriet raised her bandaged arm. "I wanted to be sure Marcel knew that Michelle had been arrested."

"What for?" Cookie leaned forward.

"She tried to stage a kidnapping of Carla Salter's baby. She hid her in the house so she could be the hero and find the child when she'd gotten enough people involved."

"That's horrible." Cookie looked at her husband.

"Wait a minute," Jenny said. "Are you supposed to be driving yet? Aren't you taking pain medication?"

"Only at night. I'm supposed to be home resting. Although, Detective Morse was at Aiden's and did tell all of us we shouldn't go anywhere alone, so I'm breaking that rule."

"I don't understand. What do the Loose Threads have to do with Michelle and her attempt on Wendy?"

"It was coincidental. Morse just took advantage of having us all there at the same time. She's concerned that whoever shot Pamela and Bobby is going to keep trying until they get you, Jenny." Harriet was trying to think of the right words to get through to her.

"Would you like Marcel to drive you home?" Cookie asked. "It sounds like you aren't supposed to be driving or going anywhere alone."

"I can take her," Jenny said. "I need to go help tear down at the festival, so I'll be going her direction."

"Are you sure? I got here fine, and I'm sure I can get back fine, too. Besides, my car is already here."

"Your aunt would never let me hear the end of it if she knew I could have taken you and didn't. Just let me finish my tea, and we'll be on our way. I'm sure Cookie and Marcel wouldn't mind bringing your car home."

"We'd be happy to," Cookie agreed. "Do you have time?" she asked her husband.

"Sure, let me know when you're ready to leave," he said and headed back upstairs.

Cookie made Harriet a cup of tea and produced some double chocolate chip cookies, all the while chattering about the festival, her garden, the weather and whatever else popped into her head that wasn't related to either Jenny or Harriet's recent troubles. When everyone was finished, Cookie brought Harriet's coat and helped her into one sleeve, draping the other one over her shoulder.

"Thanks for listening," Jenny said to her as the two women hugged goodbye.

Harriet got in the passenger seat of Jenny's silver Mercedes and waited while Jenny clipped the seatbelt around her bad arm.

"I guess you're wondering what I was doing at Cookie's house when everyone else was helping with Wendy's disappearance," Jenny started when they were underway.

"It did cross my mind. Everyone else heeded the call."

"I knew everyone else would be there, and I needed advice. Cookie and I have been friends for years. We've served on several committees together. I needed to talk to someone who wouldn't have the same emotional attachment to me and my issues, yet knew me well enough that I could trust her opinion.

"In addition, she's a clinical psychologist—she worked fulltime until they had the kids, and she still works part-time. I feel like I can tell her anything, and she won't be horrified or repulsed but will still be able to give me a considered opinion."

"I wish you felt you could tell *us* anything and we wouldn't judge you," Harriet said softly.

"This is a very complicated situation."

"It might be less so if you came clean and told the truth. Maybe we could help."

"Believe it or not, that's pretty much what Cookie said."

"Why don't you come in and have a cup of tea at my house and try it out on me? Maybe that will be easier than talking to the whole group at once."

"I suppose I've got to start somewhere."

"In the interest of full disclosure, Lauren will be coming over to check on me pretty soon," Harriet warned.

Jenny sighed as she turned into Harriet's driveway.

"Everyone's going to have to learn about this anyway, so I guess one more won't hurt."

"Just out of curiosity, if I hadn't showed up, what would you have done?"

"Frankly, my first instinct was to just leave without a trace, but I can't do that to my husband and son. I don't want to be that kind of person. Heaven knows, I'm going to have some difficult explanations to them."

"What about us? Were you going to tell anyone?"

"I was going to start with your aunt and Mavis and maybe Connie. No offense, but one of the keys to my story is the times we lived in when this started. I know the rest of you have read about it, but unless you lived it, you can't really understand the emotion."

"I promise not to pass judgment."

"I know you won't intend to, but let's not make any promises until you hear my story."

✂ - - ✂ - - ✂

The tea water hadn't even boiled when Lauren came into the kitchen through the studio. Harriet had given her a key so she didn't have to keep digging the hidden one out of the flower box.

"I see you're resting like you're supposed to be," she said as she took her coat off and hung it on the back of a chair.

Before Harriet could warn her, Jenny came out of the downstairs bathroom.

"Okay," Lauren said so only Harriet could hear.

"Fix yourself a drink and then, when we get comfortable, Jenny has some things to explain to us."

Lauren pulled a bag of ginger snaps from her messenger bag and poured some onto a plate from Harriet's cupboard then poured herself a cup of tea.

"Can we do this in your TV room so we can at least pretend you're resting so your aunt won't bust my chops for not making you rest?"

Harriet looked at Jenny, who gave a small nod.

✂ - - - ✂ - - - ✂

"If I'm going to tell you this," Jenny began when she and Lauren were seated in upholstered chairs and Harriet was reclining on the sofa, "I need to do it my way in my time. Please don't interrupt until the end unless you need clarification on a particular point."

Lauren looked at Harriet and then they both agreed. Harriet had turned on a table lamp, but the light was dim, providing Jenny some feeling of privacy.

"I know you were taught about the war in Vietnam in history class, but that period of time was so much more intense than the pages of a book can convey. In January of nineteen sixty-eight, five thousand woman marched for peace and confronted Congress on its opening day. Jeannette Rankin led the march."

"Excuse me," Lauren said. "Remind us who Jeannette Rankin is."

"She was the first woman to serve in Congress and was instrumental in the passing of the Nineteenth Amendment, allowing women to vote. Let me remind you, that amendment, was ratified in nineteen-twenty. She was in her eighties when she led the march.

"An actress named Eartha Kitt denounced the Vietnam War at a White House luncheon with the First Lady. Boys had to sign up for the draft. In past wars and conflicts, journalists were supposed to downplay any losses and keep the masses uplifted about our efforts.

"But Vietnam represented a change. It was the first time a war was televised on the nightly news. Newsmen were reporting the horrors of war along with a true accounting of the losses we were suffering. The Pentagon Papers were published in the *New York Times*, exposing the differences between what we were being told by the government and what was really happening.

"Martin Luther King was assassinated, then Bobby Kennedy. The Chicago Eight, later seven, at first including the National Chairman of the Black Panthers, Bobby Seale, were charged with conspiracy to incite rioting. Later, Bobby's case was severed, and he was given a four-year prison sentence for contempt of court. That length of sentence for contempt was unheard-of prior to his sentencing."

Jenny stopped to sip her tea, and Lauren looked at Harriet and made a slight rolling gesture with her finger, which Harriet took to mean she, too, was anxious for Jenny to get to the point.

"I'm not doing this well," Jenny said. "But what I'm trying to tell you is that these were highly charged times. Things were changing. People were protesting everything. Everyone knew someone who had been killed in Vietnam. When you protested, the police were the enemy, using tear gas and rubber bullets. Even the movies of the times were important statements. There was no such thing as pure entertainment."

Harriet reached across Lauren and pointed at the cookie plate. Lauren scooped a couple into her lap then passed the plate. Jenny waited until Harriet was settled again.

"This is the hard part. I know I told you I'd grown up in a commune and I did—part of the time, after what went down." Jenny sipped her tea again. It was obvious she was stalling.

"My brother was, indeed, a drug dealer, but he was smalltime. He sold small quantities of marijuana to his self-important friends. We lived in Lynnwood, and they acted like we lived in Berkeley. We were a blue-collar working-class town where most of the adults we knew were just trying to get by.

"Every town had a Selective Service office, and Lynnwood was no exception. Prior to Vietnam, a large percentage of the town's young men signed up to go in the army as a way of getting out and seeing the world. But now they were scared. The army might actually expect them to fight.

"Bobby hung out with a group of stoned underachievers with high ideals and low ambition. They were very full of themselves back then. Everyone had a guitar or drum and thought they were going to be the next John Lennon or Ringo Starr. They went through a phase where they were going to be artists and craftsmen.

"Back then, the nerds had slide rules and graph paper and were always working on some problem, the solution to which would end world hunger or create a renewable source of clean energy. The only trouble was, none of them was good at anything. And of course, they all grew their hair out and stopped washing it.

"I don't even remember which one of them thought up the idea of breaking into the Selective Service office and stealing the punch cards with the names of registered eighteen-year-olds. Left to their own devices, nothing would have come of the scheme except a lot of hot air."

"How many people are we talking?" Lauren asked.

"There were a dozen, not counting Bobby, but the core group was maybe half that. Then Cosmic started hanging out with them, and that's where the trouble started. What I told you about that part was true. Cosmic had an uncle who was an ex-con, he brought in another ex-con friend, and they decided to rob the bank next door."

Jenny rubbed her hands together and then rubbed them on her upper arms.

"Are you cold?" Harriet asked and started to get up.

"Sit," Lauren commanded. "I'll get one of the fleece throws from the closet."

She opened the closet door behind her chair and pulled out an assortment of afghans and throws from a box. She gave Jenny the fleece one and tossed a ragged knitted afghan onto Harriet's lap, keeping a lap-sized flannel rag throw for herself.

Jenny wrapped the throw around her shoulders and continued her narrative.

208

"What I didn't tell you the first time was what my role was."

Harriet looked at Lauren, and they both looked at Jenny, but she was lost in her recollection.

"I was fifteen, and my parents were always working, so I tagged along with Bobby wherever he went. My parents had been making him babysit me after school from the time I was nine and he was twelve. He was flat-footed, and in those days that was enough to get you a one-F draft rating, which meant you weren't prime and would be given a noncombat job to free up more qualified soldiers, but they would only do that if they ran out of one-As, which wasn't likely."

Jenny was clearly pained having to tell her story and was dragging it out as if rescue were coming, which they all knew wasn't the case. Harriet's arm was starting to hurt, but she didn't want to distract Jenny by asking Lauren to get her pain medication.

"Bobby was lacking in ambition, beyond his small drug operation, so whenever he could make me do his chores or run errands for the group, he would. At that time, I was in awe of the older kids. They used new names, like Cosmic and Paisley and Tranquillity. They called me Jonquil. It was all very glamorous, in a hippie sort of way." Her voice took on a faraway quality.

"As I was saying, Bobby made me run errands for him, and he'd started having me fetch drugs from his stash when the group ran out. A few weeks before the planned robbery, I was walking the two-mile route along a dirt road, having just made a run to Bobby's stash, on my way back to the 'clubhouse,' which was an abandoned tin hay shed on a piece of property Tranquillity's dad owned. I was stopped by a police car.

"The police took me in for possession of drugs—I later learned they'd had Bobby and his friends under surveillance for weeks. Someone had tipped them off about the planned break-in at the Selective Service office. I have no idea who. Somebody trusted someone outside the group and that person tipped off the police. Like I said, there were always a few hangers-on at the fringe of the group.

"I was a minor, and they'd watched us enough to know I was doing errands for my brother and was not part of the planned crime, but they scared me into believing I was going to jail for ten years on the drug possession charge. They let me suffer for an hour or so, and then Officer James Sullivan came in and offered me a way out. If I would become a confidential informant there would be no charges. It would be like I'd never been stopped, and as a bonus, they would pay me when I told them anything useful. He was very convincing—he even tore up the reports with my name on them right in front of me.

"My life went from the ruin of jail time to the righteousness of being a crime fighter in a few moments time. Until that point, I hadn't really thought of the break-in as a criminal event. It was a political protest—that couldn't be a crime, could it?

"Of course, once I talked to James, it became crystal-clear. Bobby and his friends weren't the new guard that was going to change our country. They were a bunch of deluded dopers. And my brother was worse. He didn't believe in their ideals, he only believed that as long as they were excited about the 'plan' they would meet more often and need more of his product."

"Where were your parents during all this?" Harriet asked.

"James told me we didn't need to worry them with all this. They were at their jobs all the time and were distant, at best. They didn't even notice that my brother had a marijuana patch growing in the woods behind our house.

"I was young and confused. My brother had played the parental role in my life for years, and now the police had me spying on him and his friends. It never occurred to me to talk to my parents about it.

"Everyone was too stoned by the time I got back to notice I was gone longer than usual. Over the next weeks, I listened, which was pretty easy, given their drug use. I dutifully told about Cosmic's uncle coming with his friend to teach them how to execute the break-in. Those two were more savvy, never mentioning word one about the bank or their plan to rob it. James was paying me, and I was starting to think of a career in law enforcement.

"Break-in day arrived, and based on my information, James and his team were ready to step in when the job was in process. Bobby and his group had given me the role of bagman. I would be the one to take the bag filled with the punch cards to the car parked in a nearby alley.

"Of course, when the time came, the whole thing went sideways. Cosmic's uncle and his friend got us inside, and then they blew a hole in the wall between the office and the bank, and the next time I looked, they were stuffing money into one of the duffel bags we'd brought for the cards.

"All of a sudden, the police started screaming over loudspeakers for everyone to come out with their hands up, which hadn't been the plan James had explained to me. But then again, neither of us had expected the robbers to blow a hole in the bank wall.

"Chaos erupted. Everyone had been given a job to do, be it lookout, bag packer, driver, whatever. They all abandoned their posts and went into the bank, where the robbers had poked a hole through the lobby wall with a pry bar and let them into the hair salon on the other side of the bank. They were able to break the glass out of the salon's back door, and Bobby's people were crawling one by one through the hole, scattering as they got out. I saw the bag I'd brought in and grabbed it before following the crowd.

"It turned out there was one more thing Bobby's group didn't know about Cosmic's uncle. He and his friend were both armed. The police breached the bank before everyone got out of the salon and a shootout ensued."

"James was the acid thrower's father, I take it?" Harriet asked.

"I guess so. We never talked about his family. I mean, why would he talk to a fifteen-year-old about his personal life?

"Like I told you before, some people, my brother included, were captured and did jail time. Without James to identify the players, they weren't able to arrest some of the people. A few were wounded, but James was the only fatality.

"As for me, I hid in the woods with Paisley. We climbed way up into a tree, and they never saw us.

"I'm not sure who, if anyone, else in the police knew my true identity. James always just called me Jonquil. Without him to back up my story, I was sure I would be arrested along with everyone else, especially since what I had told him wasn't what had actually happened. I mean, if he'd lived, he could have arrested me for obstruction or something.

211

"In any case, Paisley and I hid in the woods until dark and then hitchhiked out of town. We drifted around, doing odd jobs and panhandling for six months, before we ended up in Georgeville at the commune. It was days before I opened the duffel bag—I took it with us assuming it was evidence that could be used against us and our friends.

"When we did open it, and saw all that money, we figured they could trace us through the serial numbers if we spent any of it. When we got settled in the commune, I hid it, and then when they taught me how to quilt, I put it in the batting. The center square of the quilt was made from the shirt I was wearing.

"Before we'd left town, I'd gone back to the car, which was still hidden in the alley. I grabbed somebody's shirt, and Paisley took a jacket and some shorts. We wore the same clothes until we reached the commune. A lot of people were hitchhiking around the country in those days, so we didn't have any trouble finding rides and places to sleep and things to eat."

"The commune had a midwife, and she had a subspecialty of creating new identities. She was older and apparently had been doing this her whole career. Every month or two, she would file a birth certificate using names of people she knew, or sometimes she made names up for the parents. Later, she'd apply for a Social Security card, and even take out a modest insurance policy of the sort grandparents would buy for a grandchild. By the time we arrived, she had a fat file of valid identities just waiting for bodies to bring them to life. I became Jenny and Paisley became Donna.

"I was immersed in the commune for six years. The war in Vietnam wound down, and the commune's truck farm became successful—they were on the leading edge of the organic food movement. I realized I wanted more out of life than growing bigger radishes. They were very supportive when I wanted to get my GED and go on to junior college. When I got my associate's degree, I got a job and an apartment."

"So, how did you end up back on the West Coast?" Lauren asked.

"That was a horrifying coincidence," Jenny said. "I met my husband in Minnesota. He was in graduate school, and I worked in the registrar's office. We got married after he graduated, and his first job was in Texas. His company eventually bought a small company in Foggy Point, and he was transferred here. It was a promotion, and how could I possibly argue that?

"He had no idea I had any connection here. We moved here, and I hoped Lynnwood was far enough away from Foggy Point, and that enough time had passed, that I wouldn't run into anyone I'd known before. And until now, that's been the case. Of course, that's assuming that whoever is causing the problems now is one of the people from my old life."

"I'd say that's a pretty safe assumption," Lauren said.

"So, all that stuff you told us about your dad leaving and your mother being in a commune was all a lie?" Harriet asked. "You really had two parents who lost their daughter at the age of fifteen?"

"I know it sounds awful, but believe me, Bobby was the only one who would have cared, and he had his own problems. If they'd paid any attention to us at all, Bobby wouldn't have been growing and selling drugs, and I wouldn't have been his drug mule."

"Before, you said the robbers told Bobby's group about the bank robbery. Now you say he didn't know," Lauren said thoughtfully. "Which story are we supposed to believe?"

"You were all pressuring me, and I was trying to rewrite history on the fly so that my part of it didn't exist. Cosmic might have known, but believe me, his uncle would never have trusted the rest of the group with that."

"And you've never told anyone?" Harriet asked.

"Not a soul," Jenny said, and for once, Harriet believed her.

Chapter 30

*L*auren took the teacups downstairs and returned a few minutes with refills of fragrant orange spice tea. Jenny and Harriet sat, each lost in her own thoughts, while she was gone.

"I thought the spicy tea would go better with the gingersnaps," she said.

"Given all that you've just told us, you must have some idea who's been killing people," Harriet told Jenny.

"Yeah," Lauren chimed in. "And you must have some idea if you're the target."

"I think the shooting of Pamela Gilbert leaves no doubt Jenny was the target," Harriet said.

"Who did the shirt belong to?" Lauren asked.

"I don't know," Jenny said. "And that's the truth. All the guys wore shirts that looked vaguely alike. Everyone used that car. It wasn't like it is today, where most of the kids get late-model cars when they turn sixteen. The back seat of that old car had everything from jackets to bikinis, with bags of granola alongside Twinkies and cans of soda. I grabbed what was handy."

"My guess is someone recognized their shirt. Your centerpiece is pretty distinctive," Harriet said.

"Why would they wait so long for revenge?" Jenny asked. "All of them that got arrested would have gotten out decades ago."

"With your change of identity, they probably didn't know how to find you," Lauren suggested.

"I suppose," Jenny mused. "Still, if even my brother had cleaned up, surely, everyone else would have grown up and moved on by now."

"If they haven't, and they figured out you were the snitch, it would be a pretty good motive for revenge." Harriet said.

"Now you just have to figure out which one of the group it is," Lauren said. "I can help you with that if you can tell me the names."

Jenny clamped her lips shut and furrowed her brow.

"That could be a problem," she said.

"How so?" Harriet asked.

"Remember I referred to people as Cosmic, Tranquility, and Paisley? There was also a Cedar, a Sunshine and an Einstein. I never knew their real names."

Lauren covered her eyes with the palms of her hands, tilting her head downward.

"You're not making it easy to help you. I guess I can try to find more newspaper articles and public records regarding the robbery, although if any of them were minors, they wouldn't print their names."

"At least it would be a start," Harriet said.

"Thank you so much for being willing to help me after all the lies I've told you," Jenny said.

"You need to call Detective Morse and come clean," Harriet told her.

"I will, but I think I owe it to the rest of the Threads to tell them first."

"As long as you tell Morse before anything else has a chance to happen," Harriet said.

"Not to sound like your aunt," Lauren said to Harriet, "but you're looking a little gray. I know you think you're superwoman, but I think you need to do what everyone's been telling you and take a nap."

"I need to go get a pain pill, and then I promise, I will take a nap."

"Stay put," Lauren said. Scooter and Fred got up to follow her. "I supposed I have to feed you two little wretches while I'm downstairs, too. I am turning into Beth."

"Don't forget," Harriet said to Jenny. "This isn't over yet. You may have shared your past, but someone dangerous is still out there. You and Lauren need to stay together until you can connect with Robin or DeAnn or somebody. And I'm guessing you get it that you can't go home."

"I'll need to go get some clothes, but I promise—I won't go alone."

"That's all I ask."

"Okay, Sicko," Lauren said a few minutes later, "here's your pill, here's a glass of water. Your cookie plate is reloaded." She looked around the room and piled the extra throws on the end of the sofa. "Here's the remote control for your TV, although you are supposed to be sleeping. Your pets have been fed, and I took Scooter out. I'm done being a nursemaid. And yes, I won't let Jenny go anywhere unless she has an escort."

"Thank you," Harriet said. "I mean it."

"Yeah, whatever," Lauren said, and left.

✄ - - - ✄ - - - ✄

Harriet woke to find Mavis sitting in the upholstered chair next to her. She'd pulled a small needlepoint-covered footrest in front of the chair and had her feet up and her eyes closed. She woke with a start when Harriet sat up.

"Hi, honey," she said. "I hope you don't mind I came over. When I saw Lauren she said you were sleeping at home alone, and it worried me. I thought I'd come over and see if I could fix you a snack and keep you company for a while."

"Sure, make yourself at home."

"Let me go see what I can rustle up in the kitchen," Mavis said and went downstairs.

Harriet's cell phone buzzed, and she picked it up to check caller ID. It was Tom.

"I appreciate the offer," she said after they'd exchanged greetings and he had asked her out to dinner. "But I'm housebound."

She related the results of her doctor appointment. He suggested takeout.

"The idea of dinner with you sounds wonderful, but I think I need to follow doctor's orders this time."

216

She had barely ended the conversation when Mavis called upstairs, "Harriet? There's someone here to see you. Can you come down?"

Colm Byrne stood in her kitchen.

"Oh, my gosh."

"Did you forget our date?" he asked with a smile.

"I guess so. I wasn't sure you were serious."

"I was, but if this isn't a good time…"

"When I went to get my bandage changed, the doctor wasn't happy with my progress, so I've been grounded."

"Harriet can probably handle a short visit," Mavis said. "I was just going to fix her a snack. Would you like to stay and have a bite to eat?"

"I'm never one to turn down a home-cooked meal," Colm said.

"You two can go sit in the dining room, and I'll bring it out when it's ready."

Harriet led him instead to her formal living room and sat in her Victorian rocking chair.

"This week has been a real trip, as they used to say," he said. "I hope it did what the planners hoped for."

"I haven't heard a lot of the results because of the other stuff going on, but what I've heard has been positive."

"We were shocked when that woman was killed," Colm said. "Regardless of what people think about rock singers, we're just like everyone else. In Ireland, we were raised with violence all around us. My family lived in Belfast. We were raised Catholic. Every day, there were riots or bombings or both." He shuddered. "The lads and I used music as our way out. For a lot of years, we played clubs and parties, but eventually, we started getting bigger gigs, and finally, we made it out."

"I can't imagine how frightening it must have been to live in a war zone," Harriet said. "How do the two sides get past their differences after decades of fighting?"

"You just have to want peace more than war," Colm said. The lads in the band feel the same way. We swore that, if we ever made it big, we'd use our wealth and influence to support peace projects, and so far, that's exactly what we've done."

217

"Even if it was your friend that was killed?" Harriet asked. "When my friend was killed earlier this year, I couldn't leave it alone until justice was served."

"I didn't say it was easy," he said in his lilting brogue. "The peace project helps, but when that woman was killed, Sean had such an anxiety attack we had to take him to the emergency room."

"I'm sorry to hear that. Is he okay now? Murder was the last thing our planning committee imagined they'd be involved in. In fact, they'd rather blame it on an unfortunate case of domestic violence and move on."

"Does anyone have any idea what happened?" he asked.

"Not that I've heard. There was originally some idea it was the victim's husband, but now they think my friend Jenny was the intended target. There were three quilters who were wearing identical costumes that night. It's awful, but Jenny is hoping it's the ex-husband, too."

"But that's not what you think?"

"Oh, I don't know. With Jenny's brother being killed, and everything else that's happened, it's hard to believe the ex-husband would coincidentally choose the same weekend to kill his wife."

"It *was* a festival weekend, though," Colm countered. "More than one person may have thought that having a crowd of strangers in town would provide good cover for whatever they wanted to do."

"We're a small community. We can't go creeping around being afraid of our own shadows. I won't live that way. We'll figure out what happened."

"Be careful," he said and pointed to her arm. "Justice is one thing, but personal safety is as important."

"No one is interested in me," Harriet said, lifting her burned arm. "I'm convinced this is the result of one crazy woman and her own personal demons. It was just chance that I was standing on the stage with the quilt when she took action."

"Do you think the local police have the resources to keep you safe with a killer on the loose?"

"They're a small force, but diligent. I doubt they'd turn down any offers of money, if that's what you're asking."

"I've already brought in extra security, and giving your folks money won't help the immediate problem."

"How did you end up with those two ex-cons who attacked my friends?" Harriet asked.

"That's my fault. Well, Sean's and my fault. After all these years, and everything we've seen, we can still be naive at times," Colm said. "I had this idea that folks who come out of prison end up offending again for simple lack of a job. The band and I decided we were going to take a leap of faith and hire nonviolent ex-offenders for our road crew. Most of the time, it works out—Skeeter's evidence of that. But as your friend saw, sometimes we end up with people who aren't ready to be rehabilitated."

"At least you're trying to make the world a better place," Harriet said.

"I hope you and your friends will accept our apologies."

"Dinner's ready," Mavis called from the kitchen, ending their discussion.

✂- - - ✂- - - ✂

"This looks great," Colm said as he sat down opposite Harriet and Mavis at the dining room table.

Mavis had heated some minestrone soup from a can and made grilled cheese sandwiches. She'd also cut up celery and carrots and put them on a plate with green olives and dill pickle spears.

"We have a cook, and with the exception of concert day, when they put on a show for the backstage guests, she only makes what our nutritional consultant tells her to. At our ages, it's the only way we can stay in the game. Sometimes I think if I eat any more skinless chicken I'm going to start clucking."

"I hear you. My aunt sort of plays that role for me."

"I thought you rock stars got to dictate a long list of must-haves in your dressing room—blue Skittles, brown M-and-Ms, some exotic brand of bottled water that no one's ever heard of," Mavis said.

"I'm sure some bands take advantage of their hosts, but most people put those detailed snack requirements at the bottom of the contract so they can tell quickly if the right people read the whole thing. We all have very specialized electronics in order to produce all the effects we use on stage—video equipment, lifts in the middle of the stage, pyrotechnics, you name it. If you walk in the dressing room and see the big bowl of blue Skittles sitting next to the brown M-and-Ms, then you know they paid attention and probably did all the wiring correctly, too. We, of course, check it out, but it gives us a clue what we'll be dealing with."

"How very clever," Mavis said.

"Can I help you wash the dishes?" Colm asked Mavis when they had all finished eating. "It's hard to believe, but it really is nice to do ordinary tasks. It gets tiresome having people wanting to do everything for you. Not for who you are, but for who you are, if that makes any sense."

"Help yourself," Mavis said. "Harriet's not going to be able to help you, if you were hoping to have some one-on-one time. She needs to lie down again."

"I do want some one-on-one time, m'lady—with you,"

"I bet you tell that to all the girls," Mavis answered, but Harriet noticed her cheeks were ever-so-slightly pink.

"Thanks for staying to have dinner with us," Harriet said. She stood up and started toward the stairs.

"Can I come see you in the morning before we leave town? I'll bring something my nutritionist doesn't approve of," Colm said with a devilish smile. He wiggled his eyebrows for emphasis.

Harriet mentally reminded herself that she already had too many men in her life.

"That sounds wonderful," she said. "What time should I expect you?"

"Is eight too early?"

"Eight sounds perfect."

He stood and came to her, grasping her good hand and raising it to his lips. He went to Mavis and repeated the performance.

"Thanks again for dinner," he said to her and headed for the kitchen.

✄- - -✄- - -✄

"He's a charmer," Mavis said when he was gone, "but he does wash a mean dish."

Harriet looked at her, and they both laughed. They were once again upstairs in the TV room.

"He does seem a little slick, but I'll eat food made by his trainer if he talks to me with that accent."

"Forget the food," Mavis said. "I'd pay him to sit there and read the phone book."

Harriet laughed.

"I'm surprised we haven't heard from Aunt Beth."

"I'm not. While you were sleeping and everyone was packing up the booths and displays, Jenny and Lauren came to help, and then Jenny said she needed to talk to us all. They were going to Jorge's place. Jenny told me that you could tell me what she'd told you and Lauren. Lauren has your stuff in her car, by the way. She said to tell you she'll bring it tomorrow."

"We better make some hot cocoa, because her story is going to take a while."

Harriet was tired by the time she finished telling Mavis what she now believed was the true story of Jenny's life before Foggy Point.

"The problem," she said, "is that it doesn't get us any closer to figuring out who killed Pamela or Bobby or even who slashed Jenny's tires. We can assume it was someone associated with the robbery, but who?"

"Sounds like there are more than a few choices. I'd imagine any of the people who got shot, went to jail or both could be contenders. So, how can we figure it out?" Mavis asked.

"Lauren is going to see if she can track each of the players, but she's not holding out much hope. It's likely that more than one person changed their identity as effectively as Jenny did."

"I don't like feeling so helpless like this," Mavis complained. "We don't know what's going to happen next."

"You can stay here with me if you're worried. Nothing's going to happen to me as long as you-all have me on house arrest."

"I guess we can hope Detective Morse and her bunch will do their jobs and solve the case."

"I like Jane, but I'm not holding my breath on this one," Harriet said.

"Now, honey, you know she's doing the best she can on a shoe-string budget and her having to stay within the bounds of the law all the time."

"I guess."

"Would you like some help getting in your jammies?"

Harriet would never have admitted it if Lauren had been there, but she really did need help.

"That would be great," she said and followed Mavis across the hall to her bedroom.

Chapter 31

*H*arriet woke to the sound of her cell phone buzzing on her nightstand. She saw the image of Carla holding Wendy on the screen and grabbed it, swiping to connect the call.

"Hey," she said.

"Is it too early?"

"No, my alarm was about to go off."

"I thought you were supposed to be resting."

"Colm Byrne is bringing me breakfast."

"Wow, that's exciting," Carla said.

"I guess. But enough about me. What did you want to talk about so badly we're doing this at seven in the morning?"

"It's Aiden," she said. "He wants me to move home. I mean, to his home."

"What do *you* want to do?"

"I want all this business with Michelle to never have happened," she said.

"I'm sure, but what do you want to do now, in the real world?"

"That's what I'm trying to figure out," Carla said. "I've spent a lot of time making bad choices and being everyone's doormat. I don't want Wendy to think it's okay for people to treat you bad, and then you respond by asking them to do it again."

"So, you don't want to go back to Aiden's?"

"No, I do want to go back to Aiden's, but how do I without it being him taking advantage of me again?"

"That's a tough one," Harriet said. "You're sure you want to go back?"

"Our time at Aiden's was the first time in Wendy's life that I didn't have to worry where her next meal was coming from. And I liked the idea of being able to stay in one place for a while."

"It's not being weak wanting to provide a better life for your child. Maybe you need to talk it out with Aiden. Tell him what you just told me. Let him know how he made you feel. Let him know that if you come back, it can't be like it was, with him letting his sister or anyone else treat you like that."

"Won't he fire me for being too demanding?"

"He needs you more than you need him," Harriet told her.

"That's not true," Carla protested. "He has everything."

"He has everything *material*. The only reason his sister could influence him like she did was because he's lonely or emotionally fragile or something. He's suffered a lot of loss this last year."

"Including you?" Carla asked softly.

"That was his doing. I guess I'm in the same spot you are. Michelle has been our only real problem. I just worry that, if he ditched me so easily when his sister went off the rails, what else might do it?"

"Maybe he's right. If either of us had a sister, maybe we'd understand why he'll move heaven and earth to help her. Maybe she is a one-off, and nothing else would cause him to treat us so badly," Carla said.

"Or maybe we're being the perfect victims."

"So what am I supposed to do?"

"I guess I'm not the right person to ask."

"It helped to talk about it—thanks for listening. I guess I better go."

"Let me know how it goes," Harriet said and rang off.

"Come on, boys," she said to her furry bed buddies. "We need to get you fed, and I need to get cleaned up before our breakfast date gets here."

Scooter jumped off the bed and started dancing around her feet. Fred swatted at the excited dog then ran down the stairs.

True to his word, Colm Byrne was on her doorstep at three minutes after eight. She had just come downstairs, tucking her cell phone into the sling the doctor had insisted she wear when she was up and about. As far as she could tell, that was the only thing the sling was useful for.

"Hi," she said as she opened the door. "Come on in."

"Where can I put this?" he said and held out a white cardboard baker's box balanced on his right hand; his guitar case he held by its handle in his left.

"Follow me." She led him into the kitchen, where he set the guitar down. He opened the box, revealing four individual-sized pies. Two were quiche of some sort, and two looked like miniature fruit pies.

"Cook said if we ate our eggs, we could have our fruit pies. And her pies are to die for."

"They look great and smell even better," Harriet agreed.

She pulled two plates one-handed from her cupboard and gathered silverware and napkins.

"I hope you don't mind eating in the kitchen," she said.

"I prefer the kitchen. My dear mother always fed us kids in the kitchen. It makes me feel a little like I'm home." He rolled up the cuffs of his white button-down shirt before reaching into the box to lift out the quiches and place one on each plate. Harriet noticed the edge of a tattoo on his arm.

"Is that a tattoo?" she asked. "Can I see it?"

He pulled his shirtsleeve up, revealing a familiar stylized peace sign.

"Do you like it?" he asked, rubbing his hand over it.

"I like the colors," Harriet said, trying to think of something positive to say about the tattoo.

"This was the first one I got," he said with a rueful smile. "My friends and I all got the same tattoo when we were eighteen years old. I was the youngest in the group, and the day after I passed my eighteenth birthday, we all went and got matching ink. My mother almost had a stroke." He smiled. "It was my first big rebellion."

"The first of many, I take it?" She smiled back.

"Do you have any?" he asked. "Tattoos, that is. I can see you're a rebel at heart."

"No, my parents would have killed me. I definitely was a rebel, but I never really had the urge to be marked in such a permanent way."

"We considered it a rite of passage."

"Was that peace symbol a common image when you got it?" she asked.

"There were plenty of people with peace signs, but we had the artist modify ours so it would be unique."

Harriet knew she'd seen it before.

"Enough about me. I get bored talking about myself all the time." He reached across the table and put his fingers lightly on the back of her hand. "How are you doing? Last night you said you weren't getting better. What do your doctors say?"

"It's no big deal," Harriet said. "My burn is having a little infection trouble. They don't really know if the woman who threw the acid purposefully contaminated the brew she threw on me or if it's just the typical sort of infection you can get as a result of being in a hospital."

"She's not that clever," Colm said, and then hurriedly added, "At least, from what I've read in the paper she wouldn't be that clever. They said she was too mentally ill."

"She did seem pretty crazy," Harriet agreed, but she wondered at his choice of words.

"Speaking of mentally ill," he said, changing the subject. "Have you heard anything new about the murder?"

"No, have you?"

"Not really. Most of the people I've heard talking agree your friend was the intended target. Do you ladies have any idea why anyone would want to kill her?"

"You seem awfully interested in our small-town murder," Harriet said with a smile. "But don't worry, we'll figure out who did it."

"I'll just bet you will."

"My friend Jenny would be happy if it all just goes away. She doesn't want to know who wants her dead, she just wants them to stop."

"She doesn't like the attention?" he asked.

226

"Would you?"

"No, I suppose not," he conceded. "But you're willing to be the talk of the town if it means justice for the victim?"

"That ship has sailed," she said. "A few murders ago. So, yeah, I will find out who killed Pamela and see that they pay."

"I was afraid you were going to say that." Colm got up, went over to his guitar case and knelt down to open it. Was he going to sing to her after this weird conversational turn? she wondered as he fumbled around in the case.

Her smile froze when he turned around, a shiny black nine-millimeter pistol in one hand, a matching silencer in his other. He began screwing the two pieces together.

"What are you doing?" she squeaked.

"Oh, I think you know," he said. "I was hoping it wasn't going to come to this. I gave you every chance I could. All you had to say was you were going to let it go."

"Let what go? I don't know what you're talking about."

"Don't play coy with me. What have we been talking about? The murders, of course. And strangely, you may have saved your friend Jenny."

"You?" The quiche she'd just eaten was threatening to come back up. "What have you got against Jenny?"

"Well, now, that's an interesting story," Colm said. "It turns out your friend Jenny is my friend Jonquil."

Colm's accent had changed; his last sentence wasn't spoken in the lilting Irish she'd become familiar with. His was a distinctly American accent—Pacific Northwest, if she had to make a guess.

"Who are you?" she said.

His answer was interrupted by a knock on her outside door.

"Are you expecting company?" he demanded.

"It could be any of the Threads. They've all been spending time here since I got burned."

"It's not them. Your group is all at a post-festival meeting for the volunteers and vendors. I checked. Their cars were all in the parking lot when I left."

"I can't tell you, then. What I can tell you is if I don't answer the door, whoever it is will likely get the hidden key and come in anyway."

"Answer it and get rid of whoever it is," he barked at her, and waved his gun toward the connecting door. "And don't try anything cute, or you won't be the only one with a hole in their head."

Harriet got up, tilting her arm slightly down as she turned her back to Colm and went into her studio with him following at a distance.

"Aiden," she said in surprise. "I'm so glad to see you."

"You are?" He raised his left eyebrow. A muscle in his jaw tightened.

"Scooter's back is really bothering him. I was afraid I was going to have to wait until one of the Threads came over to take him to see you."

She took his hand i and pulled him into the room.

"This is Colm Byrne," she said. "You know, the rock star."

"I know who Colm Byrne is," he said, giving her a questioning look.

She stared into his eyes, willing him not to go into his jealous routine.

"Nice to meet you," he said, turning to Byrne with a smile. Colm nodded, but kept his distance, the gun held straight down, hidden behind his leg.

"Dr. Jalbert is my little dog Scooter's doctor," Harriet explained, realizing she was babbling but unable to stop. "He rescued Scooter from a hoarder a few months ago, and Scooter still has some health problems. He needs to check the burn on his back."

She called Scooter, who came to the kitchen door and barked to be let into the studio. Harriet turned and went to the door, Aiden close on her heels. He saw the half-eaten pies on the kitchen table and looked back at her.

"Am I interrupting something?"

"We were eating breakfast," Colm said.

"But it's okay," Harriet added, pointedly looking at Aiden and hoping he was reading between the lines. "His back is really bothering him."

"Make it quick," Colm said, his accent firmly back in place. "My busses are pulling out within the hour."

Aiden picked up the little dog and examined the burn scar on his back. There was a small remaining scab, but he knew it was of

228

no consequence. With a silent apology, he deftly scraped it open, causing Scooter to yelp and the wound to bleed.

Harriet was relieved Aiden had picked up on her ruse. While the two men were focused on her yelping dog, she retracted her burned arm into the sling, blindly stabbing the face of her concealed phone with her fingers and hoping she'd hit the speed dial number she was aiming for. She pressed the volume button down when she heard a woman's voice.

"I'm going to need to get my bag from the car," Aiden said.

"I don't think so," Colm snapped, revealing the gun. "Nice try, though. I'm not sure how she got you here, but now that you are, I'm afraid you won't be leaving."

"I have no idea what's going on here, but Harriet didn't 'get me here.' I came to check on Scooter, which is something I do every day on my way to the clinic," Aiden lied.

"Well, that's unfortunate." Colm's accent was once again gone. "I'm afraid your devotion to the dog is going to get you killed."

"What?" Aiden gasped. "What on earth are you talking about? If you're going to shoot me, can I at least know why?"

"The short version is that your friend here is too nosy for her own good."

"Come on, you have to give me more than that. If I'm just collateral damage, at least tell me what cause I'm dying for."

"I'm curious, too," Harriet said.

Both men turned and glared at her.

"This is all about her friend Jenny," Colm said.

"Jenny Logan?" Aiden asked. "What could she possibly have done to you?"

"You'd be surprised," Colm said. "She seems to have set herself up as a suburban housewife now, but she has a past you-all don't seem to know about. And see, that's the thing—we share a past that I need to make sure stays in the past.

"I've been able to hire most of the people who did jail time. They're dependent on me, so it's in their best interest to keep their mouths shut. But Jonquil and Paisley escaped scott-free."

"I don't mean to be dense," Aiden said, "but I still am not following what you're telling me. Who are Paisley and Jonquil, and what do they have to do with Jenny and Harriet, and why do you want everybody, including me, dead?"

"It's like this. I got involved with a group of people when we were all in our teens. We had a crazy idea to make a political statement, and we got involved with some people with a different agenda. They robbed a bank, killed a policeman, and we all were incarcerated for various amounts of time. Everyone, that is, except two girls, who disappeared off the face of the earth.

"After that, two things happened. I got forged papers and left for Ireland, where I played my guitar in pubs full of drunks. A funny thing happened, though. Without the drugs, I got better, and then I got real good. As soon as I started making real money, I hired private investigators to find Jonquil and Paisley. I also had a little reconstructive surgery done—my face needed to match my new age."

"I take it Jonquil or Paisley is who we know as Jenny?" Aiden asked.

"I found Paisley about ten years ago," Colm continued. "Just in time, it turned out. She was about to publish a memoir, and unfortunately, she included a chapter on me and how a drug-using excon became an Irish rock singer. I'm not saying it would have destroyed my career to be outed. It's not like I was lip-syncing like Milli Vanilli or anything, but you know, I can't take that chance. I could be run out of the business on a rail—you never can tell about these things."

"How did you find Jenny?" Harriet asked.

"Well, that's what's funny, you know? All the high-priced detectives I've paid for over the years, and a newspaper article about this festival did it for me. I wasn't expecting it. I was looking to see what they said about the band, and there was a picture of my old shirt. Well, not my shirt, but a piece of it. Jonquil was always sewing patches on jeans and stuff, and she'd use whatever material she could find. She made her and Paisley skirts from some old jeans one time.

"Anyway, there was the back of my favorite shirt, right in the middle of that quilt. It disappeared the day of the robbery. I had bigger things to worry about on that day, but when I saw the quilt, I figured out where it came from. That shirt was hand-dyed, so it was an original. There wasn't a chance it was anything else *but* my shirt."

"So, you just decided to kill Jenny without even talking to her?" Harriet persisted.

"Come on, give me a little credit. I had my PI check her out. There didn't seem to be anything I could leverage in her background, and it was obvious that, if she was confronted, she'd crack. Her brother was a bit of a problem, too."

"What do you mean?" Harriet interrupted him again, hoping whomever she'd reached had called 911 and could hear what was being said.

She wiggled her arm again as if it were hurting her, sliding her phone forward toward her hand. She used her good hand to reposition the sling, brushing her finger over the screen. The face illuminated, and she could see she was still connected.

"Ole Bobby was finally cleaning up. My guys interviewed Bobby's fellow rehab inmates. He was coming up on steps eight and nine in his process—identify people you have wronged and make amends. We couldn't have him making any amends that involved me or the band."

"If you had plastic surgery, how was he going to know it was you?" Aiden interrupted.

Colm pulled his sleeve up, exposing the peace sign tattoo.

"We all had these," he said. "And Bobby was snooping around backstage and saw mine. I offered him cash to go away, but he said he couldn't leave until he'd connected with his sister and made amends. He had a lot of guilt about involving her with the rest of us. And he was ready to do whatever she wanted him to do to make it right."

"Too bad he didn't know that what she wanted most was to bury her past deep. She had no desire to dredge it all back up," Harriet said.

"That is too bad, but there was no way for my PI to figure that out. All we can do now is clean up. You two are, unfortunately, going to be the victims of a murder-suicide."

"No one will believe that," Harriet said. "He's just my veterinarian. Why would he kill me?"

"Good point," Colm said. "You'll kill him accidentally and be so remorseful you'll kill yourself."

"No one will believe you," Aiden said and stood up.

"Don't do anything foolish, hero," Colm said. He slid the top of the gun back, chambering a round.

The door from the studio slammed open.

"Drop the gun and put your hands in the air," Detective Morse said. "It's over."

Colm not only didn't drop his gun, he grabbed Harriet by the arm and whirled her around so her back was pressed to his chest, his gun jammed into her neck.

"It's over, Mr. Byrne," Morse repeated. "This place is surrounded. Put your gun down and your hands in the air." She slowly edged along the length of the kitchen bar, causing Colm to retreat, turning his back to the windows that flanked the kitchen table on two sides.

No one spoke for a moment.

"Remember what Robin is always trying to get us to do?" Morse commented.

Harriet stared at her. When Robin wasn't driving her children all over Foggy Point, or using her skills as a lawyer to rescue her quilting friends from trouble, she taught yoga, something she was always trying to get the Threads to participate in, with varying degrees of success.

"Now!" Morse barked.

Everything happened at once. Harriet bent forward as if to touch her toes, her kitchen window shattered, and Colm Byrne fell forward onto her.

Aiden apparently had taken a step toward her because she heard Morse say "Stop." She couldn't see what was going on from the floor. She heard a metallic scrape, which must have been the gun being kicked away from Colm's hand. He was so still, lying on top of her back, that she was pretty sure he wasn't going to be grabbing it—or anything else, for that matter.

Her arm was screaming in pain—it was pinned under her with Colm Byrne's weight pressing down on her.

"Clear," she heard Morse yell, followed by the sound of feet shuffling into the kitchen.

Finally, Colm's body was lifted off her, and Aiden gently took her by her good arm and pulled her to her feet.

Chapter 32

The kitchen filled with crime scene-related personnel, and Harriet, Aiden and Detective Morse went into the dining room to regroup. Harriet's bottom lip was quivering from the pain in her arm.

"Where are your pain meds?" Aiden asked.

"Upstairs in my bathroom," she told him in a tight voice.

He looked at Morse.

"Okay if I go get her pain meds?"

Morse nodded.

"I need to ask you some questions," she said, "but I can wait until your meds kick in, if you want."

"I'm okay," Harriet choked out, and then recounted Jenny's story one more time while Morse scratched notes as quickly as she could write.

"Here," Aiden interrupted when he brought Harriet's medication and a small glass of water. He had a bed pillow clenched under his arm, and he placed it gently under her damaged arm.

"Did you suspect Byrne was our killer when you invited him here?" Morse asked.

"Not even a little," Harriet said in a shocked tone. "I was starting to wonder why he was so interested in me, though. He brought me CDs and T-shirts, and then he kept wanting to come for dinner. But he was a rock star, so who was I to question him?"

Aiden looked at her.

"You let your head be turned by the glitz and glamour of a rock star?"

"Better that than a crazy sister," Harriet shot back.

"Children, please. You can fight all you want later. Let's go back to this," Morse glanced at her notes. "Paisley. You said he found her some years ago and just in time. Did he say what he did about it?"

"No, he didn't. The implication was clear, though."

"Any idea who Paisley was?"

"You need to talk to Jenny, not me. She knows all the players. I'm sure she'll know who Colm Byrne really is when she finds out he's had plastic surgery." She yawned.

"She needs to lie down," Aiden advised. "The pain meds make you sleepy."

"I need to go get my bandage changed first," Harriet held her arm up, displaying her blood-soaked sling. "Colm bled on me."

Aiden jumped up.

"Come on, we have to get you to the emergency room." He looked at Morse. "You can come with us if you want, but she needs this cleaned right away. We need to see if his blood got into her raw wound."

Morse declined, and Aiden took Harriet to the hospital alone.

Chapter 33

"Tom's coming by after our Loose Threads meeting," Harriet told her aunt Beth the following day. They were sitting in Harriet's kitchen watching a workman spread caulking around the edges of the newly replaced window. "He's heading back to Angel Harbor."

"Is that a good thing or a bad thing?"

"I don't know," Harriet sighed. "If Aiden weren't in the picture, it would be an unqualified good thing, but even though I'm really unhappy with Aiden at the moment, I feel like we have unfinished business to deal with. But things with Tom are so easy."

"Oh, honey, you know the easy way isn't always the best way."

"Not to change the subject, but you and Jorge seem to be spending a lot of time together these days." Harriet's eyes sparkled.

"He's a lot of fun, and I think he enjoys my company, too, but there's no reason for us to push to make it anything else at this point." Beth picked up the candle that sat on the table, sniffed it and set it back down again.

"You wouldn't let me get away with an answer like that," Harriet said with a laugh.

"Oh, you hush, now."

"Hello?" someone called from Harriet's studio. Robin came through the connecting door, followed by DeAnn, Kissa on her hip.

"My, you're getting big," Beth said and took the baby from DeAnn. "You want some juice?" she asked her.

"No," said Kissa.

"She says that to everything," DeAnn explained. "She never turns down juice."

Harriet stood up.

"There's coffee in the pot and hot water in the kettle. Fix your drinks and meet me in the studio," she said, still too uncomfortable to be more gracious.

Beth had set up the studio with chairs in a loose circle and the tables strategically placed to hold teacups and coffee mugs. Carla arrived, followed by Mavis then Connie and Lauren and, finally, Jenny.

"I'm really sorry," Jenny began.

"You don't have to apologize to any of us," Connie said. "Everyone has a past and is entitled to keep it just that—in the past."

"We're sorry you had to have yours drug out for everyone to see and have an opinion about. None of us can say what we would do if we'd been in the same situation," Mavis agreed.

"We care about the Jenny we know now," said Aunt Beth, Kissa firmly planted on her hip with a sippy cup of juice clutched in her chubby hands.

"I appreciate your support, and I'm sure you all have questions. If I can answer anything, please ask me," Jenny said. "It's the least I can do after lying to you all these years."

"Since we never asked you," Lauren said, "it can't even be considered a sin of omission. It's more of a 'we didn't ask so you didn't tell.'"

"I'd like to know who Colm Byrne is," Harriet said. "I mean, we know who the invention is, but who is the man?"

"His name was Dennis. Dennis Smith."

"Boy, it doesn't get much more ordinary than that," Lauren said.

"Dennis was anything but ordinary," Jenny said. "He was the one who thought up the whole break-in scheme. He always had grand plans. And he always said he was going to be a rock star." She gave a little laugh. "At least he achieved that goal—for a little while."

"Are you in any trouble?" Carla asked.

"No. At least, not so far. When I disappeared, I mainly did it because I assumed that, with James dead, no one would know I was there as his informant. I was only fifteen when this happened, so my knowledge of the world and of how the police worked was limited. It turns out he'd documented everything. All that time, I was never a suspect. They wanted me to be a witness. On the other hand, I was in danger from my friends, so go figure—hiding from my perceived enemy saved me from my perceived friends."

"I'm sure there's a moral in there somewhere," Lauren said.

"I'm just glad it's all out," Jenny said.

"Me, too," Mavis said. "Now that we're done with the sixties festival, we've got to get busy on our quilts for the women's shelter."

"No rest for the weary," Connie said.

"Before we move on," Beth said. "Anyone interested in how the festival did? We're talking rough figures right now. It will take weeks to get all the secondary numbers in."

Everyone nodded or murmured agreement.

"I went to a meeting with the main committee. Jorge was included, since he was a major part of the profits."

A knock sounded on the door, interrupting Beth's report before it got started. Harriet looked out the bow window and saw it was Aiden. She got up, grabbing her fleece jacket from a coat tree by the door.

"I'll be back in a few minutes," she said, swirling the coat over her bound arm then putting her good arm in the sleeve.

"Can we talk?" Aiden said when she was outside.

"Sure, let's walk down the driveway so we're not in view of the Threads."

"I wanted to see how your arm is doing," he said. "It can't feel great after all the cleaning they did last night."

"No, it doesn't feel great, but I'll live. My temperature is almost back to normal, so the infection is better, but that's not what you really wanted to talk about, is it?"

"I guess not. I mean, I do want to know how you're doing, but I guess what I really want to know is has my sister ruined everything? Or do we have a chance?"

Harriet took a deep breath.

238

"Before we get started, I need to let you know that Tom is coming by any time now."

"Do you want me to leave?"

"No, of course not. I just don't want you going nuts when he drives up."

"Is that how you see me? Someone who's 'going nuts' all the time."

"I didn't say that," Harriet said.

"But it's clear that's what you're thinking."

She grabbed his arm with her good hand and turned him toward her.

"We had a good thing going for a while——" Aiden started.

"Let me speak, please. I think you'll agree, we had a great start to our relationship, but it seems like the first time things got rough, we couldn't deal with it. It's possible we could make things work again, but not if we try to pretend everything's okay and try to just pick up where we left off. We need help, but if you're not willing to change anything, we're going to be spinning our wheels."

"So that's it? An ultimatum? Get help or else?"

"I didn't say that. You know I don't come from a traditional family. My boarding school headmistresses didn't teach me much about personal relationships with the opposite sex, and we both know how well my first husband and I communicated. My problem is—I can't figure out how couples counseling will help if I don't have the other half of a couple with me."

He was silent for so long she thought their discussion was over. She'd started to turn back to the house when he spoke.

"Let me think about it." The muscle in his jaw tightened. "Will you give me some time to do that?"

"Take all the time you need."

"I'll come by in a day or two to check Scooter's back again where I had to scratch him," he said.

"I guess I'll see you then."

She watched him walk back to his car, get in and drive down the driveway. She was still standing there when Tom's truck pulled in. He rolled down his window, took one look at her face and stopped where he was. Without saying anything, he got out and carefully pulled her into a silent embrace.

END

239

ABOUT THE AUTHOR

ARLENE SACHITANO was born at Camp Pendleton while her father was serving in the US Navy. Her family lived in Newport, RI, before settling in Oregon, where Arlene still resides.

Arlene worked in the electronics industry for almost thirty years, including stints in solid state research as well as production supervision. Arlene is handy, being both a knitter and a quilter. She puts her quilting knowledge to work writing the Harriet Truman/Loose Threads mystery series, which features a long-arm quilter as the amateur sleuth.

ABOUT THE ARTIST

APRIL MARTINEZ was born in the Philippines and raised in San Diego, California, daughter to a US Navy chef and a US postal worker, sibling to one younger sister. For years, she went from job to job, dissatisfied that she couldn't make use of her creative tendencies, until she started working as an imaging specialist for a big book and magazine publishing house in Irvine and began learning the trade of graphic design. From that point on, she worked as a graphic designer and webmaster at subsequent day jobs while doing freelance art and illustration at night. April lives with her cat in Orange County, California, as a full-time freelance artist/illustrator and graphic designer.

CPSIA information can be obtained at www.ICGtesting.com
Printed in the USA
BVOW080252090713

325428BV00001B/153/P